MW00883606

KEEP EVOLVING

A Paradise Lot Novel

This book is a work of fiction. The characters, incidents and dialogue are drawn from the author's imagination and are not to be construed as real. Any resemblance to actual events or persons, living or dead, is fictionalized or coincidental.

Paradise Lot Copyright © R.E. Vance (2015). All rights reserved. First edition. Published 2015. **www.Paradise-Lot.com**

The right of R.E. Vance to be identified as the author of this work has been asserted by the author in accordance with the Copyright, Designs and Patents Act,1988. All rights reserved. No part of this publication may be reproduced, stored in a retrieval system, or transmitted, in any form, or by any means, electronic, mechanical, photocopying, recording or otherwise, without the prior permission of the publishers. This book is sold subject to the condition that it shall not, by way of trade or otherwise, be lent, resold, hired out, or otherwise circulated without the author's prior consent in any form of binding or cover other than that in which it is published and without a similar condition being imposed on the subsequent purchaser.

Requests to publish work from this book should be sent to:
ramy@paradise-lot.com

Cover Design: Stuart Bache: bookscovered.co.uk

Cover images © Shutterstock.co

For Wee John

A Paradise Lot Novel

The GoneGod World

R.E. Vance

KEEP EVOLVING

Prologue

The gods are gone. All of them.

I've had the same dream every night since they left. I'm running from a devouring darkness that rushes over the world like a tidal wave of emptiness. I run on charred earth, unsure if the darkness or fear will get me first. In the distance, I can just see a pinprick of light ahead. If I can get to it, I will be safe. My legs burn and my lungs heave. I run and run toward the light, but before I reach it, the world stops. Not like a ledge or a shore; the world just stops. Null and void. And I know, in that way you do in dreams, that I'm standing at the end of everything.

I turn around. If I'm going to die, I want to see it coming. The darkness slows down as the rushing wave breaks into a creeping black fog. It knows I'm trapped. It's savoring my terror.

Just before the darkness envelops me, a burning light grows from the Void.

Like the darkness, it blinds.

I am surrounded by light and dark until a hand reaches from the burning halo and pulls me somewhere else.

That's when the dreams differ, because every night she takes me somewhere new.

↔

Tonight, we walk on a sandy beach that reminds me of where I proposed to her. This is more secluded though—

there's no other sign of life. An imperfect memory of a place made perfect by time and imagination.

I'm in linen shorts and little else. Bella is in the same sleeveless sundress that she wears on all our nightly rendezvous. It's the dress she wore the night we got engaged; the one she wore when we drove up to PopPop's cabin for what would pass as our honeymoon.

The dress she was wearing the day the Others killed her.

The hem is dry despite her being ankle-deep in the ocean. She's standing next to me, so close that we could hold hands. But we never do. Even though I want it more than anything, we never touch. I don't know why.

"Hi, Bella," I say. She doesn't look at me, her eyes fixed on the blue, cloudless sky. "I thought you hated salt water. What was it you used to say? 'Salt's a preservative and I don't like the thought of anything preserving me.' "

"Dust to dust," she says, still staring at the same spot in the sky. A single cumulus cloud has crept in from beyond the horizon.

"Yeah, yeah—'dust to dust.' Mummify me, I say. I want to be this beautiful forever."

"I stand by my words," she chuckles, looking at me for the first time that night. "I wanted life to use me up, and when it was done with me, I wanted to fade away into whatever came next."

"And did you?"

"Nothing comes next. You know that."

Yeah, I do. Everyone knows that Heaven is closed and Hell doesn't exist.

"So what are you? A ghost, haunting my dreams?" I ask. The words come out bitter and angry.

Her mood darkens and in a distant voice she says, "Ghosts aren't real. Not anymore."

"Well, they kind of are," I say. "Have you spoken to your mother recently?"

A smile creeps across her face as she shoots me her "You better behave" look.

"Be nice. You promised." Her smile fades and she is looking at the horizon again. The lone cloud has been replaced with a gray, ominous skyline. She points. "There's somewhere you need to be."

I hear the distant roll of thunder as the wind picks up.

"There is nowhere I want to be," I say, raising my voice so she can hear me over the wind.

A fork of lightning strikes the sand beside us as a gale force wind blows in from the sea, far too fast to be natural. The once blue sky is now blanketed in grays.

"I didn't say it was somewhere you wanted to be. There is somewhere you *need* to be," she says, flattening the wrinkles of her impossibly dry dress.

"I don't want this to end. Not yet."

"Oh Jean-Luc, I don't want you to go either." She captures me with her intense cerulean blue eyes and, in a serious tone I've seldom heard her use, says, "Jean, there's a storm coming. The thing about storms is that they always end. Remember that, and remember your promise."

I nod. My promise. A promise I made to the dream of my dead wife one lonely night in the middle of nowhere. A promise that I would go to Paradise Lot and help Others. A promise I plan to keep.

The storm is getting stronger. I need to wake up. "Will you be back?" I ask her this every time I have to leave.

"Whenever you sleep," she always replies, smiling. "Someone has to save you from your dreams."

I know she will. She always does.

"In this life and the next," I say, just before my body

3

jolts as the real world comes into focus.

↔→↔→↔→

My mobile phone was ringing. I glanced at the clock. Three in the morning. Only one person would call me at this time: Penemue.

Part One

Chapter 1

Of Angels and Men

I parked in front of the Paradise Lot Police Station, to where I had been summoned—if such a lofty term could be used for being roused from a perfect dream at such a GoneGodless hour—to bail out a certain guest of mine. My head throbbed from lack of sleep. I hated being woken up; I hated being taken away from Bella.

From outside, the station looked like any other: red brick building; a boring backlit sign with the name in big blue letters; a flex-face shield above the door. Typical—until you went inside.

The first indication that the Paradise Lot Police Station, and by extension the world, was different was that the entrance had been unceremoniously enlarged. Whereas the doors were previously wide enough to accommodate three humans standing shoulder to shoulder, now they were big enough for an elephant.

The next indication that it wasn't your typical cops' HQ was who manned the front desk: Medusa. As in turn-you-to-stone lady-of-legend and friggin' Queen-of-the-Gorgons Medusa. As I walked in, at least seven of her thirty or so snake dreadlocks looked up. "Jean," she said, not taking her own eyes off the computer screen, "what brings you here at …" One of the snakes looked at the clock on the wall. "Three in the morning?"

"Same old, same old," I said. She giggled and pulled out a form for me. I avoided eye contact as I took it from her. I wasn't afraid she'd turn me to stone—she could, if she was willing to burn through a couple years of her life—it was just that some habits die harder than others. It didn't matter that in this *Brave New* GoneGod *World* she no longer guarded the Golden Fleece, or that she, like all cops, had taken a vow to serve and protect. Nor did it matter that she was mortal, with all the insecurities, doubts and fears that entailed …

She was still friggin' *Medusa*.

Her giggles faded, and a shy hand took the signed form back. A few taps on a keyboard later a hurt voice said, "Officer Steve will be with you in a moment." I got the feeling one of her snakes was eyeing me, which was confirmed by a disdainful hiss.

I reminded myself that humans didn't look at her out of the same superstitious habit as me. Hell, most Others probably avoided looking at her for the same damn reason. Medusa, like all Others, was newly mortal—thirteen years to be exact—and I guess she went through all the existential angst any teenager did. After all, wasn't not being seen the basis of countless teenage vampire novels?

Oh, hell …

I forced myself to look up. Medusa worked with her head down, but a large green snake that stemmed from the top of her skull edged forward. Its forked tongue flicked a couple of inches from my face. Partly because I was still half asleep and partly because the snake genuinely looked like it was smiling, I petted it on the head.

Medusa looked up immediately, and my heart fluttered in fear as our eyes connected.

I did not turn to stone.

And really looking at her for the first time, I noted that the Medusa of legend had a bad rep. She wasn't hideous— hell, she wasn't even plain. High cheekbones housed perfect little dimples on a kind face.

Unused to eye contact, she turned away with a bashful flutter—and that's when I noticed she possessed a more than ample, perfectly formed bosom that heaved quite seductively with every breath.

Medusa was hot!

Hot enough that any serious suitor would consider a bath of snakes just to get used to scaly skin crawling all over them. Plus, Astarte, the succubus who lived in my hotel, had informed me that between the sheets, the snakes were quite the erotic apparatus—for both parties.

"Oooh," Medusa said, shivering at my touch, "Marty likes you."

"Marty?" I asked, retracting my hand. "You named him?"

"Only the mains," she said. "This is Johnny, Alfie, Rocky, Jimmy, Cory, Georgie, and you've already met Marty. What, don't you name yours?" she asked.

"What? My hair?"

"No, silly," she said, her eyes sliding down my torso.

"Oh! Oh … Ahh, I suppose I did, once. Well, not me, but, my wife. I mean …" I stuttered, feeling my face burn red.

Medusa broke my awkward stammering by touching my sleeve.

"I like your jacket," she said.

There was something about my jacket. It existed in that sweet spot of representing different things for different people. It was black and collarless. To some, I looked like a hipster priest, my white T-shirt acting as the clerical collar. Others saw me as a sort of fashionable monk, back from years in the mountains. Astarte said the jacket reminded her of an ancient demon called the Judge who separated the righteous from the wicked—and then burned the righteous. Sounded like a great guy.

Medusa looked at me expectantly. Oh, hell … I suddenly

felt like I was back in junior high. What should I do? Maybe I should compliment something about her? Perhaps one of her snakes? If so, which one? And if I picked one, would the others be offended? And would they be venomous?

The switchboard beeped—and I was literally saved by the bell. Her snakes hissed at the computer as she buzzed me through to the back.

"Officer Steve will meet you through there," she said, disappointed.

Just before entering, I turned to say goodbye. I was met by a head full of snakes, all of which simultaneously winked at me.

Hellelujah!

↔

Officer Steve met me at the door, shifting from four legs to two and standing erect before me with an ease that implied every creature could do so. Being one of the Billy Goat Gruff brothers, Officer Steve had a cubicle shaped more like a stable than an office space.

Serious, efficient, smart and diligent, the Gruff brothers made perfect cops, despite looking like your typical—albeit very large—goat. Officer Steve was the youngest and thus smallest Gruff, which meant he was the size of a lion.

"Hi, Steve," I started, but he lifted a hoof, indicating that he needed a minute. Then his hoof fanned out into finger-like appendages, which he put into his overcoat to search for a pen in pockets not designed for hooves.

As he fumbled in his pockets, I surveyed the room and was greeted by the hustle and bustle of Paradise Lot Police Station. Just like any human station, this one was filled with angry cops and even angrier cops. Except here, the average beat cop had fangs. An annoyed valkyrie led a cuffed dark elf to an interrogation room, a despondent three-headed cerberus booked several stoned fairies. A minotaur detective with a pinstriped tie sat in his nipple-high fuzzy cubicle, filling out paperwork. Several broken pencils littered his desk, all destroyed by powerful hands more used to war hammers than No. 2 lead pencils.

When the gods left with only a "Thank you for believing in us, but it's not enough. We're leaving. Good luck," Others were forced from their homes to live on the mortal plane. Some fought this change, but most Others accepted their new lot in life, trying to make the best out of a bad situation. Paradise Lot Police Station was an example of them trying. The station was filled with legends trying to fix the problem created by our mutual gods. But even legends have limitations and these guys had been utterly defeated, not by mortal combat but by a far more formidable foe—human bureaucracy.

Officer Steve finally managed to pull out his pen. Clicking it awake, he asked, "Jean-Luc Matthias?"

"Oh, come on, Steve, we spoke less than an hour ago on the phone. What's more, we've met over a dozen times before."

The Gruff gave me a blank look, his pen hovering over his clipboard as he waited for my answer.

"Yes, yes—I'm Jean-Luc Matthias," I said, annoyed, doing my best to iron out my frustration as I reminded myself that the Gruffs were just doing their best in the GoneGod world.

The Gruffs, more diligent than most, studied human customs, determined to fit in as best they could. But since they were creatures of story, they preferred tales to dry explanation, finding particular comfort in the legends of

Sherlock Holmes. Hence the London Fog overcoats, heavy wool hats and smokeless pipes. At least they were trying.

Officer Steve ticked a box and handed me a form to fill out.

"What happened this time?" I asked as I filled in my information.

"Fighting, I'm afraid," the Gruff brayed in a British accent. Damn Sherlock.

"Again?" I said, surprised—Penemue was an arrogant pain in the ass, but a fighter he was not.

"Indeed, but this time it is a bit more serious. You see, your feathered friend was engaging in fisticuffs outside the Palisade."

"What?" I said. "What the hell was he doing there?"

"Not a clue. But he's been roughed up pretty bad. When we arrived on the scene, three HuMans were pinning him to the ground like a butterfly on display. They're all locked up now."

Damn—this was far more serious than his usual drunk antics. The HuMans were a gang of Other-hating wannabe bad-asses. If you imagined the illegitimate children of Nazis and nutbar survivalists, you'd just be scratching the surface of what kind of scum these guys were. And the Palisade served as their headquarters. No sane Other would come within five blocks of the place. But then again—Penemue was suffering from something he called "Mortal Madness." I guess in that way he wasn't really that different from the rest of us.

I shook my head. "Damn," I said aloud. "Where is he?"

"This way, sir," the Gruff brayed, reverting to four legs.

We took four steps before an ominous voice bellowed, "Hold—I wish to speak with the human." Only one creature possessed a voice made from thunder—the archangel

Michael.

Hellelujah … it had to be him!

Chapter 2

Even Angels Have Their Wicked Schemes

After the GrandExodus and the initial years of fighting subsided, Michael retired from his role as archangel, Advocate of Man, Slayer of the Great Dragon and Leader of the Host of God, to begin his career as a police officer in Paradise Lot. We'd had our run-ins in the past, and he didn't like how I ran the One Spire Hotel. He didn't like the kind of Others I let in and how willing I was to ignore some of their more questionable ways. There was a time, early on, when he visited the hotel daily, citing some violation or other that I was ignoring. It wasn't until I countered with "Let he who is without sin cast the first stone" that I finally got the archangel to leave me alone. Since then, he only came around when there was a complaint.

Still, despite him being such a hardass, I had to hand it to the archangel. He could have been a demigod here—what with all the denominations of Christianity vying for him to be the head of their various churches—but instead he chose to enter the police force in one of the slummiest, dirtiest parts of the world, insisting on starting as a beat cop before quickly working his way up the ranks. For that, if nothing else, I could respect him.

The archangel strode into the main area, each movement exuding strength, each gesture demanding respect. By the GoneGods, he was power incarnate. "Human Jean-Luc," he didn't so much as say, but rather boomed. He was addressing me with my species, which meant that whatever he had to show me mattered. Using one's species as a prefix put a formal twist to any conversation. It was like using "Mister" or "Missus," and was a habit employed by many Others. I, for one, welcomed the habit, finding it useful in avoiding embarrassing situations like confusing gnomes for dwarves, harpies for valkyrie, or elves for vulcans—not that I'd ever met a vulcan … yet.

"Look, if it has to do with Penemue, I—"

"No, Human Jean-Luc. My business with you this evening has nothing to do with the fallen angel or his debauched ways," the archangel bellowed, each word coming down like a hammer. "Come. Follow me and all shall be made clear."

↔

Michael led me to his office, its door widened to accommodate his massive size. Head to toe, the chief of police was eleven feet high and built as if Mr. Olympia were carved out of granite. He walked in, sat on the steel frame that acted as his chair, and gestured for me to take the seat opposite him. He started fumbling with his desk drawers, his massive fingers struggling to flip through files.

As I waited for Police Chief Michael to find whatever it was he wanted to show me, I noted that on his office wall hung various awards and one framed newspaper clipping from the local rag that showed an unimpressed Michael accepting a plaque—the headline reading, "Archangel Climbs Police Ranks at Record Speed." Well, with such a colorful resume, there wasn't ever really a doubt, was there, that he'd rise quickly in the ranks of the local PD.

Still, to display so many awards was quite prideful and very unangelic. I pointed to the awards and said, "Pride cometh before a fall."

Michael stopped fiddling and looked behind him. "Indeed," he sighed with recognition. He raised the tips of one of his multiple pairs of wings so that I could no longer see the display from where I sat. "But I have been told that they make me more … more … human."

"A worthy quality?" I asked, knowing how he felt.

"A useful one," he said, finally getting out the folder and slamming shut his drawers. He settled on the steel-frame chair, then looking past me and out of the window he said, "Your car registration will soon expire. Be sure to renew it lest I am forced to impound it."

I looked behind me and through the window at my 1969 Plymouth Road Runner. He could read the registration sticker from where it sat a hundred feet away in a dimly lit parking lot at night? Hellelujah.

"Did you really call me in here to talk about my car?" I asked. In my mind I debated the possibility of that being the case. After all, he was an Other cop and registrations were exactly the kind of bureaucratic plight that they took very seriously. It was right up there with sorting the recycling and paying overdue library book fines.

"No, human, there is this … ahh … *poster* I wish to show you," he said, the word *poster* stumbling out of his lips. He fumbled with a folder before his angelic dexterity won the day and he managed to pull out a flyer. On it I read:

KEEP EVOLVING

In today's confusing mortal world,
Others of all species are welcome to attend

COPING WITH MORTALITY

We'll answer pestering questions like:
"Why is Sleep Important?"

and

"Headaches—Biological Inconvenience, or Wrath of an
Angry Demon?"

and many, many more!

"So?" I asked, rubbing my eyes. I looked over at the clock ticking on the wall. Three-thirty a.m. If I could get home in an hour, I could hang out with Bella for another three hours before my day started. "What does that have to do with me?"

"The address," Michael answered.

I looked down at the address—One Spire Hotel, followed by a date and time. I took a double look, rubbing my eyes again. *Damn, Jean-Luc, wake up.* "Holy crap," I said, my brain finally confirming what I read. "This is for tomorrow. I mean, tonight. This is supposed to start in like fifteen hours." I failed to hide my surprise.

"Indeed," Michael muttered. "And crap is anything but holy," he added, folding his arms over his chest as he waited for my explanation.

"Well, hell—it's a seminar to help Others cope with mortality. It's a *good* thing. The kind of service that Paradise Lot needs. And if you're going to stop it from happening because of some ridiculous minor infraction, you're being … being … really anal," I said. What I failed to add was that I had no idea this kind of thing happened in Paradise Lot, let alone in my hotel. That was exactly the kind of thing the archangel would latch onto.

Michael waved his hands in a dismissive gesture. "Where would one get a flyer such as this?"

"I don't know." I really didn't. "Various help centers, the hospital, anywhere public service announcements are made. Hell, a police station should be handing out stacks of them." My voice dripped with sarcasm, which I hoped sufficiently hid the fact that I really didn't know.

My gambit seemed to work. Michael announced to no one in particular, "I am satisfied with your answer." He opened a second folder and removed a single photograph.

He threw the rest of the folder's remains in front of me, scattering photographs that displayed a scene of carnage in a glossy finish. I hadn't seen this kind of gore since I left the Army. The photos were of three humanoid creatures that were impaled into the side of a building, pressed so forcefully against the wall that they hung to the wall like macabre graffiti. Bits of bone stuck out where the flesh could not stretch enough to accommodate their new form. If it wasn't so horrific, I might have thought this some comical rendition of a three dimensional creature being flattened by a rolling pin. Their bodies were mangled so badly that it was impossible for me to tell what kind of creatures they were, but given that their blood was bright yellow, I ruled out human.

I leafed through the photos, one after another. Something about them bugged me. Sure, there were the mangled bodies, but whatever had killed them did so by slamming them against a wall with such force that it literally flattened them, though the red brick wall on which they hung was completely unaffected. You'd think that there would be some cracks in the wall, crumbled stone, anything. "What could have done this?" I asked.

Michael shook his head. "We are not sure. All we do know is that *time* was burned to do this, which means that either this was some ancient grudge settled or we have a—"

"Fanatic on our hands," I finished.

The archangel nodded.

"How much time?" I asked.

"Again, it is hard to tell. If I were to use such force, I would burn through a month, perhaps six weeks."

"A month!" I said in surprise. When the gods left, ejecting their OnceImmortal subjects to the mortal plane, they effectively cut them off from their source of magic. Every Other only had a certain amount of time to live. Others could trade in some of that time to tap into their once-upon-a-time limitless magic. The more powerful you were, the more time you had, but still … rational Others didn't use magic, choosing to preserve the precious little time they had left. Can you blame them? Eighty years, for a creature that has known thousands of years of life, is precious little time indeed.

But then there were the Fanatics, Others so unhinged by mortality that they burned through time in a self-destructive, suicidal rampage without consideration or care. The result was catastrophic. During the Nine Year War, a Fanatic valkyrie took on an entire platoon on her own, aging with every swing of her golden axe. The result? Seventy human soldiers slain before she was too old to lift her weapon.

"A month is not a 'grudge,' ancient or not," I said. "Why give your enemy the satisfaction of knowing they took so much time from you? No, this has Fanatic written all over it."

Michael nodded. "Still, of all the tortures I have witnessed, not even the Devil killed with such brutality."

"The Devil doesn't exist. Not anymore," I said, handing him back the photographs.

Michael boomed, "So you keep telling me. But I've met the demon, and I can assure you that he's real. Anyway, the victims were cynocephaly. In your travels, have you ever met any?"

"Humanoid bodies, dogs' heads," I confirmed. Michael nodded. "Yeah, I knew a few just after the war. They served as guards when Bella and I ... you know. But I haven't seen a cynocephalus in years. Why?" I asked.

"Because we also found this at the crime scene," he said, his voice uncharacteristically soft. He handed me the photo he had removed.

This one wasn't of a crime scene. It was an old black and white photo of Bella, standing with the Ambassador. They were both smiling and so filled with hope that their mission of peace would work. Although I had never seen this photograph before, I knew when and where it had been taken. They were standing in front of old machinery that would have made a 1950s *Frankenstein* set director drool with envy. Ancient lab equipment that was more alchemy than scientific, clunky mechanical gears meshed together and sparks of electrical current jumping from antenna to antenna—not that you could see the electricity move in the photo. I just knew because I'd been there once, helplessly watching Bella's death from behind a steel door.

Hellelujah—I wanted to be reminded of that place as much as I wanted to be drawn and quartered. Actually, I would have preferred the drawn-and-quartered option. At least that one included a foreseeable end to the pain.

Instinctively I reached up and grabbed the fake-silver chain with a twisty-tie wrapped around it. I rubbed the plastic between my fingers as I held the image for a long time, staring at the unwavering smile she wore no matter how bad it got. I guess that's why the Ambassador chose her—he needed a human counterpart to help his mission to broker peace between humans and Others, and Bella was, well ... Let's just say that few humans were as kind and as good as she was.

"Have you seen this photograph before?"

"No ..." I said, having to clear my throat. It stung to see her so happy when in just a few short months she would be dead. "How did you get this?"

Michael studied my face, as if looking for some hint of a lie in it. He must have found none, because he said, "It probably means nothing. After all, Bella and the—"

"One of these guys had it?" I asked, rising from my seat.

Michael nodded. "We have no way of knowing who originally possessed the photograph. We suspect it belonged to one of the victims, who most likely knew her during her time as a diplomat."

I nodded. "Like I said—some were guards, but no one I ever got close to."

"Very well, Human Jean-Luc. I thank you for your time," he said, standing.

"What? So that's it? You found a photo of my wife ...

my Bella … and a flyer with my hotel address on it, and you just, 'Thank you for your time,' boom, boom. Thunder, thunder. Come on. You've got to give me more than this."

"We'll keep you posted if anything comes up. In the meantime, should you remember anything, please do give us a call." He handed me one of his cards.

"I have your number," I said, leaving the card on his desk. "Just tell me if the hotel is in danger. I have guests and—"

"We do not believe so," Michael interrupted. "We believe that this is retribution for the cynocephaly failing to protect the Ambassador. But like I said, this is an ongoing investigation. We will keep you posted."

I gave Michael my best *Oh, really?* look, to which he answered, "I promise." A promise from an Other was as good as gold, and a promise from an archangel was even better.

I nodded and made to leave, pausing at the door.

"Yes," Michael bellowed. "Did you forget something?"

"The photograph. Can I have it?"

"It is evidence," he said. But when I didn't move he sighed and said, "After the investigation is closed I will see what I can do."

"Thank you."

Chapter 3
Do Caged Angels Sing?

I stepped out of Chief of Police Michael's office, my heart fluttering with anguish. Bella was the last person I expected to see at four a.m. in a police station, and I was struggling not to break down. But it was more than that. Someone had a picture of Bella. It drove me crazy thinking that some nutbar would be looking at her, thinking about her. I supposed that the photo could have belonged to one of the cynocephaly. Hell, it was even likely. The now expired Ambassador was somewhat of a celebrity amongst Others and his picture hung on many walls, like a velvet painting of Elvis. The Ambassador had done much good before some Fanatics set an explosion that ended his life, and there were many Others who still remembered him for trying.

However, if the photo of my Bella belonged to the killer, that meant he could have been part of the plot that ended Bella's and the Ambassador's lives all those years ago. After Bella died, I tried tracking down the group responsible, but all leads went cold. In the end, after spending three years hunting for her killer, all I had was a river of blood and was no closer to finding her killers. A part of me really hoped that the photo belonged to those elusive Fanatics and that our paths would finally cross. I would relish the second chance at avenging my dead wife.

But that probably would not come to pass—I'd spent all my second chances when Bella took me back. Twice. The first time was when I returned from my stint in the Army. And the second, well ... that was when she began haunting my dreams. Hallucination or not, Bella saved me.

I would have to put aside all thoughts of payback. That

was the old me. The new me was about helping Others. And right now, an Other was waiting for me to bail him out of jail.

Back in the main area, I approached Officer Steve and said, "OK, you can take me to Penemue now."

The Billy Goat Gruff stood on his hind legs, pulled out his clipboard and asked, "Jean-Luc Matthias?"

↔

Penemue sat in the drunk tank, expounding on the glory days of immortality lost, which was—according to him—another symptom of Mortal Madness. That, I was expecting. What I did not expect were the half dozen HuMan gang members that sat in the tank with him.

Penemue, unlike Michael, was just an angel (it's funny how natural those words were—*just an angel*, like that wasn't special enough), which meant that he was only eight feet high and had one pair of wings to Michael's three. He was well built, with the physique of a finely tuned bodybuilder, although these days Penemue was looking more like Homer Simpson than Arnold Schwarzenegger—if, that was, Homer had long beautiful blond hair and wore a tweed vest.

When we walked in, the leader of the HuMans perked up. "Come on, Officer. Let us go … We weren't fighting. Cross my heart," he said, making a little X over his heart. Their leader was a boy of eighteen affectionately known as EightBall. He had all the tell-tale sign of the HuMans: shaved head covered in tattoos of symbols that once meant something—the cross, the Star of David, the crescent moon, the Wheel of the Dharma, the nine-pointed star and a half dozen other symbols from dead or dying religions. As for his name, my guess was that it had something to do with the vertical infinity symbol tattooed right between his eyes. In the right light, it kind of looked like the number 8. To those with a limited imagination, his dark complexion combined with the tattoo made his head look like an eight ball. "We weren't fighting. We were having a disagreement, that's all," EightBall repeated.

Penemue sighed. "The boy is correct. We were merely having a disagreement as to whether or not I should exist. A debate that has raged on long before the GrandExodus, although for less literal reasons."

Officer Steve ignored this, pulling out keys and unlocking the cell. "I formally discharge Angel Penemue into your care," he said.

Before he could open the cell door, EightBall reached out and grabbed Officer Steve's hoof. "How come the pigeon gets out and we don't?"

"Because," Officer Steve said, withdrawing his hoof and pulling at the door, "the telephone numbers you provided either did not work or the person answering refused to come and collect you."

"Awww, come on, Baa Baa Black Sheep," EightBall said. Several of his fellow gang members chuckled at the insult. "We're just a bunch of poor kids abandoned by our parents, out looking for love in all the wrong places. Show us some love, Mutton, and let us out."

At EightBall's words, Penemue turned to the boy and said, "Not *abandoned*, young human. Orphaned. I tried to tell you, your mother and father would have never done such a thing ... Do you know why they named you Newton, young human? It is because—"

But before Penemue could finish, EightBall—whose real name was apparently Newton—punched him square in the nose, causing little streams of light to bleed out of his nostrils.

So *that* was why they were fighting—Penemue was doing his thing. Angels were created with a single purpose in mind—their one true "thing"——and Penemue's thing was knowing all that was written. That included the abstract, metaphorical writing of one's deeds on one's soul. And with Penemue's perfect memory it meant he could tell you everything about you, your parents, your extended family and all your relatives going back to the beginning of time, with an eerie precision. Sadly, Penemue's thing tended to freak the hell out of people.

The youngest Billy Goat Gruff produced a billy club from out of only the GoneGods knew where and in a stern voice bleated, "That's enough out of you hooligans. One more peep and I'll lock you up and throw away the key." Clearly the Sherlock that Steve studied was more Victorian than modern.

The gang burst out into laughter before settling down. "Look here, copper," EightBall said between chuckles, "he started it."

Penemue nodded. "Indeed I did. My apologies, young Human New—ahhh … EightBall."

Officer Steve huffed and opened the cell. Penemue, still stinking drunk, stumbled out. "Let's try and have a week where I don't see you in there. Think you can manage it?" the Gruff said, temporarily abandoning his Victorian English vernacular. I had to admit, I was impressed at how natural he sounded. Officer Steve got on all fours and walked away— hellelujah, he sounded like a cop; in the right light, he even looked like a cop … until he got on all fours and trotted away and reminded everyone he was a large goat.

"Come on, you giant lug," I said, trying to lead Penemue away. The angel used his wings to help balance himself, feathered tips pressing against the police station's linoleum floor.

"Hey, priest," EightBall said before we could walk away. I looked over as the young boy gestured for me to come close.

I should have walked away, ignored the kid, but instead I tugged at my collarless jacket and said, "Priest? I'm no priest. But I think you know that already."

"Yeah, we do," EightBall said, gesturing for me to lean in close. He looked around to see if Officer Steve was listening. "We know all about what you do, priest. We know where you and the pigeon live. And we know how much you love them freaks. The boys and I used to turn a blind eye to you insulting the human race by helping those rejects out, but no longer. Pigeon got us fired up and now we're going to fire *you* up. Soon as we get out of here, we're coming and we're going to rain holy, righteous hell on you and your hotel."

I sighed as if bored. Only two things got through to a kid like him: fear and respect. And since respect took time, I went for fear. "Fine ... but will you do me a favor?" I said in a steady, even tone. EightBall looked at me curiously. "When you come, just make sure you take me down first. I don't want any of your blood on my hands, and if I see you hurting someone living under my roof, well then ..." My voice trailed off, letting his imagination finish the thought.

EightBall looked at me, confused, a hint of fear touching his eyes. For a moment I thought maybe that was enough, that him seeing how deadly serious I was, how unafraid I was, would deter him from attacking. Like I said, I knew his type. EightBall's eyes hardened. "OK, old man," he said, nodding slowly, "I can do that for you. You go down first." He backed away from the bars, rejoining his gang on the

26

bench.

Hellelujah—so much for a peaceful resolution.

Chapter 4

Trains, Planes, Automobiles and Wings

Getting Penemue into the backseat of my old Plymouth was damn near impossible. In the end I had to rest him on his stomach. It wasn't far to the hotel and we could have walked it, but have you ever tried to act as a crutch for an eight-foot-tall, four-hundred-pound angel? The last time I tried, I nearly passed out from the effort, even though Penemue used his wings as crutches.

The arches of his wings jutted out the driver's side backseat window, while his taloned feet hung out the passenger's. It wasn't the best I could do, just the best I was willing to do. The angel had, after all, woken me from a very pleasant dream.

"Drambuie," he said as I pulled out of the police station parking lot.

Drambuie was a sickly sweet honey whiskey and it was the only thing the fallen angel drank, claiming it was the closest thing mortals had to Ambrosia. If you've ever had a Drambuie hangover, you'll know that the last thing you'd ever want to drink was Ambrosia. I honked at no one in particular as I hit a speed bump way too fast. The angel groaned, and I smiled at my over-developed sense of passive aggression. Like I said—pleasant dream.

"I think you've had quite enough of that stuff for one night," I said, taking a fast turn. Another groan from him. Another smile from me.

Penemue lifted one of his wings, pulled at a little canteen of Drambuie and began downing it. Seeing that turned my passive aggression to *aggressive* aggression. I reached in the back, yanked the canteen from his grimy claws and threw it out the window. "Hey," he protested. "I was drinking that."

"Yes, you were," I growled. "And what good did that do you? I'm bailing your ass out of jail at four in the morning, we got a gang of testosterone-jacked teenagers who want to turn you into a pincushion of light—and you want to drink some more. What's wrong with you?"

"The same thing that is wrong with all of us. Mortal Madness! For which death is the only known cure."

"Shut it," I said.

"Indeed," he said. A hand popped out from the back with another canteen in it. "Drink?"

"Drink? What? Where did you get that from?" I said, grabbing the second canteen and throwing it out the window.

"I have more than one wing, Human Jean-Luc," Penemue said matter-of-factly. "And layer after layer of feathers. I could stay dry in a tsunami. Did it once in a river of blood …"

"Penemue!" I barked. "Are you even listening to me?"

From my rear view mirror I could see the angel's face turn toward me. Our eyes met in the glass. "Jean, please. I hear you. All of Paradise Lot hears you."

"Why!"

"I wanted to play pool," Penemue said. "Figured I'd be good at the angles."

That was too much. I pulled the car to the side and threw the gear into Park. I turned to face the fallen angel and said, "I supported you when you were homeless. I covered for you when the cops came 'round looking for all the library books you stole. I lied for you when your makeshift distillery blew up and I took care of you when you sprained your wing playing Santa Claus and got stuck in a chimney."

"St. Nick, and it was an industrial shoot and I was trying

to escape a pack of guard dogs with a taste for the divine."

"Whatever!" I shouted. "The point is, you were laid up for three months while I fed, watered and Drambuie. I think I've earned enough credit to know why! Why would you mess with them? Why would you go to the HuMans' headquarters? Why? Why? Why!"

"Because …" Penemue hesitated. "Because I wanted to apologize."

"To who?" I asked.

"To Newton. EightBall, I mean."

I had expected a lot of clever answers from the angel, but the thought that he'd apologize to anyone for anything left me flabbergasted. Eventually I asked, "For what?"

"For what?" Penemue echoed. "Let's see … Perhaps I wanted to apologize for burning down his house. Or perhaps it was because I felt guilty for stealing his future and turning him into an orphan. Or perhaps I wanted to say sorry for killing his parents."

That last comment shut me up. The two of us drove in silence until the angel eventually broke it. "Killing his parents, Jean-Luc. Even for a human, you are daft. During the GrandExodus, I fell on his home and killed his parents. For that, I felt I at least owed him an apology, even if it is thirteen years too late."

So that was what this was all about. Others were just as shocked by the gods leaving, so much so that most didn't show up in the best of moods. In Australia, scores of bunyips came out of the sea. In Japan, yūrei descended Mt. Fuji. Giants wandered out of Stonehenge, and in Oxford angry dwarves walked out of some poor guy's chimney. And those were the nicer arrivals. Sadly, in most places Others showed up in a more Biblical fashion.

Volcanoes spewed dragons and tornadoes were filled

with shrieking banshees. Oceans boiled and skies turned blood red. In Paris, the earth opened up, swallowing the Arc de Triomphe de l'Étoile as ghouls and orcs streamed out in droves, attacking everything and anything that was unlucky enough to have been nearby. In Greece, minotaurs leveled the Parthenon. In China, the Jade Emperor's army wiped out entire villages before their rage finally subsided.

And as for Paradise Lot? Well, the sky opened up and legions of angels fell onto my city like comets. One of those comets killed PopPop, making me an orphan. Another comet did the same to EightBall.

More fluorescent tears streamed down Penemue's face as he spoke. "When I was ejected from Heaven, I fell—and not for the first time, mind you—onto this cursed city … and right onto the apartment building where young Human Newton's parents resided. I didn't mean to, but as anyone who has fallen can tell you, one does not always have control over one's trajectory." He spoke the last sentence with a pompous air, trying to hide his shame.

"For days, I stood out on the Palisade," Penemue continued, "trying to work up the courage to speak to the young boy. When I saw him this evening, laughing with his friends, I thought to myself that today would be the day I apologized—but before I could say anything, the gang of boys just attacked, and … well, you know the rest."

I didn't know what to say. Penemue's guilt for accidentally killing EightBall's parents was consuming him. This was not the kind of guilt that went away with a confession or even self-destruction. Believe me, I know. This kind of guilt stalked you, nipping away at your heels little by little until you were driven mad. And there was nothing I could say or do to console my friend.

Penemue looked up and said, "Did you know that young

Human Newton was considered a child prodigy? At the age of eight he could play the entire Fifth Symphony with nary an error. His parents were so proud that they saved every penny they could to encourage his talent. Who knows what he could have accomplished had I not stolen his future from him?"

"It's not your fault," I said. "It's *theirs*." I jerked my head at the car roof, indicating the gods. "For leaving. For the way they left."

"Perhaps ..." he said, his voice drifting off. "But I do have wings, and had I been just a little bit faster or more aware, I might have fallen elsewhere." And with that fell more fluorescent tears, until the twice-fallen angel fell once more into sleep.

Chapter 5

Lust or Love

We drove home, a soft snore emanating from the backseat. After hearing Penemue's confession, I knew that the EightBall problem wasn't going away. Beyond the little annoyance that the HuMans were a violent group of Otherphobes who would start targeting the One Spire Hotel, this was an issue of penance for the twice-fallen angel. How could he blame himself for their death? It wasn't his fault that he was evicted from Hell without warning. And it wasn't his fault that his entry to the mortal realm happened to be over Paradise Lot. But those were rational arguments for a much larger problem, and as one who has more blood on his hands than a thousand good deeds could wash off, when it came to seeking redemption, rationality was not the nail on which you hung your coat.

Redemption is reliant on being forgiven, and I seriously doubted that EightBall would ever forgive Penemue. Even if he did, Penemue would never forgive himself. Although I felt for my friend's plight, I had a more practical issue to deal with—EightBall would come for him, and soon. Penemue was a fallen angel with a massive amount of power, both physical and magical; I knew that he would suffer a thousand strikes and still not be tempted to lift a finger against a human. So was his way. So was the way of so many Others hated by my fear-mongering species. He might even welcome the attack, seeing it as a blood-for-blood kind of deal—like I said, redemption wasn't rational. But Penemue was only *one* of the Others who lived at One Spire Hotel, and what he did put them in danger as well. His confession, although noble, was also selfish.

I nervously thumbed the industrial heavy-plastic twist-tie I'd coiled around a plain silver chain I always wore. Other than being designed to hold together electric wires in all temperatures, there was nothing special about it except that once-upon-a-time I used it as an engagement ring when I proposed to Bella. At seventeen, I was in a hurry and didn't have any money to buy a real ring. That night I knew it was now or never, so I raided the house until I found the twisty tie. Then I got down on one knee on a beach near Paradise Lot and proposed. Lucky for me, Bella thought the twisty-tie was the most romantic thing ever. I don't know why and don't care. All I know is I was damn lucky to have found Bella. I had to hand it to the twisty-tie makers, they knew how to build something to last. I touched the last tangible symbol I had for Bella as I thought about Penemue's current dilemma. I had always found cruising a great way to clear my head. But even after taking the really long way home, I had nothing. After circling the block three times, I parked in front of my hotel and left the slumbering angel in the car— no point in trying to carry his celestial ass. Besides, the thought of trying to get him inside made my already sore head throb.

As I walked inside, the bell above the front door faithfully jingled. With a whoop, I sat behind the secondhand IKEA desk that served as my reception. Whatever would happen next, I would deal with it—if not only to protect my friend, but also the other Others living in my hotel. After all, I once made a promise to this girl whom I love very much.

I surveyed my desk. Bills, bills, bills and more bills. Electricity, water, gas, unpaid taxes—hell, one of them was a garbage-collection bill for unnatural biowaste left in a dumpster by the demigod CaCa who lived in my basement. There was a particularly vile letter from the landlord stating, in no uncertain terms, that he'd "rain holy hell on my ass" if I missed another rent payment. Well, screw him … He was a racist, or rather an Otherist, and I was the only human stubborn or stupid enough to take on this place. Given his limited options, I knew he would always choose to rent to a late-paying human than a prompt, responsible Other. Before Hell was shut down, there was a special kind of place for assholes like him.

Speaking of Hell and assholes, what happened to all the human souls that didn't return after the GrandExodus? Not a single human returned. Ghosts and ghouls came in legions, but the actual Heaven and Hell occupants—not one came back. Why? No one knows. There are two theories as to what happened to them: either they were taken with the gods, or they were extinguished. But whenever you start to think about why the gods did what they did, questions only lead to more questions. Screw it—I didn't have time to engage in a solo philosophical debate. With my growing debt, there was a real chance I couldn't keep this place open for another month, let alone the rest of the year. Unless I found a way to pay some of these bills off and a steady flow of income, I was sunk. Bella—damn it—how did you manage to keep this place above water?

"Ahem," a voice said behind me. I didn't need to turn around to know it was Judith, my once human, but now poltergeist, mother-in-law. I had once joked with Bella that if anyone hated me enough to come back from the dead to haunt me, it would have been her mom. Seems the joke was on me, because that's exactly what she did. After the GrandExodus happened and the magic ceased, Judith rematerialized. Suddenly all those moments when I'd go cold for no reason or socks went missing from the wash made sense.

"Judith, I'm sorry if I woke you," I said, "but it's five in the morning, so if this can wait ..."

The ghost gave me a disapproving look. "It's doing it again," she interrupted, her voice dripping with disdain.

I didn't need clarification—she was referring to Astarte, the succubus who lived in room 5. For the uninitiated, a succubus is a creature that feeds off of sex, literally sucking your life's energy out of you. Like a vampire, but with orgasms. Lots of orgasms. Of course, these days she no longer fed directly from sexual energy—but that didn't mean she still didn't get what she needed from sex. She used her talents to earn money, which she used in turn to purchase what she needed to survive—food, water, shelter. Lingerie. As far as Astarte was concerned, very little had changed in this new GoneGod world.

Judith sucked air through her ectoplasmic teeth. "All that groaning, it is simply unnatural." Bold words from a woman who floated.

"Fine, fine," I said, "I'll talk to her."

"Please see that you do," Judith said, turning to drift upstairs.

↔

Judith watched from her door as I knocked on room 5. From inside I could hear continuous sounds of moaning and groaning as several voices continued their nightly pleasure, undisturbed by my knock. I banged on the door again, louder this time. The voices stopped for a moment; there was a rustling pause, then the moaning quickly reached its previous crescendo.

"Astarte," I yelled.

Before I could knock again, the Other opened the door.

When she saw me, she leaned against its frame as if presenting herself to me. She was wearing a nightgown that accentuated lean, small hips that subtly suggested that if you were horizontal and near them, all would be right with the world. Lush, brunette tresses rested perfectly on her shoulders. She wore an elegant, lacy tank top just transparent enough that a hint of her dark nipples peeked through from atop her small, perfect, perky breasts.

I looked past her and saw several writhing bodies, all intertwined in the ecstasy embrace she hosted. She closed the door just enough so that I could no longer see the bodies, but wide enough that I could hear all the bliss going on inside. From within, a distant voice said, "Astarte, where are …?" The voice drew in a breath before slowly exhaling with a flesh-filled "Oh …"

Astarte gave me a knowing smile as I tried to focus on her. She pulled out a cigarette from only the GoneGods knew where and placed it between ruby lips—lips that could do a lot more than hold a cigarette. Lips that most men would sell their left foot to have on theirs. Fire from her lighter illuminated rosy cheeks that bracketed her sensual nature with a false sense of innocence.

There was nothing innocent about Astarte.

"No smoking inside, Astarte. You know that," I said, doing my best to not look at the A-cup angel's breasts. I reminded myself that there was no evidence that she was actually a *she*. And without the tell-tale signs of gender, this Other skirted the edges of male-female perfectly. Breasts that may or may not exist underneath a loosely fitting nightshirt. A long sensual neck with enough bulge to it that it might be an Adam's apple—but, then again, might not. Arms that were muscular but tender, hair that was lush but somehow masculine. Not that being androgynous did anything to

37

diminish this Other, who was wildly tantalizing. I had no doubt that there were many who saw Astarte as male, female and Other, and reminded myself that I only saw Astarte as a *she* because, well … I like boobs. There, I said it.

"Yes?" Astarte said, taking a long drag on her cigarette.

"Come on," I said, "you know the rules. Put it out."

"Oh my, Jean—always with the rules." She let out a sensuous puff of white smoke that just made you wish you were in her cloud of heaven. I shot her a look that said it wasn't working. I was lying. She opened the door just wide enough for me to see four other bodies all writhing and reeling, and dropped her cigarette into a lipstick-stained wineglass. "Happy?" she asked as she blocked my view again.

I nodded and said, "There's been a complaint about the …" But before I could say "noise," a loud groan bellowed out of the room, making my point for me.

Astarte chuckled. "I told her she could join," she said, looking at Judith behind me. "One without legs could be an interesting … asset."

Judith snorted with disgust and floated through the door.

Astarte chuckled and then, looking me up and down, she gave me a disapproving look. "You look like hell."

"Headache and Penemue," I said. I didn't need to say more.

"What has that devil done now?" Astarte chuckled, her posture too perfect. When she stood, her back arched just enough to push out her breasts, accentuating them so that any sane human wondered exactly what they must look like underneath that delicate sheath of lace. But it was more than that. The way she held herself made every article of scanty clothing hang on her in such a way that pronounced every curve, every dimple, every bump, driving her admirers to a maddening frenzy of lust. She did not light a cigarette, she ignited it. She did not brush back her hair, she sculpted it. She did not smile at you, she *inflamed* you.

Everything about her screamed desire, and by the GoneGods I was not immune. I looked at her and wanted nothing more than to embrace her for a few perfect moments of unbridled ecstasy. But that was just it. It was not love, it was lust. It was not passion she inspired, but desire. And if you could see her in that light, you could see that the way she held herself—the way she gestured, walked, spoke— was an unnatural lie designed to capture her quarry. She was a predator, and your desire was her prey.

Still—she was beautiful.

"Picked a fight with the HuMans," I said in answer to Astarte's question, figuring it was best to warn my guests of what might come.

"Oh, darling," she sighed. "Is it serious?" The words slipped off her tongue with a hint of a Parisian accent coloring her voice. I doubted she ever spent any time in France and I was pretty sure that her accent was the side effect of me once confessing a particular love for the way French women spoke. The introduction of the accent had been subtle, and if it weren't for my experience with Others, I might have never noticed. Still, despite noticing, the accent was a nice touch to her seductive dance. Hearing her speak aroused me in ways that made me doubt why I remained loyal to the dream of my wife.

I nodded.

"What are you going to do about it?" she said, her tone demanding. Once-upon-a-time, Astarte was a demigoddess, worshiped by thousands, lusted after by more. She was used to getting her way, commanding people to do her will. Some habits die hard.

I thought about telling her to shove it and deal with her own battles. That I was done fighting their battles for them. But I could see that her forcefulness came from fear. After living thousands of years unable to be hurt, the fear that some kids with a baseball bat would come knocking on your door took on a completely different nuance. It wasn't her fault that Penemue got drunk and did what he did. And it wasn't her fault that she was a lover, not a fighter. "You could offer them a freebie?" I joked.

Astarte laughed at the suggestion. I mean really laughed, clutching her stomach, her cheeks turning rosy red. Her laughter seemed to turn off the sultry sex-goddess and leave a vulnerable, beautiful, real woman in its place. I don't think she'd ever looked as lovely as she did at that moment. "Oh, Human Jean," she said, "you are a delight. An evening with me would change them forever, but I fear that I am not what they want."

"What? Do you think they'd turn you down?"

She gave me a look that a thousand cold showers couldn't reverse. "No one turns me down," she said. "But after ... well, that's another story."

Astarte was right. She wasn't what they wanted, and once the blood was rerouted back to their big heads, they would resume their path of carnage. I nodded. "Well, I'll figure something out. Until then, will you keep it down?"

"Cross my heart," she said, crossing something far too low to be a heart. "Now if you don't mind, I really must say goodnight, unless of course you want to join ..." She pushed the door open, revealing bodies which would have required an autopsy to figure out where one body stopped and another began.

"Thanks," I said, summoning all the willpower I had,

"but lust isn't what I need right now."

Astarte glared at me before opening the door wide, revealing the full glory of the orgy inside. "Why not?" the succubus said in a harsh tone. "You say it like there is something wrong with Lust. What would you prefer? *Love?*" She laughed at the word. "I could never be so cruel. Love is not the doe-eyed virgin you believe her to be. Love is always hungry. Love is always wanting. Love is not rational. Love does not compromise. And Love is not happy simply possessing you. She wants to own you. Control you. Be you. The first murder was because of Love. And I promise you that the last of your kind will die for her.

"Love is the single-minded hunter who consumes its prey, sucking it of all its worth, and then seeks another. Love is only happy when you are on your knees, begging her to stay. And Love will walk away, leaving you to your self-pity just to feel your 'need.'

"Love is addiction, leaving you always wanting more.

"Love is a disease for which there is no cure.

"But Lust ... Lust is the tender paramour that wants nothing more of you than what you are now. Lust does not seek some idealized fictional version of yourself, nor does she try to mold you into that false creation.

"Lust is present, Lust is attentive and Lust is now.

"And when now is over, Lust moves on, harming you no more than a pleasant memory harms a child.

"But most importantly," Astarte said, pulling out an envelope of money from only the GoneGods knew where, "Lust pays your bills.

"Now tell me, Human Jean, what's so wrong about Lust?"

"Well," I said, feeling myself blush, "when you put it that way ..."

Chapter 6

The Head of the Pin is Crowded

Given the fun, fun, *fun* of the last four hours, I decided that a couple hours of sleep would be a good idea. I lay down under my duvet—extra fluffy—and closed my eyes, thinking that being bone-tired was all I needed to fall asleep. Stupid. Like sleep would come to me now. Sure, the woman of my dreams, both literally and figuratively, was waiting for me once I drew back the curtain of night, but come on! After an evening of dealing with Penemue and the imminent threat of the HuMans, appeasing my tyrannical ghost of a mother-in-law and summoning every ounce of self-restraint to not join an orgy with a succubus that I knew would have rocked my world with fifty shades of rainbow. Every fluid, hormone and muscle was revving at maximum, and nothing short of a baseball bat to the head would put me under. And I doubted that would work.

So I did what I did every night I couldn't sleep. I played with myself. No, not like that. Amongst my many quirks, I collect old toys. I have almost the entire collection of the original Transformers, a bunch of He-Mans, some GoBots, an Etch A Sketch, an entire village of Smurfs and a bunch of other toys that went extinct as soon as your phone let you fling about angry birds. Tonight I staged a battle between Voltron and the G.I. Joes, letting my subconscious mull over all my problems while the Red Lion flanked Snake Eyes.

As Red Lion pounced I thought about the HuMans and Penemue, about my bills and complaints about the noise. I thought about everything that was wrong except the one thing that was really bothering me. You see, dealing with the Others that lived in the One Spire Hotel was like being a stage manager for the cast of *The Muppet Show*, and over the years I'd gotten used to that. As for those pictures that Michael showed me—well, I'd seen worse. Much, much worse.

So why were the Defenders of the Universe and Joes at each other's throats? Because of Bella. I hated seeing her there, with her wide hopeful smile as she stood next to that damned Ambassador.

Questions swam in my head. Where did the photo come from? Why was it in Paradise Lot? Did it have anything to do with her death? What did it have to do with me? And what the hell was up with that flyer? "What is 'Coping with Mortality' anyway?" I cried out loud, the last question spilling out of me.

A flicker came from the right eye of my Castle Grayskull just before its little plastic drawbridge lowered and a three-inch-tall golden fairy walked out, rubbing her eyes.

"Sorry I woke you, TinkerBelle," I said to the golden fairy.

I had no idea if her real name was TinkerBelle, and since she couldn't speak, she had no way of telling me. But in the six years we'd lived together, she'd never once complained. She either was unaware of *Peter Pan* or saw the name as a compliment. As for why I named her TinkerBelle ... well, how many three-inch-tall golden fairies do you know?

Her dragonfly wings fluttered and she flew until she was close enough to me that I could see her annoyed face—which I suspect was the point.

By way of an apology, I said, "Penemue got arrested again." Tink gave me a knowing look that said she knew that wasn't everything. A look that said, *And ...*

"OK, OK." I lifted my hands up in front of me in a defensive stance. "When I was at the police station, the archangel Michael showed me some pictures."

Tink did two flips in front of me before fluttering up to my face and jutting out her arms in a bodybuilder's stance, puffing out her cheeks.

"Yeah, him."

Tink never left the hotel, staying out of sight whenever an Other came around. But it was more than being shy that kept her out of sight. As far as I understood—and I admit I didn't know much—TinkerBelle was a legend of a legend. A myth of a myth. To Others, Tink was as unbelievable as Medusa, Loch Ness and Big Foot had once been to humans. And I was the only living creature that knew of her existence. I met Tink at the lowest moment of my life, and I don't think I would be standing here if it wasn't for her immense capacity to forgive. I owed the fairy a lot—I would see myself die from a hundred thousand paper cuts before I let any harm come to this fable of a fable.

Tink gestured, *So what?*

"Well ... one of the photos was of Bella."

Tink's eyes widened in surprise. She pointed toward her wrist before taking a picture with an imaginary camera.

"When was it taken?" I guessed. Tink nodded. "The day she died."

Concern painted across her golden face. Her eyes narrowed and she shrugged, pointing at me and then at her own head. "How do I know?" I asked. Again, Tink nodded. Hey, what can I say? After years of playing charades with the fairy, I was pretty good.

I told Tink all about the photo and how I recognized the place from its background—modern equipment surrounded by ancient gears and apparatus, like she was standing in an updated version of Dr. Frankenstein's lab. Bella died in that place exactly one year after the Ambassador came to this very hotel and convinced her to join him on his crusade of peace. The devil and his promises.

Tink listened, but it wasn't until I mentioned the *Keep Evolving* flyer that she put up a hand, gesturing for me to repeat myself. "Yeah—he showed me this advert for a seminar that I am supposedly throwing at the hotel."

And are you? she gestured. Don't ask me how she did it or how I guessed it—sometimes I think she cheated and burned a bit of time to telepathically give me the answer.

"No," I exclaimed.

She shrugged, rolling her eyes. "Yes, I'm sure," I said.

Her hand hit her forehead in a *Duh!* gesture, and her wings stopped fluttering and started flapping. Like bird's wings. Or angel wings.

"How could I be so stupid?" I said. There was only one creature brazen enough to organize an event at my hotel without informing me. Angel Miral. "You're a genius!" I said.

Tink blew on the backs of her fingernails before wiping them on her chest. She whisked off to the left turret of Castle Grayskull, pulling the drawbridge back up as she entered her home. With a flicker, the castle went dark.

"Goodnight, Tink," I said, putting on my black collarless jacket and heading for the door.

I was off to confront Miral. I always thought angels were supposed to offer humans comfort and care, but to me they were all just a pain in the ass.

Chapter 7

White Wings, White Coat

Miral worked at St. Mercy Hospital, which was a twenty minute walk from the hotel. I would have driven there, but Penemue still snored away in the backseat of my car. Better to walk. Besides, dawn was nearly here, and with the light, Paradise Lot came to life.

↔

Paradise Lot was located on an island roughly half the size of Manhattan. Although once-upon-a-time an affluent human city, given how violently the Others appeared over its skies, the island quickly became an unofficial refugee camp for Others. After the war, humans upgraded Paradise Lot from an unofficial Ellis Island of sorts to an official Ellis Island-*cum*-refugee camp-*cum*-Gaza Strip where all the Others got official-looking documents which did not allow them to travel, vote, own land or legally marry. They could, however, use the ID to pay taxes.

"Give me your tired, your poor, your huddled masses yearning to breathe free, the wretched refuse of your teeming shore. Send these, the homeless, tempest-tossed to me, I lift my lamp beside the golden door!"

Yeah, right. More like, "We welcome all you OnceImmortal creatures of myth and legend. We give you the least of what we have to offer. Please do not ask for more."

Any way you cut it, Paradise Lot was a slum. The only difference was that in this slum, winos had angel wings and the homeless slept in discarded lamps.

That said, for those who could afford it, Paradise Lot

did have the kind of establishments that appealed to and their particular tastes. The Stalker Steakhou example, was a restaurant that catered to werewolv__ and other Others that liked to actually hunt their meals. Then there was the Red Rooster, an extremely impractical place to go unless you knew how to perch. For culture, you could watch an Eleven play at Adawin's Playhouse—that is if you had the time to spare. The average play lasted three weeks and made Japanese kabuki feel like you're watching the latest *Fast & Furious* movie on fast-forward.

And then there were the Others' places of worship. Churches, mosques and synagogues, as well as temples, shrines and sanctuaries of the ancient or forgotten, were open day and night, welcoming all practitioners if they were willing to dedicate themselves to the single purpose of praying the gods back.

The gods have yet to answer and in that way, not much is different between the GoneGod world and its silent past.

↔

I got to the hospital and walked into the emergency room where Miral worked. It was, as always, filled with a nice cross-section of Paradise Lot's inhabitants. Fairies, pixies, gargoyles, and a nymph with both arms badly broken. They were all vying for attention from the understaffed, overworked nurses and doctors.

The average Other wasn't very good at standing in line, as was evident by them crowding some poor fairy receptionist who kept insisting they fill out a form first. Unfortunately, the average Other wasn't very good at filling out forms either, as most of them only knew how to read or write in an obscure language that no one but their kin could read.

And then there were the Onces.

Onces were the ones that once-upon-a-time were somebody—or something. They were the dukes and duchesses, the princes and princesses of Olympus, Tartarus, Hades and the several dozen other realms that once-upon-a-time meant something. And now that they were lowly commoners, just as mortal as the next guy, well—they didn't take kindly to being asked to sign their name. Some laws of nature were all too true—the higher you are, the harder you fall.

"I am Asal of the Vanir," cried out a half-man, half-donkey creature. The fairy receiptonist stared at the onocentaur, evidently unimpressed. The Once snorted, continuing nonetheless. "Yes, the very Asal of the Vanir who stood against the invading Æsir."

The receptionist, still unimpressed, handed his human half a form and said in a detached voice, "And I am Elsvir the Reception-Desk Fairy who once stood against an invading horde of asses who think they're better than everyone else. Next!"

Asal stomped his hooves and brayed, "Well, I never … If it wasn't for me, you would be speaking orc garble, eating babies for lunch and enjoying the obsessive drumming those deformed Northerners never seem to get enough of." The onocentaur shuddered at the thought. "As a reward for my deeds, the All Father assigned me to be Kvasir's steed. For nearly a century I carried Kvasir, the wisest of all men, on my back before—"

"The form," the receptionist said.

"But I drank from the Mead of Poetry."

"Next."

Normally I'd leave a Once to their rants and inevitable

humiliation, but Asal looked so sad, his donkey ears drooping, his human face downtrodden as he stared at the form. Besides, he held the paper upside down. I grabbed it from him and said, "Here, let me do it." Sometimes it really sucks that there's no Heaven, because if there was, I'd get a palace for sure.

He looked down at me—not hard given that he was basically a horse—and said, "Finally, a mortal that understands protocol."

"Indeed," I said, stretching out the word to an unnatural length. Sarcasm.

"Yes, indeed!" the onocentaur responded with much enthusiasm. Sarcasm was wasted on Others. "The name is Asal of—"

"Of the Vanir, yes, I've heard."

"So you know of my deeds." The gleam in his eye was positively palpable, and I'm a sucker for a pathetic smile. I nodded. Why not? It probably made his week.

He hee-hawed and dug his hind hooves into the carpet and bowed, right leg tucked behind his left foot in an elegant bow. "Young master …?"

"Jean."

"Jean … I am forever in your debt. Should ever you need the services of Asal, the great Ass of Kvasir, all you must do is call out my name."

"Thanks," I said, pointing at the form, "but right now the only service I need from you is to answer a few standard questions."

↔

I had just finished Asal's form when the room went quiet. Ever been to a party when suddenly everything went quiet and someone broke the silence with "An angel passes by"? Well, it's more literal than you'd think. An angel did pass by. Rather, walked in. Miral walked into the waiting room, her every step holding a dancer's polish. Her dovelike wings hunched over her shoulders, forming a doctor's coat, tiny linoleum name tag with the words *Resident on Call* pinned to them. As soon as she entered, all of the waiting Others ran up to her, hands—and claws, tentacles, etc.—outstretched. Miral ignored them all, looking over the crowd—not hard to do, as she was seven feet tall—and called out, "Sparkles. Miss Rainbow Sparkles, of Coca-Cola?" A sickly-looking pixie fluttered up from her seat, gripping her stomach as she flew over to Miral.

"Miral," I said, chasing after her, "I need to speak to you."

She did not turn around as she headed to her office. "Need, Jean, is very much a matter of perspective. Is your need greater than theirs?" she asked, pointing to the overrun waiting room. Her voice came out even and steady, her every word spoken with a refinement that mirrored her grace of movement.

"But—"

"But *nothing*," Miral said, extending her hand so that the sickly pixie could rest on it. "My experience is that *need* is often mistaken for *want*. What I want is more time. What I need is more help." And with that Miral turned on her heel and left the waiting room to examine the pixie, and me to reflect on my shame. Damn, the angel was good.

↔

After being shamed by Miral, I decided that I would give her a bit of what she needed by helping. I clicked a pen and

,standing in the middle of the waiting room, announced, "OK, I'll fill out forms." For the briefest of moments I felt what it must be like to be Mick Jagger. The Others didn't just come over—they rushed me, each one of them shoving their form in my face, begging that they be first. I literally had to stand on a chair to get out of the crowd. Then, summoning my most commanding voice, I said, "One at a time."

That had as much effect as telling a group of seagulls not to eat the discarded bread. The rush only got more overwhelming, and it didn't stop until I yelled, "I will only help those who are quiet! … And sitting!" For good measure I pushed through the crowd and went over to the only Other that had not rushed me—a satyr with a nasty gash on his head.

The Others obeyed. Literally. Every one of them went quiet, sitting down not on an empty chair but exactly where they had been standing.

"On the chairs."

A whirlwind of wings, feet and hooves filled the room as the Others played a version of musical chairs.

Hellelujah!

When they were quiet and somewhat patient, I went around filling out forms. Most of them were complaining about stomach cramps and headaches. Some complained of fatigue. Truth was, most of these Others weren't really sick, they were just bad at being mortal. They still tried to live by the same rules that governed them for thousands of years before, and this new world was so cumbersome with all the things they had to remember. Things like eating, hydrating, sleeping. Shitting. You'd be surprised how many Others suffered from self-imposed constipation pains simply because they couldn't live with the daily indignity of a morning poo.

I must have filled out two dozen forms when Miral walked in and announced, "Fellow Fallen—those of you who have swollen stomachs and aching heads, please follow my associate to the mess hall and bathrooms." Half of the Others left. "Those of you with dry tongues, please head over to the water fountain and drink. And those of you with blurry vision, go home and sleep."

The room cleared out, leaving behind the nymph with the broken arms and the satyr with the nasty head wound. Both of whom went off with other doctors, leaving me alone with Miral.

"I do that twice a night," she said with a cunning smile, and led me to her office.

↔

For the second time today, I sat across a desk from an angel. "Thanks, Miral," I started. "I won't take much of your time. I just wanted to ask you—"

"Jean, what would you say if I told you I have a way to solve all your problems?"

I blinked twice. "I'd probably tell you that you're spending way too much time watching infomercials."

"No, silly," she said, pulling out a flyer with the words *Keep Evolving* on it. It was the same damn flyer they found from the crime scene.

"Aha! I knew you were behind this!" I cried out, proud of my detective skills, then remembered it was really Tink who figured it out. Still, Miral didn't have to know that.

Miral rolled her eyes, pulling out a manila folder and opening it in front of me. I was hesitant to look. The last time an angel gave me a manila anything, I didn't like what I saw. This was no different. In it was a bunch of empty boxes to be filled out for the OIF—the Other Integration Fund.

"Oh, great. More forms," I said, closing the folder.

She opened it up again. "They are accepting another round of applications. And I know that your bills are mounting up. This will save you."

The OIF was a government-run initiative. A human government initiative, which meant a lot of hoops to jump through, a lot of paperwork to fill out with a shit-ton of *measurable*s and *deliverable*s. Not to mention milestones and action plans. I danced with them once before and all I got in the end was sore feet. Miral, like so many Others, didn't get human bureaucracy. It seems that Heaven didn't really have paperwork.

"I told you, I already tried with the OIF. They pulled the funding as soon as Bella … you know …"

"Yes, because all you did was offer Others a place to sleep. Bella, she offered seminars, talks, classes. You barely offer clean sheets."

Now it was my turn to roll my eyes.

"Don't you see?" Miral continued. "This is a second chance. If the One Spire combines forces with St. Mercy Hospital, throwing weekly seminars on coping with mortality, the OIF will reinstate your funding."

"I don't know," I said. It would be great to get a bit of cash coming in. As it stood I was barely making ends meet. I shook my head. "I've been down this path before and—"

"You're already doing it. I've called the OIF. They said that all you need to do is throw one seminar a week. That will be enough to gain access to the funding." She pointed at the flyer. "We got a full house."

"Resistance is futile," I said in my best Borg voice.

"Resistance is pointless," she said, evidently not a *Star*

Trek fan. "I've taken care of everything. All you have to do is set up and—"

"Don't say it," I said.

"Bake cookies."

"I hate baking," I protested.

"Think of it as penance. Now, tell me—what did you want to see me about?"

Chapter 8

Blessed Be He

I told Miral about Michael and finding the flyer. I also found myself telling her about Penemue and the HuMans, about Judith and Astarte and the damn headache I'd had since waking up that morning. Hell, there must be something about women with wings; they can always get me talking. Once I started, I opened up to the angel, telling her about every pain, problem and pathetic thought that rattled around in that empty canister I called my skull. It felt good to get it all off my chest, and with every word I spoke, I felt my burdens lifting.

I told her everything except about my dreams of Bella. Some things were private, damn it, and angel of mercy or not, she did not have full reign over all that occupied my mind.

After I finished unburdening myself, I went silent, expecting, hoping, praying for some kind of ancient divine wisdom that would cure all. But she didn't say a word. She just stared at me for a long, long time before finally standing up and walking over to her cupboard and offering me a Tylenol.

"This is for your headache," she said.

I took the pill and said, "The murders? Any thoughts on that?"

"Either it is a Fanatic, or her killer returns. Only time will reveal which it is."

"Time. You're the once-captain of God's army and a being older than solid objects, and all you can tell me is 'Be patient'?"

"Indeed. And it gets better than that. For the rest of

your problems I recommend faith," Miral said as she ushered me out her door.

"Faith in what?" I said. "They're gone, remember."

"Even when they were here, faith was never about them. It was always about having faith in yourself," Miral said, giving me a knowing smile.

"So that's it? Faith and patience."

"Yes." Then, as if as an afterthought, she added, "Oh, and let the cookie dough sit for at least half an hour. That way the cookies will come out all the more fluffy."

↔

I left Miral's office, annoyed at having no more answers to any of my problems, and headed into the reception where I was greeted by a low, reverent murmuring.

"It is he—the Form Filler."

"Do you think he will come to our aid?"

"Approach with caution."

"Do not make eye contact."

"Beware his mighty pen."

"Be humble. And remember to SIT!"

Several Others approached, heads hanging low, eyes averted, clipboards outstretched. Hellelujah!

A blue-tinged jinni at the head of the line rushed over. He knelt before me and said in a reverent voice, "O wise and wondrous Form Filler, if you should bless us this early summer morning, we would ever be in your debt. I shall whisper your name in seashells and cast them in the ocean so that all the creatures of the beneath will know your name."

A garden gnome no taller than six inches scurried up the wall, his tiny climbing spikes dotting the wall. When he was eye level he said, "And I shall enter the beehive in the central park and slay the pollen lovers' queen in thy name."

And with that, all the Others offered me various honors. It wasn't until an ahuizotl barked "And I shall offer a human sacrifice!" that I intervened.

"No, no, no! There'll be no seashell throwing, no bee slaying, and certainly no human sacrifices." I pointed at the Aztec demon dog to emphasize how serious I was about not killing people. The dog lowered his head in embarrassment and frustration, partly because I refused his gift, but mostly because he didn't have an excuse to rip apart a human.

I looked at my watch—seven a.m. I was exhausted, overworked and in desperate need to bake four dozen chocolate chip and macadamia nut cookies. I simply didn't have time for this. "Hellelujah," I muttered, grabbing the jinni's clipboard.

↔

I must have gotten through eight more clipboards when the lights flickered. Just outside the sliding glass doors of the reception, I saw an Other standing there, staring at me with an uncomfortable intensity. His arms were longer than normal, as were his neck, fingers and teeth. Hell, everything was just a bit too big, too long, too prominent for what could have passed as an otherwise normal human frame.

Our eyes met. He smiled, the edges of his lips almost literally touching his eyes. Massive, blocky teeth reflected the hospital's fluorescent lights, and I got an eerie *The-better-to-eat-you-with* sense from this Other.

A popobawa hung upside down from the ceiling and I noticed it was writing its own name in the correct place. "You," I said, looking into the horizontal slits it called eyes. The thing focused on me and the horizontal slits rotated until they were vertical. I shuddered. "Can you write?" I asked.

"Yes," it clicked.

"English, I mean."

"Yes." It blinked. Well, not blinked so much as rotated the slits that were its eyes another three hundred and sixty degrees.

"Good, you are the new ... Master Form Filler." I handed over the clipboard in an exaggerated, ceremonial passing-of-the-mantle that resembled a half-hearted signing of the cross followed by what probably looked like me chasing away an invisible bee. The creature beamed. I don't mean "smiled," "danced with joy," or "clicked in glorious triumph." I mean it actually emanated light like a firefly.

"I shall not fail thee, O Great Master of Master Form Filler."

"Yeah, yeah," I said, handing him my pen. "May the ink flow ever freely."

↔

I approached the sliding doors. Up-close I noticed that it wasn't just this new Other's physical features that made him odd—it was his smell, too. Over the years, I've learned that humans as a species have a distinct smell. The same is true of Others. Each species has its unique scent; to describe a human smell over an Other without experiencing it is like explaining color to the blind. Humans, with our pheromones and sweat glands, our stomach acids and diets, smell human. Which is to say, mortal. Others, although thirteen years mortal, had yet to have those biological processes permeate them on a cellular level. There was no mistaking an angel's smell. Or any other Other for that matter.

But this Other—this "Grinner"—he didn't just smell human. He smelled very human. As if he over-sweat, over-ate, over-shat. His pheromones were double-timing to get maximum effect. More didn't mean better or worse. He just smelled wrong.

The automatic doors didn't slide open, which could only mean one thing. This grinning Other was burning time. The thing about magic is that it doesn't play nicely with modern technology. Burn time in front of a computer and it will shut down. Lights will flicker and TVs will go on the fritz. And automatic doors won't open. You know how the old pacemakers couldn't be near microwaves? Same concept here. And the stronger the magic, the more time burned, the bigger the problem for the electronics. I've seen airplane navigation systems fail, hospital main and backup generators cease and radios shut off.

I gripped at the sliding doors and tried to force them apart. They wouldn't budge.

"Human," this Grinner guy hissed, his voice holding a serpentlike quality.

"Yeah, that's me," I said, pulling at the door.

He sniffed through the glass and grinned so wide that his eyes actually moved inwards to make room for the edges of his smile. "Yes … Indeed," he said, backing away from the door. When he got about three meters away the automatic doors finally budged, opening at a maddeningly slow pace.

I pulled at them, squeezing through, and said, "Hey, you … I want to ask you something." But in the moment I took my eyes off him to squeeze through the door, he vanished. As in, into thin air. And in the early morning light I could have sworn I saw the half-moon crescent of a Cheshire Cat smile fade away.

Chapter 9

Being Human Is Easy ... If You Have the Cash

I didn't like what happened in the parking lot with that strange Other so willing to burn time, but what was I going to do? Using magic wasn't a crime. Yet. I guess I could call Michael and tell him I saw someone suspicious, but even then, what would I say? "That Cheshire Cat gave me the heebie-jeebies"? I had no idea if this guy was related to the homicides or not, but something in my guts said he was. As I walked home, I imagined what that conversation with Michael would go like:

"Human Jean-Luc, what did you see?"

"An Other."

"An Other?"

"Yes, an Other ..."

Awkward silence.

"And?"

"And, ahhh, he looked menacing."

"How so?"

"Well, he smiled."

"Smiled?"

"Yeah, but it was a really, really creepy smile."

"Oh, a creepy smile you say. Well then, that does it! Guilty! Thank you, Human Jean-Luc. Once again you have saved the day. Oh, by the way, here is the Key to the City."

No way was I going through that. And what's more, it was racial profiling—rather, Other profiling—assuming that this guy was guilty of some crime simply because of the way he looked. It was like arresting a guy because he had a beard. There was enough of that going around with everyone assuming vampires were evil, ogres stupid and angels good, and I wasn't going to be a part of it.

Luckily, I had two Others older than most mountains living in my hotel. If one of them told me an Other like that was not to be trusted, well then …

My thoughts were stopped dead in their tracks by the sight of an old man who was standing right next to my 1969 Plymouth RoadRunner. He was eying Penemue's taloned feet with unnatural concern. He looked at the feet, as if trying to glean something about the essence of the being to whom they belonged, before nodding in approval and then touching their soles, causing the slumbering angel to stir and withdraw his feet into the backseat of the car. Either the old man possessed an unhealthy foot fetish or he was of the gutsiest pranksters in the world to dare tickle the feet of a sleeping fallen angel.

Either way, I couldn't just stand there. "Hey," I said walking up to him. "Leave him alone."

The old man caught my gaze with his hazel eyes, and what hit me next was something that I struggled to understand. Warmth. Comfort. Peace. But even that was an oversimplification of what happened, because warmth implies temperature; it was so much more than that. I read somewhere the best sleep of our entire lives happens when we are in the womb. Growing in the belly of our mothers was where we experienced the deepest, most all-encompassing sleep that we will ever have. Think about it—we're in a perfectly dark room that is at the ideal temperature for our developing body. We are constantly being fed while we rest, in blissful ignorance of all the troubles of the world. The soft heartbeat of the person who loves us more than life itself is constantly beating in the background, reassuring us that all is well. All is safe.

And that was what I felt standing before the old man.

Or rather, I should say—the old Other.

My military training kicked in as I reminded myself that this creature was manipulating my emotions with some serious kind of mojo. Hell, if this Other kept it up—given how old he already was—he'd turn to dust before my very eyes. If, that was, I still stood to witness it. Summoning all my will, I did what I was trained to do in such situations— counter whatever was happening with the opposite. In the once-upon-a-time world of magic, opposites negated one another, and it was a matter of whoever had the stronger will that won. I flooded my mind with images of PopPop's funeral, the horrors I'd seen while being a soldier in the war and of Bella's body being ripped apart.

Popping out of his spell, I growled through gritted teeth, "You stop that right now."

I reached out to throttle him, but a giant clawed hand held back my arm. "He can't help it."

I swung around to see Penemue awake and holding me back. The previous night he had been all banged up—bloody nose, black eye, torn vest. And although his tweed vest was still torn, the rest of him was healed. He looked as good as new. Better than new, because somehow the years of self-abuse were washed away and he looked more like his former self. "He can't help it," Penemue repeated, eying the old man. I noticed that Penemue's blue iris glistened behind an unescaped tear. "It is his nature. His innate ability." The angel let me go and, putting a fist over his heart, bowed. "I thought you left with … them."

"No," the old man said. "I am no god. I am, however, a traveler seeking shelter." Turning to me, the old man lowered his head slightly and said, "I understand your establishment is friendly to me and my kind."

I nodded and from the corner of my eye I saw Penemue

wipe away a milky white tear. Speaking in a language I did not understand, Penemue said something in a low tone. The old man turned to face Penemue, who immediately dropped to his knees, bowing his head in a gesture of contrition. The old man gave him a knowing smile and touched his head.

Penemue stood and, putting a fist over his heart, turned to me and did something that he never even came close to doing in the four years we'd known each other. He apologized. "Human Jean-Luc, for all the trouble I have caused you, I am sorry. It seems that we have a very special guest staying with us tonight. Please afford him all the hospitalities you have shown me." With that, he unfurled his wings and said, "I shall be up in the attic contemplating my sins should either of you require anything from me." Penemue took to the sky, leaving me alone with the old man.

Hellelujah!

↔

"Sorry about that," I said, not really sure what I was sorry for. The drunk angel? Yelling at him outside? I suspect I was apologizing for a lot more. I took him over to the mess that passed as the hotel's welcome desk. "We've got some issues here in Paradise Lot to work out, and …" I clicked a ballpoint pen open and handed him a check-in form.

"You've been hurt." There was something about his tone that told me he wasn't talking about bruises or broken bones. And, equally, there was something soothing about his words. Like he understood my pain and was sure that all would work out in the end.

"Stop it," I said, looking at him. Deep wise wrinkles crawled out from the corners of his eyes that must have been forged by a lifetime of laughter and tears. He had heavy-set hazel eyes that rested under a silver brow, and he gave off an air of confidence that simultaneously conveyed strength and compassion. He wore a subtle smile that said he'd had more good times than bad ones, and his calloused hands told me that he knew what a hard day's work felt like. Everything about this man was comforting and strong. Even his smell made me feel safe and secure. He smelled like … like … Old Spice and cigars?

Holy crap, this man smelled like my grandfather, PopPop. Hell, everything about him screamed "PopPop," from the way he waved his hands, to his hunched shoulders that, for PopPop at least, was a result of gravity and arthritis slowly pushing down his spine.

PopPop was always my inspiration, someone who when I was growing up I desperately wanted to be. When he died, I cried for seven days straight, ready to die from misery— probably would have had Bella not been there to feed me. And now, this man—this Other——stood before me, reminding me of PopPop in the most visceral of ways.

Except he wasn't PopPop. He just looked like him, smelled like him. Felt like him. "Stop making me feel better. It is not real. Innate ability or not, I don't like feeling manipulated."

"As you wish," he said, and his eyes began to glow.

"What are you doing?" I said as my general irritability returned to me.

"Preventing myself from making you feel better."

"How?" I said. It wasn't just his eyes that glowed—his whole body became bioluminescent.

"How else? Magic."

"What?" I said. "Are you burning time?"

He nodded. "A bit. It is the only way to stop making you feel better. As the angel mentioned, I cannot help who I am.

64

My presence has always been a calming effect on those near me. I can no more change that part of me than you could change the color of your eyes."

"Well, stop that!"

"What?"

"Stop burning time," I ordered.

"But earlier ..."

"It's fine," I sighed, still not happy with being made to feel happy. "I'll deal with it. Just don't burn any more time."

"As you wish," the old man said, and his skin stopped glowing.

"Thank you."

Immediately the feeling of my PopPop came back and I felt ... better. Safe. Almost content. I had heard of Others like this one before—Others who were the equivalent of emotional chameleons, camouflaging themselves in your feelings and desires to help or protect them. This innate ability was something that they had little control over, which meant I had to be careful around him. After all, you never see the knife in your back coming from the ones you love. But still, judging from Penemue's reaction and taking into account who the angel was, I suspected that this Other's intentions were less than nefarious, if not outright good. I reminded myself of something Bella used to say: *One can survive without trust. But living means having faith in others and Others.* Damn you, Bella.

"OK—fine," I said, fighting back a smile. "Mister ...?" I said, tapping the form.

"Joseph. Just Joseph. 'Mister' was my father." He laughed at his joke. When I did not join him, he frowned and said, "Oh well, I am very funny in Valhalla."

"I'm sure you are, Joseph," I said, writing down his name as I suppressed a chuckle. "I'm sure you are."

I handed over the room key and Joseph eyed me suspiciously. "Aren't you going to ask me more questions?"

"Like what?" I asked.

"My purpose for staying—"

"None of my business," I said.

"A deposit?"

"You'll pay when you check out. Or you won't. I figure those who can afford to pay, do. Those who can't—well I'm just happy to offer them a few nights here."

"Are you really?" he asked.

"No," I mused, "but I made this promise, and …" I stopped fighting the mojo again.

He nodded like he understood and said, "How about what kind of Other I am?"

"No," I said.

"Oh," the Other said, widening his eyes. "Why not? In my short time as a mortal, it seems the question most asked by humans."

"It's like asking what your religion is—or was—or how much money you got in your bank account or if you're straight or gay. Leaves too much room for profiling, and I'd rather judge you on what I see than what I believe."

Joseph nodded, slowly eying me up and down. A small smile crept over his face and he said in a slow and deliberate tone, "When I heard of your little haven, I didn't believe it. But now … like you said—what you see …"

He stood there for a long moment, not moving, like he was trying to unravel something he didn't understand. "Well," I said, breaking the silence, "if that's it, I'll be …"

"Your name?"

"Excuse me," I said.

"Your name—you never told me your name."

"Oh, right. Jean," I said, straightening my collarless

jacket. "Jean-Luc Matthias."

"Ahh," he said, smiling, "you're just missing the 'Mark.' " Again, he chuckled at his own joke.

"Excuse me?" I asked.

"John, Luke, Matthew and Mark."

"Oh yeah—right," I said. "My mom was a devout Catholic and apparently the day I was born she wanted to spread the good news." I lifted my hands in a half-hearted gesture of *Surprise!*

"And did she? Spread the news, that is?"

"No. She died giving birth to me, kind of killing the good news aspect and any faith I might have had, and ..." I said, and as the words came out of my mouth, I put down my pen in frustration. His mojo was loosening my lips, and I hated it. "I've only told that story to one other person and she's dead. Your innate ability, or whatever it is, is throwing me off. I just met you. I don't even know if I trust you. So what do you say if we call it quits on the questions?"

"I am sorry," he said, his expression momentarily sad. But as quickly as his smile left his face it returned, and he said, "Would it help if I told you a secret?"

"Not really," I said, still annoyed at falling under his spell yet again.

"But it would make us even." He gave me a hopeful look.

I sighed. "OK, fine." I'd played these kinds of games with Others before. Secrets, riddles, Guess-my-name ... it always ended the same. They'd say something ridiculous and look at you like they just laid out the secrets of the Universe.

He produced a plain wooden box no bigger than a Rubik's Cube from his pocket. He opened it and showed me its hollowed, empty innards. "I stole this three thousand years ago, always planning on giving it back. But then they left, and now there is no one to give it back to."

See? Told you. I gave him the same expression one gives a cat when presented with a dead bird.

"Don't you want to know what it is?"

"It's a box," I said.

"Yes … and no." He paused, waiting expectantly.

"OK, fine—what is it?" I said.

"A lot of things, and nothing at all," he said with a deadly serious expression. Oh brother, give me a break! A smile crept on his face, and he started laughing. "It's a box. Just a box. You should have seen your face. 'A lot of things, and nothing at all' … Really, Mister Matthias, lighten up."

"Oh?" I said, returning his smile.

"But I will tell you this—the box has belonged to some very interesting mortals over the ages. Pharaohs, prophets, would-be gods. And all of them thought that if they could just fill it up with the right kind of—what did you call it?—*mojo*, they'd change the world. Not always for the better, mind you." He handed me the box.

I examined the plain wooden thing that looked like it was constructed by the slow kid in wood shop. The thing hadn't even been sanded down, and slivers of wood splintered from the edges. Holding it, I felt nothing. I tried to hand it back, but he refused.

"No, you keep it," he said. "Maybe you will be able to do more good with it than they ever managed to."

"I can't accept this," I said.

"Please, I insist."

What I didn't say was *But it's a piece of useless crap*, opting for a more cordial, but empty, "Thank you." I opened my top drawer and put it inside.

He smiled. "Think nothing of it. Should the fates smile upon us, maybe we will find time for me to regale you with tales about those who thought they could change the world with a plain wooden box."

"I'd like that," I found myself saying. What was strange was that—mojo or not—I meant it. I really would like to hear this odd creature's stories.

Damn—it was proving very difficult not to like this Other.

Chapter 10
Home Is Where Your Heart Is

The One Spire Hotel was seven rooms, plus an attic and cellar. Currently five guests resided here—six if you included the fairy that lived in Castle Grayskull. In less than twenty-four hours, my world went from crushing debt, a prostitute succubus's constant orgies, a pissed-off ghost of a mother-in-law and drunk fallen angel, to all of the above plus a Fanatical Other in town, homicidal gangbangers hell bent on destroying my hotel, a soothing Other that—despite Penemue's reaction to him—I didn't fully trust and a pissed-off archangel of a cop.

And I would go on a month-long trek to the Himalayas with all of them if it meant I didn't have to bake.

I hated baking.

No matter how hard I mixed, how vigorously I beat or how committed I was to stirring, my batter was still lumpier than the poxes on a Capulet's ass. Despite carefully measuring, no two cookies were the same size, and in spite of my precise timing, every single batch of the chocolate chip and macadamia nut cookies came out rock hard. And what's more—it took me the whole day to whip up the monstrosity of cookie hell I planned on feeding my guests.

Welcome to mortality. Lesson one: not all cookies were created equal.

Hellelujah!

↔

After the cookies were baked, I put on my black collarless coat and set about to make the One Spire Hotel's little dining room suitable for a seminar, which meant covering the three tables with freshly laundered sheets and lining up all the chairs to face the front.

As my pièce de résistance, I displayed my burnt cookies on two silver trays and placed an old metal music stand in front of the room to act as a speaker's podium.

Then I took a step back and surveyed what "making the most of what I got" meant. Insufficient lighting, a cramped space and burnt cookies.

Way to make them feel wanted, Jean-Luc.

"What did you expect me to do?" I found myself saying to a Miral yet to arrive. "Lay out fresh flowers, maybe put on a little Kenny G in the background for musical accompaniment? Remember, I didn't want to do this in the first place." I was practicing. If you knew Miral, you would too.

"Actually, this exceeds all expectation," Miral said as she walked in, her flawlessly white wings wrapped around her shoulders like some kind of superhero cape. Little rain droplets ran down her wings like water on a duck's back. "Not a hard feat when you have none."

I swear to the GoneGods that I was a man of extreme military training who was always acutely aware of my surroundings. At any given time, I could size up a room, tell you how many exits there were, the number of possible combatants, where the surveillance equipment was hidden, and I had abnormally wide peripheral vision. Beyond that— there's a friggin' bell above the front door. None of my alarms—internal or otherwise—went off. "How the hell did you do that?"

"Hell," she said, raising an eyebrow, "is exactly why I learned to do that."

She surveyed the room while practicing mortal

techniques at diplomacy. In other words, compliment the good things, gloss over the bad. She didn't do a good job. I guess when you had the word of God on your side, tact wasn't one of the skills you needed to develop. "Not exactly the heavenly halls, but I guess you tried. Given who you are and what you are capable of, I should be happy that you remembered the cookies." She picked one up, bit into it and spit it out. "Or perhaps not," she scowled.

I looked at my watch. Five minutes until the time on the flyer. Five minutes and so far it was just me and Miral. Not that it meant anything. The concept of time was one of the many things Others struggled with.

"Have faith," she said, taking her place behind the podium.

"You already said that."

"Then," she said, with a smile, "you should listen," and nodded to someone standing behind me.

I wouldn't have believed it had I not seen it with my own eyes, but in walked my mother-in-law and current poltergeist Judith, side by side with Penemue. Judith gave me her requisite scowl but didn't say anything. Once-upon-a-time she was a staunch Catholic—I guess being in the presence of a couple of angels resulted in best behavior. She held the arm of an unusually sober and well-groomed Penemue, who guided her to seats in the front. He nodded at Miral with an unearthly reverence and sat next to Judith. I got to hand it to the big guy, I don't know if I could be so cordial with the one who stood at the gates of Heaven while I was being cast down to the pits of Hell. Then again, the gods leaving meant that Miral was an outcast too, and I suspected his nod carried with it a silent empathy for her.

The front door bell rang and a familiar hand touched my shoulder. I turned to see a rough-looking woman of about five-foot-nothing, wearing an old Victorian dress with a hat that had lost so much of its vibrant color that it was practically sepia. She looked like an old photo.

She folded her old Victorian umbrella that was so filled with holes it was more a showpiece than anything of use and, pulling out a handkerchief, wiped away some of the rain from her brow.

"Sandy," I said. "Good of you to join us."

"Jean, there is not much time and we must dispense with pleasantries," Sandy barked. But when she saw Miral across the room, her tone became far more affable as she walked over to greet her. "Miral, darling—how are you?"

Once-upon-a-time, when Bella ran the One Spire Hotel with a hell of a lot more success than I did, Miral and Sandy were her first employees. Both had moved onto bigger and brighter things—Miral using her preternatural brain to complete medical school in three years, and Sandy using her cooking skills and former werewolf nature to open the Stalker Steakhouse. As the two conversed, looking over the place, I couldn't help but feel self-conscious. There was no doubt that I was barely holding Bella's dream together.

When the pleasantries that she apparently did not have time for ended, Sandy returned to me and in a curt voice said, "Is my cell ready?" As a once-upon-a-time werewolf, Sandy never got used to the fact that she no longer transformed with the Moon. I guess after years of running on all fours for three days a month, she couldn't let go. So once a month Sandy came to the One Spire Hotel to be locked away in the basement where she sat there, not changing. I had to admire the little woman—she'd been locking herself up every full moon for over three hundred years because she wanted to make sure she wouldn't hurt anyone, and she wasn't going to stop now.

"Everything is ready down there. Even got the combination lock like you asked. But, Sandy, you don't need to lock yourself up. Not anymore …" I started.

The teeny-tiny woman snarled, "Not a word, Jean-Luc, I am here to be locked away. It is, after all, that time of the month."

"Tell me about it, girl," Astarte chimed as she shuffled past us into the room.

"Sex-slave of Satan!" Sandy barked.

"My, my—we are in a mood," the succubus said without missing a beat, sending the former werewolf out of the room and down into the cellar. "Give me the Black Death over a Victorian prude any day. At least the dying screw like it's their last day on Earth," Astarte said, following Sandy with her eyes.

↔

The little bell in my reception chimed continuously as a flight of fairies, a frustration of dwarves, and hodgepodge of goblins walked in, followed by a kitchen of trolls, a charge of ogres, a quarry of gargoyles and a dust of pixies.

There was barely enough space for the nearly three dozen Others. Hell, if it wasn't for the fairies and pixies hovering midair and the goblins hanging from the ceiling lamps, the event would have had to turn Others away. The seminar began with the more mundane subjects that covered the importance of eating regularly, drinking and sleeping enough and shitting daily. Many of the Others nodded in agreement, asking questions like "How do you know when you're full?" and "Which bodily fluids are acceptable to excrete in public and which aren't?"

This was followed by the slightly more complex

concepts of money and time, how to read time, count money and the basics of social etiquette like not cutting in line and why being late was bad. Like I said, pretty straightforward stuff.

This went on for a couple hours—you'd be surprised how many details there were to cover, things I pretty much just did without ever stopping to think about it—and all was drawing to a close when one particularly big-eyed pixie asked Miral what happened to Others when they died.

In the years that I had known Miral, I'd never seen her flustered. Not once. Not even close—until that night. "Well, ummm, I suppose … the prevalent theory is that nothing happens," she floundered. Then, as if needing to clarify herself, she repeated the key word: "Nothing." Angels suck at tact.

"What do you mean, nothing?" The pixie sparkled, a dark azure and crimson purple dust emanating from her being.

"I mean that when you die it all just kind of goes black," Miral said. "Like sleeping, except you never wake up." Miral forced a smile.

"But I only have a thousand years," mourned the pixie.

"A thousand years—I only have eight hundred and sixty-three," cried a gargoyle.

"Sleep is death," lamented a fairy who vowed never to sleep again.

The frustration of dwarves started jumping up and down in place—their version of public protest—while the goblins flung big mounds of green mucus at one another.

"Calm down," Miral pleaded, "calm down!" but even her angelic countenance wasn't enough to calm this crowd. Death, whether imminent or a ways away, was terrifying. But suddenly needing to face mortality when thirteen years ago you were once-upon-a-time immortal … That was several dozen shades of dark scary shit.

Things were getting out of control, and I was considering throwing them out, starting with the dwarves, when a soft voice pierced the clamor. "Death is the door through which we must all walk through, one by one," it said in barely a whisper. As if feeling the words rather than hearing them, everyone immediately calmed down and listened. "Death is final and forever, and it is the only experience that each and every one of us shall share. The sooner we all accept this, the better we shall respect the time we have," Joseph said, calm and even.

The crowd not only calmed down, but they also bowed. Even Miral and Penemue lowered their head in reverence. One of the dilemmas that faced Other unification was that one type did not necessarily respect another. With long memories and tens of thousands of years of history, each type of Other had at one point or another gone to war. It seemed that no two types did not have some kind of historical beef. And yet, everyone in this room regarded Joseph with equal reverence. I'd never seen anything like this before. Innate ability or not, magic or not, this Other had some serious cred.

I wished Bella was here—she would have been floored.

"Death," Joseph continued, "is the bridge that ties the AlwaysMortal humans and the OnceImmortal Others. Death is what binds us together, our only shared experience. For that reason, if nothing else, death should not be feared, but embraced."

↔

The rest of the evening wrapped up with each and every

Other insisting on meeting Joseph before leaving. The dwarves smiled, the goblins climbed, the pixies sprinkled him with their dust. The fairies sang to him and the trolls offered him rancid meat which he humbly accepted. Hell, not a single Other left until they got a chance to show their respect. Even Penemue saluted Joseph before leaving, and Judith—well, let's just say she didn't scowl at me as she left. She didn't smile either, but I'll take whatever little victory I can get. And it was then that I realized what it was that I wanted. What it was that all of us want. And I knew I had figured out what EightBall wanted, too. In excitement I ran over to the fairies and asked them for a favor. They listened intently and replied that they were happy to help for seven vials of glitter and two bottles of Elmer's Glue. A steep price, but one I was willing to pay. They agreed and left.

I turned to my now empty breakfast room and saw that Astarte, Miral and Joseph still remained. Astarte approached him and, for the first time that I knew of, she didn't try to seduce the Other, but rather spoke to him in a quiet voice. I don't know what they said to each other that night and I suspect I never will, but whatever it was, when Astarte left the room I could sense in her a feeling of hope. Seeing Astarte, I remembered the smiling Other outside the hospital, but tonight was such a wonderful evening that my questions could wait until the morning.

Miral was the last to leave. She bowed deeply to Joseph, thanking him over and over. I tried to catch her attention, but like Astarte, the emotional experience of meeting Joseph had obviously taken its toll.

Alone, I turned to the Other and before I could stop my mouth, I said, "What are you?"

"I thought you deemed it rude to ask."

"I do, but did you see what you did here tonight?

Seriously, I have to know ... What are you?"

Joseph laughed. "How easily we break our principles, claiming that necessity deems it acceptable."

"As much as I love your quotable wisdom, I've got to know," I said.

"I'll tell you what. I'll give you three guesses. That way you will not be breaking your own vow to never ask."

"And if I get it?"

"Then you'll know."

"And if I don't?"

"Then you won't."

"Oh, come on!" I protested. "OK, fine, but if I don't get it, then you've got to tell me."

The Other shrugged and said, "Let's cross that bridge when we get there."

"OK, fine. Let's see ... You're unique. But we knew that much already. Perhaps you're a legend?" Joseph's eyes lit up at that, "There are stories of humans that were chosen to perform great deeds for the gods. Hercules, Achilles, Benkei ... and let's not forget the prophets who got to visit all the various heavens and hells ... Human?" I hazarded.

He shook his head. "I'm afraid not."

I considered who he could be. My second guess was that he was a god that had chosen not to leave. I couldn't ask. I didn't know how. How do you ask a being responsible for creation itself what they are? The thought hung at the edge of my lips, begging to get out.

"No," he said. "I'm not that either. But we established that with the angel already."

"But I didn't say anything."

He shook his head. "You didn't have to. Your hesitation said it for you." He put up his index finger, indicating one last guess.

I racked my brain for some commonality that Others shared, whether in their myths or legends, but nothing came to mind. My thoughts went on like this for a long time. So long that I was beginning to feel rude for keeping him awake, even though Joseph still had the same patient look on his face. All I really knew about him was that all Others respected him and that he was always cordial to everyone. I finally settled on, "A dragon using a glamor in order to look human, maybe? Or a shape shifter?"

"Which is it? A dragon or a shape shifter?"

"A shape-shifting dragon," I offered.

"Cheeky," he said, shaking his head.

"Damn it!" I said. "Fine, but that middle guess didn't count. You've got to give me one more. Please."

Joseph chuckled. "This is why I so love human beings. Always demanding what is fair and bargaining for it. Fine. One more guess—but I suggest you sleep on it."

"But—"

"But *nothing*, Jean-Luc," he said with a soft smile as he headed upstairs.

On the landing below his, I bid him goodnight. He walked to the base of the next set of stairs. The lights flickered and Joseph looked at them with concern.

"It's just the rain," I said. "Messes with the electrics of this old building. I can't afford to get it all fixed up."

He sniffed the air. "There's a storm coming," he said, continuing up the stairs. "Thing about storms is that one way or another, they always end. You would do well to remember that."

"You know," I said, shaking my head, "you're the second person today to say that to me."

"Sounds like you know some very wise people. Have a good night, Jean-Luc Matthias who is just missing the

Mark," he said, laughing again at his own joke. "A good night, indeed."

"Goodnight," I returned, although the comment hung empty, shallow after a night of so much good. But I was exhausted and too lazy to think of anything more to say. Had I known that Joseph would be dead in less than three hours, I might have tried harder.

Chapter 11

Just When It Was All Going So Well

For the first time in a very, very long time, I went to bed excited—not only to see Bella, but to wake up the next morning. Whatever was happening in Paradise Lot—Fanatic, gangs of HuMan Otherphobes, bills, orgies and pissed off mother-in-laws—I actually felt hope for the morning. Dawn would come, and with it things could get better. Much, much better. I was excited. Happy even, and I didn't think sleep would come easy.

I was wrong. On all counts.

I closed my eyes, sleep taking me before my head even touched the pillow. The darkness came rolling in, a tidal wave of nothing, and—like every night—I ran. But this time there was less terror and more excitement to see Bella. My wife may be dead and the memory of her may haunt my dreams, but a piece of her was that memory, and that memory—like Bella—wanted the world to heal. I needed to tell her that someone had finally arrived with enough respect, kindness and wisdom to be the glue to hold us all together.

I ran to the edge of everything where Bella always saved me moments before the darkness came. That night she took me, not to the beach where I proposed or the cottage where we first made love, but to our first apartment. And not the happy move-in days. Marriage is hard, and we were mac-and-cheese poor, and this was the apartment we moved in to after PopPop died. It was also the apartment I left her alone in when I joined the Army.

Typically, my brain would guide us to happy places, and on an eve when I was particularly happy, I just assumed I'd go somewhere happy. But then again, misery is a habit and my brain was probably compensating. Stupid brain!

"You look well," she started, looking around at the apartment before finally settling her gaze on me. "Chipper, even."

"I feel good," I said, sitting on our two-person sofa, if the two people were toddlers.

"Does it have to do with that new guest? Joseph?" I wasn't surprised that she knew his name or sensed that my peace came from his presence. After all, she was my delusion. Therefore it stood to reason that she knew everything I did.

I nodded. "He has a wisdom to him. The Others listen to him. Humans listen. I really feel he can change things for us. For the better."

She gave me her *Poor naïve Jean* look, and said, "I hope you are right, but please, don't pin your hopes on him. Remember, we've been here before."

"Sheesh," I said, "I thought *I* was the negative one. Where are we? The Bizarro World?"

She chuckled and said, "Trust the Unicorn, but don't put all your hope in him."

"Unicorn?" Then it hit me. In order to be loved by all, Joseph needed to be a legend of legend—like TinkerBelle—which meant he needed to be an Other that appeared in all traditions. A unicorn was one of them. "A unicorn! Of course … Why didn't I think of that?"

She stepped toward me, her hand outstretched, but with every step she took the farther away she got. The room began to stretch out, elongating, pulling her away. Still, she strode toward me, but it was like she was on one of those super long moving walkways you get at airports. Bella was walking against the roll and losing.

I stepped forward to close the gap, but I too was being

82

pulled away from her. "What's happening?" I asked.

"I'm sorry," Bella said, putting her hand over her lips. "I had hoped for more time." She blew me a kiss—you know, that cute thing you do with your lover—and I did my part by pretending to catch it. Except instead of it being a mime, my entire body was hit by the shockwave of her kiss, knocking me clear out of my bed.

↔

I woke up on the floor, all my toys shaking as a slow-moving waterfall of dust fell from my ceiling. Tink was out of her castle, flying over to me, a look of worry on her face. "What … what happened?" I said, my mind still waking up.

Tink pointed upstairs and then put her body into a cannonball before exploding out her arms and legs in all directions. She followed this up by whirling around, gesturing for me to leave my room. The look she gave me told me that we were under attack.

Hellelujah!

↔

I made my way to the outer hall. The second floor was completely untouched. For a moment I thought that maybe, just maybe, there *was* no explosion. But the shockwaves alone told me I was lying to myself. I ran upstairs, where Astarte met me on the landing and pointed to Joseph's room. I took a moment to prepare myself for what was beyond the threshold and opened the door.

There was something decidedly unbelievable about explosions. Not that I didn't believe in them. I did. The GoneGods knew that I'd survived more than my fair share of them. But still, through all the explosions that I'd had the misfortune of being near, I just couldn't get used to them.

First of all, there was the sheer chaos caused by a bomb. The scattering of debris, whole objects broken into smaller pieces along unnatural lines in the most unnatural places. I'd seen a car blown in two, its hood upside down in a trench only a meter off of the strip of road it had been driving along, its trunk hanging in a tree like some sort of deformed metal bird's nest. And that was a car. A soulless, unfeeling hunk of metal.

I'd also seen what happens to a body, human and Other, when it was caught in a blast. One moment there was a whole being, and the next moment its foot was several meters away, its sole on the ground, stump pointing upwards, while its toes faced away from the blast as if it were trying to run away and had simply forgotten to take the rest of the body with it. A wing in the hands of an angel, her other wing flapping futilely as she tried to get off the ground. The suspended entrails of a yeti hanging from cedar branches like poorly hung Christmas decorations, the yeti looking at it with a look of admiration that seemed to say, "Look at what I made."

I'd seen all that and worse, and still I wasn't prepared for what waited behind the door.

↔

The room was empty, its bed, side table, closet and chest of drawers all missing, presumably littering the road out front. From the threshold, I could see the bathroom sink embedded in the building across the street. The outer wall had been blown out in a nearly perfect square that did not encroach on the floors above or below. The explosion should have torn holes into the inner walls, damaging the hallway and adjacent rooms. As far as I could tell, the only damaged area was in the room. It looked like someone took a giant vacuum cleaner and sucked out everything.

What's more, the area where the bathroom once was should have been covered in water, its pipes still spouting. But from the mouths of broken pipes water gushed up only an inch before hitting some invisible shield and spreading out like a garden hose pouring water on glass. It defied physics.

I tried to cross the threshold but instead hit an invisible shield at the door. I pushed, but I didn't have the strength to get through. Then I realized the whole room was being held together by a force field that was in the room, like a balloon inflated in a box. In the middle lay Joseph, his arms over his chest like he was being swaddled by an invisible blanket. "Joseph," I cried out, banging against the force field. "Joseph!"

The old man turned his head slightly. Upon seeing me, he smiled, before a look of pain ran across his face, his lips curling. He took a deep breath and mouthed one word.

"Push."

I didn't need to be told twice. I pushed with all my might. The force field didn't budge. Astarte and four scantily-clad bodies came to my aid and our combined effort caused the wall to move, but it wasn't until Judith joined that we finally caused it to pop.

Water started spouting everywhere. I yelled at Judith to go to the basement and turn it off. She gave me her typical derisive look and headed downstairs. As soon as that was taken care of, I stepped further into the room. Then, turning to Astarte and her guests—noticing for the first time that they were all humans—I said, "You got to get out of here.

Out the back door and, please, call for help." As five naked bodies ran out the door, I added, "And for the love of the GoneGods, put on some shoes."

Then I ran over to Joseph. Little droplets of rainbow-colored blood trickled out of his eyes and from his lips, but still the Other smiled. In a voice far too casual for what just happened, he said, "Sorry about that, Jean. Magic is so much easier to turn on than off. But I think I did it. Didn't I? The hotel, the Others, they are all right, yes? Did I manage to contain it?" He coughed. I put my hand against his chest and nodded.

"Yes. No other part of the hotel was touched," I said. "Because of you, no one was hurt, Joseph. You did it." I looked down at Joseph and saw that his arms were pressed so tight against his chest that his ribs were compressed to make space for his forearms. His legs were mangled, broken in several places and pushing up against his torso. His neck was also pushed against his body, like a turtle trying to get back in its shell. The features of his face were flat and tight; blood dripped out of the corners of his eyes and into the tributaries of his wrinkles. He looked like he had just been pulled out of the belly of a snake, after every part of him had been crushed within the serpent's contracting muscles.

"Good," he said, and even though it caused him great pain, he managed a chuckle. "You still have one last guess."

I couldn't believe he still wanted to play our stupid little game at a time like this. "Forget about that," I said. "Can you heal yourself? Spend a bit of time so that you can have some more here? With us. With me," I said through the glassy, shimmering lens of trapped tears.

He shook his head. "I'm afraid you'll have to use your guess now. I doubt I'll be here to answer you tomorrow."

"Oh, come on!" I said. "There's got to be something

you can do. Maybe *I* could do something." I looked at his injuries but was hesitant to touch him, lest I make them worse.

"Yes, there is … You can guess. Have you had time to think about it?"

"Yes," I said, frustration pouring out of me. "A unicorn. You're a unicorn."

Joseph smiled. "Good guess. How did you know?"

"It came to me in a dream."

Joseph nodded and said, "Your dreams are very wise. You should always listen to them."

A tear finally escaped, its stream running hot down my cheek. I clamped my eyes shut. "Who did this, Joseph?" Struggling to keep my rage caged up inside, I asked again, "Who?"

"It has finally arrived, Jean-Luc," he rasped. "The storm. It is finally here."

End of Part One

Part Two

First Interlude

There is this girl whom I love very much. That is what I say to her the day I propose, getting down on one knee and handing her a twisty-tie. I'm only seventeen and it seems like a romantic gesture. Besides, it is all I can afford. She accepts it with far too much enthusiasm, jumping up and down on the sandy beach.

We are bound together; we are forever.

"Do you love me?" she asks as we fall to the sandy floor.

There is no ceremony, no formality, just a frantic rush to get our clothes off. She gets on top of me and I slide into her with no resistance and as her warmth envelops me, I say "Yes," panting between thrusts. "You know that."

"I do," she says. "But tell me."

"I love you."

"No," she says, our bodies no longer moving, "not like that." Her eyes lock onto mine and I am drowning in their beauty.

"How, then?"

"Tell me," she repeats. "Really tell me."

I smile, pushing myself up. I want to be deeper within her. I want to be a part of her. "OK," I say. "In this life and the next, I will love you forever." Cheesy, corny or whatever else you want to call it, I mean every word.

"I love you, too," she says, riding me, our bodies pulsing faster and faster, two teenagers in love, galloping into the future together.

That night we make love for the first time. Don't get me wrong—we have known each other before, but that night is different. Her soft, firm breasts are delights I have known before, but that night they are ecstasy. Her nipples are attentive to my touch, hardening as my fingers caress them. Her warm body against mine is familiar, but somehow new. Renewed. She kisses me, but unlike the thousand kisses that have come before, her lips are electric.

↔

Our love is condemned by her mother, Judith. She hates the idea of her precious daughter marrying so young. Even more than that, she hates the idea of her precious Bella marrying me. She refuses to sign the papers that will let us marry before we're eighteen. That's OK. We have our whole lives, and eighteen isn't that far away. Bella will be seventeen in two months and I will celebrate my eighteenth birthday with the ringing of the New Year.

My PopPop, on the other hand, is happy for us and even though Judith has forbidden Bella to come over, PopPop never tells.

Not that we have to keep up the charade long. Judith dies without warning. Bella finds her curled up on the bathroom floor, clutching her knees like a newborn. A heart attack. Just one of those things. God's will. Nobody's fault. Fate. Destiny. Pick your poison. Whatever it is, Judith is dead.

Through tears and frustration, we realize that we are free to marry early, but we choose to respect her mother's wishes. We wait until Bella's eighteenth birthday. It is a sad ceremony—a large black and white picture that sits in the first row is a poor substitute for a mother. As my bride-to-be says her vows through tear-filled eyes, I think that I would give almost anything to have Judith here to make my Bella happy.

Be careful what you wish for.

Bella and I are looking for places to go in the city that we can afford when PopPop comes into the kitchen. He's looking at us, a devilish smile veiled behind wisps of steam.

"There are two bundles of wood in the trunk of the car. It's cold up by the lake and without electricity or a bathroom, and you'll have to use a flashlight at night …"

At first we're confused, but then we notice the keys to my PopPop's old Plymouth RoadRunner sitting on a map to his cabin.

"Newlyweds should save their money for important things, like good wine," he says with a wink.

So we go up North to spend our honeymoon in a cabin without heat or electricity. That night, we make love in the living room, as close to the fireplace as possible, neither of us feeling the cold.

↔

It's midnight when it happens.

First we hear the message:

"Thank you for believing in us, but it's not enough. We're leaving. Good luck." The voice I hear is soft and calm. Reassuring but firm. And from its tone, I get this strong feeling that whatever has been done cannot be undone.

Bella and I look at each other, confusion painted on our faces.

"Did you hear that?" she asks.

"Yes."

"What was it?"

"I don't know," I say, pulling her in close. I put my hand

under her shirt and cup her bare breast. "And I don't care."

"But ..."

"But *nothing*," I say, pulling off her shirt.

She lets me, but she's still thinking about the voice. "Don't you think it's weird?" she says.

I suppose if I weren't a teenager with raging hormones, I would think it strange. But there are perfect, perky nipples reflecting the embers of the fire. And I am very badly in love. I pull back the wool blanket and run soft kisses down her torso, murmuring, "What's weird? Tell me about it."

"The voice ..." she says, her own voice trailing off as my tongue finds her special spot. "It was so ..."

The thought is lost and we are together again.

↔

After making love for a second time, we are content. Our bodies exhausted, we fall into a deep, dreamless sleep. But not for long. An explosion wakes us.

Not just an explosion, but a cascade of detonations that erupt all around us. It is not coming from the road or the nearby town. The sound is coming from the sky.

Naked, we run outside and look up. The evening sky is filled with fire that rolls through the night like a river bursting through a dam. And from the flames fall what look like meteors. A hundred thousand comets fall from above and ignite the world around us.

Isolated in the woods, we do not know that the Others are arriving, and that everything we once knew and loved is being ripped away from us with their arrival. All we know is our world is burning.

I guess, in a sense, that is all we need to know.

↔

We drive home on empty country roads, more out of curiosity than fear. We are young. We are in love. We are immortal. Sure, the sky is on fire, but how will that hurt us?

Without warning something hits the Plymouth, causing me to lose control. I twist the wheel against the spin and pump the brakes. We slide to a stop, facing the opposite direction. That's when we see it.

A monster. There is no other word for it—not in those first days, at least. The monster has a woman's body, naked breasts heaving in the moonlight. Her head is covered with a hundred squirming tendrils, each ending with the head of a snake, and her legs—oh God, she has no legs! Did I run her over and sever them from her body?

But then she rears up and shoots into the sky. Her body stops at least nine feet above the ground. It looks like she is standing on top of a podium. The podium moves as she lowers her body and it is then we see that her torso ends where the body of a giant snake begins. *Medusa*, I think, and it turns out I'm not far off. I will later learn that we've just met a far less famous member of the gorgon race.

The creature looks at us. Fear fills her eyes. What the hell does she have to be afraid of? *She's* the monster.

Bella opens the door, pulling out the flashlight. I grab her arm. "Don't," I say, but she ignores me and steps outside.

She approaches the monster like one might an angry dog, palms out, steady tone, eyes locked. "We're not going to hurt you," she says. "We just want to help." Even back then, Bella was always so kind. So good.

The gorgon's features soften. Then she starts to cry. What the hell? Monsters cry?

Bella continues to speak softly, offering the gorgon a granola bar. The creature takes it with care before devouring it down greedily. "Where did you come from?" Bella asks, but before the monster can answer, we hear a shot, followed by the roar of a pickup truck. Without hesitation or looking behind her, the gorgon slithers into the forest.

The pickup truck stops next to us and the driver steps out, rifle in hand. Two more men get out the back and a third darts out of the passenger's side door. All but the driver chase after the monster.

"What's happening?" I ask.

"Didn't you hear?" the driver says. "We're being invaded."

"By who?"

"Aliens, the news says. But I say they're demons. This is the End of Days and the angels' trumpets are sounding, boy!" And with that, he's off. Shots can be heard, but Bella and I do not stick around to see what's going on.

It will be two days later when I will pick up a local paper and see the driver of the truck and his friends standing around the gorgon's dead body. They've strung her upside down from a tree like a fisherman might a shark. They are smiling, thumbs out, beers in hand, the article caption reading: *Local Heroes Kill Snake Lady, Save Town.*

↔

We get back to the city and head home. Not that there is a home to greet us. PopPop's house is one of the hundreds hit.

Please. Please don't be home, I pray.

But there are no gods left to answer my prayers. PopPop is dead. And when the local Army starts recruiting, I join, leaving Bella alone in the crappy apartment we rented in the worst part of town.

↔

There is this girl whom I love very much. Eventually an uneasy peace settles throughout the city and, as a result, soldiers are sent home.

I am so happy to be discharged because, like I said, there is this girl and on the day I proposed to her, I promised that in this life and the next I would love her forever. I plan to make good on that promise.

↔

She meets me at the airport and takes me home. Only thing is that home isn't home. It is this old three-story building with seven rooms, an attic and a cellar.

"Welcome to the One Spire Hotel," she says with a grand gesture as we walk into its tiny foyer. The room is filled with desperate Others, broken by the GoneGod world. Each one of them has been mortally wounded by the loss of their home. A wound, Bella tells me, that will eventually kill them all.

"Poetic way of looking at it," I say.

They look up when Bella enters the room. An angel, better dressed than most, sees me and comes over. "Jean-Luc, I presume? I am Miral, former captain of the Lord's army and now assistant to the human called Bella. Welcome home." The angel extends her hand, but I do not take it. I might have left the Army, but the Army has yet to leave me.

"Jean-Luc," Bella admonishes, "honestly." She apologizes to the angel Miral, who takes it with grace and kindness.

"There is a problem with tonight's event," Miral says to Bella, pulling her aside. They go off to discuss what needs to be done.

A shorter woman wearing an old Victorian dress comes into the room. She pokes my side and says, "The name is Sandy. I am a werewolf. Treat me like you did the angel and I will rip out your throat." Sandy extends a hand and, a little bit afraid of the five-foot-nothing woman, I shake it. She nods and whispers, "Your wife's the *real* angel, helping so many Others by giving them hope. You better not muck it up. Otherwise, I'll …"

"Rip out my throat?" I offer.

Sandy nods her head. "Glad we understand each other."

Bella returns and informs Sandy that the caterers canceled. Sandy offers to rip out their throats, but Bella says she has a solution. She hands me an apron. We need four dozen chocolate chip and macadamia nut cookies.

"But I just got back," I say.

Bella shoots me her best *So what?* look and says, "Don't burn them," a bit of anger in her voice. As she walks away, Miral looks back at me, a devilish smile touching her lips.

"I hate baking," I protest feebly. "Could this day get any worse?"

"Oh," Bella says, "that reminds me. Remember my mother, Judith? Well, she's back …"

"What?"

"Welcome back," Bella says and trots off to deal with some crisis or other.

↔

Days turn into weeks, and even though I do not trust the

Others, I am inspired by how much they love Bella. Paradise Lot is filled with hope, and it is mostly because of my wife.

As for me, I am happy just to be with Bella. I've even made an uneasy peace with Judith—or rather we don't speak, which is an improvement.

Everything is going smoothly. I want this to last forever. But it seems that the Devil has other plans for us.

Chapter 12

Unleash the Dogs of War

There weren't many cops walking the streets of Paradise Lot, and when something big happened—like let's say an explosion in the only human-run hotel—they still didn't come running. There was just too much baggage in a place like Paradise Lot: too many ancient beefs that spanned millennia, too many creatures with claws and fangs, and too many once-upon-a-times with enough time on their hands to turn you into a pillar of salt. Given that, I figured I had half an hour before anyone official-looking turned up.

A lot can happen in half an hour.

Penemue and Astarte knelt by Joseph's body, both offering prayers from their respective ancient traditions. Penemue hummed as golden tears flowed from his face and Astarte washed the body with a cloth, using the pools of water from pipes that no longer gushed. I guessed Judith must have found the main—at least one thing had improved. Both of them were just as devastated by the loss of Joseph as I was. I couldn't watch anymore, and looked around the blown-out room. One of the problems of this GoneGod world was that you could no longer blame some silent entity, saying something meaningless like "He works in mysterious ways" or "Joseph was called for a higher purpose."

But there were no signs and no clues. No one to make sense of this for me. All that remained was a room with two Others paying respects to an empty, soulless body.

Judging from the way the explosion happened, time was burned. A lot of it. This ruled out EightBall, and ruled *in* my Fanatic theory. There was only one body in the room, which meant the Fanatic was still breathing, and the one thing I'd learned from dealing with Fanatics was that once they started, they didn't stop until they were dead—which usually meant a lot more explosions.

I looked over the angel's shoulder at Joseph. His features were slowly returning now that his body was no longer being crushed down by the Fanatic's magic. I forced myself to look at his hollow, empty eyes. His arms were folded over the same double-breasted suit he wore earlier today, his coat pockets turned inside out and empty. Whatever happened here was more than revenge or a fight. The Fanatic was looking for something, something that Joseph owned or left behind …

Just as the thought entered my mind, the lights flickered.

"He's still here."

"Who?" Penemue said, but without answering him I ran out the door and down the stairs, sure that when I got into the reception I'd be met by that friggin' unnatural smile.

The last thing I expected was a bat to the back of the head.

↔

Whoever took a swing at my skull wasn't very experienced. For one thing, if you are looking to knock a person out, you have to hit the point where the skull meets the neck. A good hit will take someone down, and if the angle is just right, you have a good chance of permanently paralyzing them. If you are looking to *kill* the guy, aim for the crown, angling your swing downward. That's the most likely way to get enough impact to crush the skull, and even then, you've got to go at it repeatedly to actually break through to the brain.

All that to say that the skull is friggin' hard and few are harder than mine. So when I was hit flat on the back of my head, all it did was knock me down, sending shooting stars across my vision and giving me a mind-numbing headache. I turned to see a scruffy HuMan holding the bat.

"Batter up!" He chuckled at his pun through crooked teeth.

"Good one," a voice said. "Looks like someone ruined your hotel."

I looked up to see EightBall and several more HuMans, laughing as they surrounded a less-than-pleased Judith—she must have come across the HuMans on her way up from the basement. They should have been in jail for at least another two nights.

The kid, as if reading my mind, pointed to my attacker and said, "BallSack's mom bailed us out. Guess not everyone's given up on us, yet."

Little opportunistic bastards—when the explosion happened, I guess they decided to take advantage of the situation. Hell, they were probably planning on taking responsibility for it, a nice little press release sent out by the *HuMans Weekly* newsletter.

"EightBall," I said, getting to my feet. BallSack took another swing at the back of my thigh, but I stepped to the side. The kid missed, the momentum causing him to fall forward. Ignoring him, I locked eyes on EightBall. "I know you're not going to believe me, but your timing couldn't be worse."

"I should have suspected," Judith said in an unforgiving tone, "that you would know miscreants such as these. I warned my daughter not to marry a man like you."

"Really, Judith," I said. "Now?"

EightBall and his three thug friends started laughing. "Daughter? Married? Don't tell me that you married this ghost's daughter? What is she? A white sheet with the eyes cut out?"

"You would be safer not to speak of my Bella in such terms," Judith growled as the chair from behind my desk flew right at one of the thugs standing next to EightBall. It hit him square on the head, knocking him to the ground hard. Way to go, Judith! Got to hand it to her, when she's pissed, she's dangerous.

Things started to shake around the room. Judith was about to go into a tantrum and that would cost her time. A whole bunch of it. As much as I'd like to spend less of it with her, I couldn't let her burn herself out.

"Judith," I said, "please calm down. Time, remember? We talked about this."

She met my eyes, fury in hers, and for a moment I thought she was too far gone in her poltergeist's rage to calm herself down, but then my mother-in-law took a deep breath and the room stopped rattling.

BallSack got to his feet and tried for another swing at me. This time I was ready for it, planning on taking the brunt of the blow on my side. But instead of swinging, he let the bat drop. I turned to see a petite woman in an old Victorian dress—complete with bonnet and all—leap into the fray, her teeth flashing red as they sank into his side. Sandy! Her bite was definitely worse than her bark.

Everyone looked down at the five-foot-nothing doily of fury and I took the opportunity to punch EightBall square in the nose—I can be just as opportunistic as the next guy. He went down, but got right back up, pulling a switchblade from only the GoneGods knew where, and lunged at me at the exact moment when reality decided to go out the window.

↔

Have you ever worried that gravity will suddenly disappear, causing you to float off to oblivion?

Yeah, me neither. Until the moment when EightBall lunged at me, blade in hand, and the air in the room lost all of its weight, causing me to feel naked even though I was fully dressed.

The practical effect of suddenly losing gravity was that EightBall's feet lifted off the ground, the momentum of his attack propelling him forward at a pace that would embarrass a turtle. EightBall flailed his arms wildly as he tried to gain balance in a room where up and down became abstract concepts. He looked like a man falling sideways, his face a hodgepodge of confusion, shock and fear.

Not that I blamed him. We all wore looks of surprise as our feet left the ground. The rest of us had all been standing relatively still, so the effect on us was that of simple levitation. We looked like a bunch of astronauts floating in a low-gravity environment—except that, as far as I knew, the One Spire Hotel had not teleported to the Moon.

At least we all were breathing normally. Thank the GoneGods for small miracles.

EightBall hit the wall on the other side of the room with a silent thud as the kid mouthed, "What the hell?" All of us tried to scream, but we were on Mute, our mouths contorted in shock as nothing came out. Sandy's neck was outstretched as her lips formed an O shape from which no howl emerged. And I'm ashamed to admit it, but I joined right in with the silent chorus of horror.

I guess Hollywood got it right—no one can hear you scream in space.

Only Judith was calm. Having no feet to speak of, she was used to floating around, so I guess not much changed for her. Despite the obvious panic we were all in, she still managed to give me a look that clearly blamed me for everything that was going on. To her, I was a criminal, so why not add "broke the laws of physics" to my Rolodex of felonies?

"Human," spoke a voice, breaking the silence, and flat-soled heels clicked on the ground. "Yes ... Indeed."

↔

"Holy shit!" I tried to scream, throwing up my hand in victory. "I was right!" I mouthed as Grinner walked in. What can I say? Celebrate every victory you can ... Trust me, they are few and far between.

Even in this silent room I could smell him.

"Answers," he said, his voice somehow penetrating his spell, "so many answers, but never the right questions." As he walked past me, he sniffed before grabbing my arm and spinning me 'round and around. I felt sympathy for my clothes in the tumble dryer, and swore at that moment to always hang them up.

Spin, spin, spin—I saw the others floating around. Some of them had managed to latch onto one another, only making them larger objects in motion. 'Round, 'round and around—I saw Grinner go to my desk and look through my papers. He stopped at the form that Joseph had written his name on.

"Joseph," he said to no one in particular, "of all the names the Universe had bestowed upon you, Joseph is by far the most human." He paused and cocked his head. "The stench of mortality has finally taken you. Perhaps Joseph is a fitting name to have been your last."

'Round and around—and I saw Judith about three meters away, rolling her eyes vertically in opposition to my horizontal spin.

'Round and around—Grinner opened the top drawer, a look of delight spreading his grin even wider as he saw the box. "How simple the mortal mind is. What is plain is discarded as worthless? And to think the gods chose you as their pets."

'Round, 'round—Judith was no longer across the room, but right next to me. I don't know if she was trying to help, or just wanted to get me killed, but either way, she pushed me in the direction of Grinner with a force that must have been backed by a bit of poltergeist fury. I was flying right toward him and did the only thing I could do—I stuck out my leg. The result was a roundhouse kick that would have had Bruce Lee eating his heart out. I connected with Grinner's friggin' smile, knocking him on his ass. Hard.

He dropped the box.

Wait a minute, he dropped the box! As if my realization made it happen, all of us came crashing down on the ground at the same time.

I grabbed the plain-looking thing and tossed it to Sandy with a "Catch!" She caught it in the air with her mouth and ran off on all fours like a Labrador at the park.

She leaped outside and I had just enough time to see her hand the box to Penemue—he must have flown down from the hole formerly known as Joseph's room—and him unfurl his wings before ten tons of invisible earth took me to the ground.

Well, at least the world had stopped spinning. Thank the GoneGods for small miracles.

↔

It happened so fast. Penemue couldn't have been more than

a few feet off the ground before Grinner trotted past me and pointed to the sky. Penemue fell hard, his wings outstretched but weighed to the ground, and Grinner picked the box up where it had fallen. I tried to push against the invisible force that held me down, but all I managed was to move my head around and survey the room. Every one of us was lying flat, even Judith, like we were all under a blanket made of lead.

I looked over at Grinner's face and I could see age lines starting to form around his lips. He was burning through time and if I pushed him a bit more, I might send him into a rage, let him burn himself out. Of course, I ran the risk that he'd burn himself out by lifting a mountain and dropping it on our heads.

"You!" I screamed out. "Yeah, you! Cheshire Cat!"

Grinner looked down at me and, with a light skip, came over. He held the box in front of my face and said, "Cat? I am no cat ... but the beasts please me. They shall be welcome in my new kingdom."

"Ahh, screw you! New kingdom, my ass ... You're just a two-bit worthless Other that the gods decided to leave behind. Maybe if you were worthy, they would have taken you with them."

He pushed down his index finger like one would flick ash off a cigarette, and the force that held me down doubled.

I couldn't breathe. I could feel the strain as my innards flattened out, vying for space in my torso.

I pushed against the massive, invisible weight. *Come on, you Fanatic, the clock is ticking.* "Is ... that ... all ... you ... got?" I grunted as I pushed myself up.

He redoubled the force and I crumpled to my knees. I fought it and I could actually see the strain on his face. I was resisting. But then he lifted his hands over his head, the box plummeting straight to the ground and landing, miraculously, in one piece. Grinner gave it no notice; he looked like he was literally pulling down the sky.

I fell flat on my back.

"But an answer I shall give," he grinned. His eyes betrayed a bit of surprise at how much of a fight I managed to put up against him. He displayed the same shock a lion might when coming up against a particularly feisty lamb. "For I am here to answer the second question each one of you asked when you finally understood that your gods were really gone. But before I do, there is something I need from you. I need you to dream."

"Like I said, screw …" I tried to finish the sentence but suddenly I was very tired. Very, very tired.

He was sucking out the oxygen. I tried taking shallow breaths, slowing my heart down, but it was impossible. There wasn't enough air to keep me awake. I started to fade.

↔

There is this girl whom I love very much. Every time I sleep, she rescues me from the darkness that chases me, and tonight is no different. Except whereas she is usually happy to see me, this time she greets me with a frantic concern.

"Wake up!" she screams. "You have to wake up!"

↔

"Huh?" I said, opening my eyes, fighting the fatigue.

"She waits," Grinner hissed, "go to her."

So tired, I … I …

↔

"Oh, hello, Bella," I say as my wife comes into view once more. "It's so good to …"

But Bella does not let me finish.

"Wake up!" she screams again. "Wake up! Wake up!"

↔

"WAKE!" a thunderous voice screamed from outside my hotel, and with it the air returned to normal.

I woke to see Grinner no longer concerned with me, his head turned to the entrance of the hotel. Whoever was outside must have scared the bejesus out of him because for the first time since I'd met the Fanatic, he wasn't smiling.

"You? You are gone," Grinner said, his concentration broken just enough that I was able to stand. It still felt like my black collarless jacket was made of ball bearings.

Standing just beyond the threshold of the reception was a young black man with a military buzz cut. He was maybe in his early twenties and wore jeans and a simple white, button-up short-sleeve shirt. "I am here," he said.

"To fill the Void," Grinner said, his tone implying an answer rather than a question.

The young man shook his head. "It is no longer our world to meddle with."

"No," Grinner retorted. "That is why they left. To start again and to let us start again."

"That is not so," the young man said, his eyes starting to glow.

I grabbed the box and put it in my pocket. I stood, only for the world to spin around. After being denied oxygen for some time, even the most ineffective bat-swings to the head can do some damage. As the world grayed out, I saw the two major-league Others face off in what must have been one of the most epic battles this world has ever seen.

Too bad I didn't get to see any of it.

Chapter 13
Spiteful Angels

"Jean," Bella says in a hurried voice, "you shouldn't be here. Not like this."

I can hear her voice, hear her breathing, but in the enveloping gloom, I can't see her. Which can only mean one thing—I failed to outrun the darkness. "Why not? This is the end, right?" I say. "My last dream of you before I go."

"I don't know." Her tone is softer now.

"I do."

"How do you know?"

"Because you're here. I always knew that in the end— my end—you'd be here to help me go over to the other side. Not like how I wasn't there for you." I can't finish the thought—*how I wasn't there for her as she bled on a cold, strange concrete floor.*

"Oh, hush. You were there. Believe me—it was you I saw before my end," she says. "And if this is your end then I am glad to have found you. There is nowhere else I'd rather be."

I feel the warmth of her as she draws in closer, and I lean into it. I know that she is just a dream but I am so happy to be with her.

Silence. But in the black, it is not just silence. It is the absence of sound. And I have never been very good at the absence of sound.

"So, what do we talk about? I mean, how does one spend their last moments alive?"

The darkness is pierced by a chuckle. "I don't know. Remembering the good times, I suppose."

"Ahh, the good times? So many to choose from. Do you

have anything particular in mind?"

"Yeah," she says, "I do … but since you're the one dying, why don't you go first?"

"OK," I say, "how about your thighs locked around mine. Like that time on the beach …"

"Jean!" she says, a hand lightly hitting my chest. "It's always about sex with you. I was thinking of something a little more … sweet."

"Like what?" It is strange how this feels so much like the old times and—dream or not—I can't think of a better way to clock out than this. "OK, you go first."

"You'll just think it's silly."

"Bella," I say, "I'm dying because a creature with a Cheshire Cat smile has literally sucked the air out the room because he wants some plain-looking box an old man gave me. I don't think there's anything you could say or do at this point that I'd think was silly." I am surprised at how calm I am. If I had known dying would be so easy, I would have tried it a long time ago.

"OK," she says, "… watching TV."

"I'm about to kick the bucket and the only memory you want to share with me is watching TV? I was expecting something like maybe the first time I told you that I loved you or when I proposed. Is there a particular show you have in mind? Because if it's *Sex and the City* I'm outta here."

"No, silly," she laughs. "Those were grand moments that punctuated our lives. The special moments. But they're not what I miss the most. I miss being with you, lying on a couch and doing nothing. I miss being bored next to you. I miss hearing you breathe and feeling the warmth of your body. I miss watching TV."

"Oh," I say, noticing a light off in the distance. It looks like the evening's first star, a pinprick in the blanket of night.

I ignore it. "I miss that, too."

"Look," she says, pointing at the dot of light, "it looks like this isn't the end, after all."

"Are you sure it's not the light at the end of the tunnel?" I say as the dot grows larger. It gets closer and closer until I am, quite literally, hit by light.

↔

Light getting shot into your brain makes gulping a cold Slurpee feel like a reasonable thing to do.

I barely opened my eyes to see Marty hissing about an inch away from my nose. Then I focused on the rest of her. Medusa was sitting at my side, a hand over my head. Judging by how warm my skull was, she burned a bit of time to save me.

"How long?" I asked, the words catching in my throat.

"You were out for an hour," she said.

"No, not that. How long did you burn to wake me up?"

Medusa turned away, not answering. I guess it'd gotten around how much I don't like time spent on me.

"How long?" I repeated, immediately regretting the harshness of my tone.

"About a day," she said, still not looking at me.

I grunted. Partly because I was still in pain, partly because my hotel was destroyed, but mostly because I hated time being wasted on me. Immortal creatures who no longer have forever should save their time for things that matter. Like living, not helping a stupid hotelier with his headache.

Medusa hunched away and from the glare Marty gave me I figured I hurt her feelings. Great job, Jean, she was just trying to help.

I started to formulate my apology, but couldn't think of

111

anything to say other than, "I'm sorry. I guess I'm a bit grumpy given everything that happened. Seriously. I'm really sorry. I shouldn't have snapped at you like that."

She turned to face me, but Marty looked away. I guess my apology wasn't acceptable to everyone.

"How is everyone else?" I asked, rubbing my head.

Medusa smiled at me, but her snakes continued to scowl. "They're all fine. As far as we can tell there was only one fatality—the Unicorn." She looked down when she mentioned Joseph. "But other than him, everyone is OK. You were hurt the worst." As she said the last words, she put up her hand to touch my head.

I winced at her touch, but was thankful to have someone looking after me and so I leaned into it a bit too much. Hey, can you blame me? I was in a lot of pain and my world was crumbling and she was being really, really nice to me.

I looked around my hotel. The mess Grinner had made was amplified by the presence of the police who were bagging and tagging just about everything. Hell, a couple of pixies in Barbie-sized police uniforms were bagging my phone. Talk about thoroughness. It bordered on comical and I might have started laughing had not a gurney appeared, carting out a body. Joseph's body. I watched with silent anger as they took him away.

I would get this smiling Fanatic if it was the last thing I did.

"Joseph," I muttered to myself as they carted his body away. Turning to Medusa I asked, "Was anyone else hurt?"

She batted her eyes at me and said, "So sensitive … Everyone's OK. Penemue is hiding in his loft, I think because he doesn't want to bump into his former adversary Michael. The HuMan hoodlums have made themselves scarce and Werewolf Sandy has given her statement and left.

Everyone is in good physical health, although they are devastated by what happened to the Unicorn." Medusa's own eyes glistened at the mention of Joseph. "You know, I met him once. A long, long time ago …"

"What happened?" I found myself asking, wanting to know more about the Other I had spent less than a day with. I wanted to honor Joseph's memory, know everything about him.

"Well," she started when a thunderous voice spoke.

"Miss Gorgon, I'll take it from here," a voice boomed from just outside.

Medusa immediately stood to attention. Then looking down at me she said, "Ahh, I got to go do police stuff. There are a lot of things to report, and I haven't seen a mess like this since Atlantis started to sink." Hurt still glistened in her eyes. "Maybe I can tell you the story about the Unicorn the next time I see you?"

"That would be nice," I said.

"Then coffee?" she asked. Before I could say anything, she smiled and said, "Great, I'll call you." With that she left, I endured another scowl from Marty and she was gone.

Hellelujah—I got a date with a gorgon.

↔

The archangel hunched down to fit through the One Spire Hotel's front door—not that there was much of it left—and crossed the threshold. The faithful, tougher-than-nails little bell above my front door chimed as he entered. I've really got to figure out how it survived all this carnage. What was it made out of? Adamantium?

As he entered, police officers of all species saluted him with hands, claws, talons and tails. He crossed the room and, seeing me still on the ground, knelt in front of me. By the GoneGods he was huge. Like André-the-Giant-crouching-in-front-of-a-newborn-baby kind of huge.

"What happened here?" he demanded.

There was something in the way he asked that made me realize that he had no clue. Like I mentioned earlier, angels—arch- or regular—aren't very good at tact. Michael spoke like someone who had just come onto the scene, despite having a good hour or so to investigate and figure things out. I mentally tallied my tenants—Sandy, Judith, CaCa, Astarte and Penemue—what did any of them really know? Joseph stayed at the hotel and was killed. As for other Others—the ones who lived nearby—they must have just seen some powerful Others destroying the street. So who did that leave? EightBall? To him it would've just looked like two Others that got into a fight. Just another reason why Others didn't belong.

But then again, what did I really know? Some Other that looked like my PopPop showed up with a box right before some wacko iced him? That wasn't much to go on.

"I don't really know …" I began. I told him everything I knew about Joseph, the weird Grinner guy and what I saw of the fight before I passed out.

Michael took it all in, listening to every word I said with a preternatural concentration. When I finished telling him all I knew, he looked at me for a long time—and for a second I feared that he knew I had left out the part about the mysterious box Joseph had given me that Grinner so obviously wanted, and that was currently in my pocket. I mean, Michael didn't look at me so much as *in* me, like he was solving some puzzle that was written on my soul. At least that's what it felt like to me to be stared at so intently by the archangel. Judging from the scowl that eventually crept on his face, I doubt he got the answer that he was looking for.

"So ... the Unicorn and this—what did you call him?"

"Grinner."

"Yes, this Grinner—just showed up at your place. Why? What connects you to them?"

I sighed. "Honestly, I have no clue!"

"Liar!" Michael boomed and the whole room shook. "After centuries of being a hidden legend, the Unicorn chooses to resurface in your hotel of all places and you have no idea why? You are hiding something, human. And I want to know what!"

"Hiding? Liar? You've got to be kidding me! Why would I lie? What could I possibly be hiding? I have zero idea why Joseph came to my hotel and have even less of an idea why anyone would hurt him. I swear to you. I don't know."

Michael huffed, dissatisfied. "Does this have anything to do with our conversation this morning?"

"Again—I don't know. Maybe? I have no evidence that what happened is connected, but then again, there's nothing saying that it isn't."

"Are you sure?" he said, staring me down with his angelic eyes. I swear to the GoneGods I could see flames flicker in them.

"Look, Michael, you know more than me. Frankly, I don't see where you get off being all alpha-angel on me. Weren't you the guy who told me that a Fanatic was in town? Weren't you the guy who drew a connection between that chump and my hotel?" His look didn't lighten up and I found myself getting more defensive. "What do I really know? I mean, up until today I didn't even know unicorns existed ..."

Michael closed his eyes in utter frustration when I

mentioned the Unicorn. He took in a deep breath before poking a taloned finger on my chest. Through gritted carnivorous teeth, he said, "If I find out that you have anything, anything at all, to do with this, I swear to …"

"God?" I offered.

I don't know what's wrong with me. In school they said it was because I had a problem with authority. The Army said the same thing. Bella thought it was because of my fragile ego. Penemue thinks it's because my skin is too sensitive. Astarte offers sexual suppression as the reason. Whatever it is, I don't like being poked. I hate it.

Still … I really wish I hadn't said what I said.

Michael roared, if you could call it a roar. I mean, I'd heard lions roar. I'd even heard a raging bull-dragon roar. But what Michael did was something much, much more. He broadcasted his ire, he pronounced his anger. He trumpeted.

He grabbed me and took to the sky, taking my front door frame with him. I didn't know what was happening until I was high enough that they'd only be able to identify my body with dental records. I'd tussled with angels before and I knew that if you hit the sweet spot where the wing met the body, they'd go down. I'd taken down one or two using that technique, but even if Michael stood perfectly still, exposing the area with a big red X on it, and I had a missile launcher, I seriously doubted I could take him down. There was a reason why Michael was Michael.

"YOU INSOLENT LITTLE TALKING MONKEY," he boomed. "WHO IS RESPONSIBLE FOR ALL THAT TOOK PLACE LAST NIGHT? TELL ME!"

I was terrified but had enough sense left in me to remember that he was an angel of the highest orders. And you didn't get that way by being a renegade. Now that his god was gone, the only orders Michael had to follow were of the kind that said dropping a human from three hundred feet in the air was illegal.

"I already told you that I don't know! Now put me down," I said, pretending that I wasn't crapping myself. "You and I both know that you're not going to kill me."

"Oath-Breaker," he whispered. "Other-Slayer. Do not presume that I am unaware of who you are. The path to redemption is long and filled with peril. You are correct that I will not drop you. But that does not stop me from telling your Army commanders where their precious little AWOL soldier went. What is the statute of limitation on desertion? Do you know, Oath-Breaker? Or maybe I don't tell them where you are, but rather inform some of the less tame Others where you are. There are many who would like nothing more than vengeance against the once great Exterminator. Tell me, how long do you think you will survive without an army to protect you? You have forty-eight hours to tell me who is responsible for the death of the Unicorn."

My face drained of all color. After Bella died I re-enlisted for a time before things got really bad. At the time, humans were no longer at war with Others, but Special Forces were put in place as a counter measure to the "less-agreeable" Others. Black Ops kind of thing—take out this terror cell, assassinate this uppity Other. Typical stuff we humans have always done to protect our interests. Only thing was, after a few missions I couldn't stomach it anymore and just left. Didn't tell Command—hell, they thought I was dead anyway—didn't even bother to get my stuff. I just left. That's a pretty serious offense, but at the time, I couldn't have cared less. I thought I had kept my secret pretty well, but if Michael knew, who else did? I was scared. Terrified.

But then it hit me … Michael must have known for a while—probably figured it out not long after I got back that second time. Maybe got suspicious when I never changed the name on the lease from Bella's to mine, or stopped signing for things in my full name or used Penemue's name on the utility bills and car registration. And despite knowing, he still hadn't turned me in. I needed to know why.

But more importantly, I needed to call his bluff.

"Oh, come on," I said. "You've got to get better at threatening! You're the original Boy Scout. You don't break rules or even bend them … for whatever reason, you haven't told the Army yet, and you're not going to tell on me now."

Michael smiled. And not a happy kind of smile. More like a "Got you!" kind of smile. I mean, I'd seen the Devil smile and it scared me, but this took "intimidating smile" to a whole new level. My body literally curled up, trying to get into the fetal position and die.

But Michael wouldn't let me off so easy. "You are correct, human. Yes, I must now obey mortal laws. But they are not the highest order. There are principles that negate their necessity. The path of redemption, for example, cancels the need to obey many mortal laws, and I, as a guardian of such principles, must give those who have proven themselves worthy a chance to do so unimpeded. That is why I have never told the mortal armed forces where you hide. Yet, if you should encumber this investigation, then I shall consider you to have strayed from the path and, therefore, no longer exempt."

A subtle pulse of luminosity passed through his eyes. "As for my other threat—do you know which principle is one rung lower than redemption, but still above mortal law? Righteous revenge. I am sure there are many Others that qualify, do you not think?"

I gulped. He had me there. During my fighting days, I killed just as much out of pleasure as necessity, and his moral compass would not twitch one bit by helping some Other get revenge on me over some of the terrible things I'd done.

But I was surprised to see that my—what did he call it?—path of redemption offered me some leeway with him. Seems I'd been doing some things right … not that it would do me any good now.

The shock of his threats was so all encompassing that I didn't notice that the whole time we were speaking, he was lowering us. He dropped me and I yelped as I fell all of three feet, before tumbling ungraciously on my ass smack dab in the middle of the PD's investigation.

"Jean-Luc Matthias, should any information concerning the events that transpired last night come to mind, please call the number on this card." He dropped a business card with MICHAEL ARCH, CHIEF OF POLICE written on it in bold letters. "Thank you for your cooperation. Let's wrap it up, boys."

The Billy Goats Gruff bleated and the eldest said without a hint of irony or suggestion, "Let's go graze Miss Dolly's backyard."

Hellelujah—I was absolutely, totally and unequivocally screwed.

Chapter 14

Even Angels Have Wicked Schemes

With Michael gone, the police wrapped up their investigation and left. I headed to my room and tapped on Castle Grayskull, nervous that one of the cops might have accidentally found the hiding fairy. She was, after all, a myth of a myth, and finding her would be like finding the back door to Narnia.

"Tink?" I said. "Tink ... are you OK?"

At first there was nothing, but then the left eye of the turret flickered and the three-inch-tall golden fairy popped out. She hit me square in the nose. I don't know if a punch from a Lego-size fist should hurt, but it did. My eyes were watering.

"What did you do that for?" I asked.

She shook a fist at me.

"Look, Tink, I had no idea this was going to happen or how to stop this."

A pang of guilt hit me—earlier, my instincts told me that Grinner was bad news and I ignored them. In another life, I would have never let it go, especially not to bake some cookies for Miral's event.

"It's not like I asked for this. I didn't ask Joseph to move in here, I didn't pick a fight with that maniac. So you can be as angry at me as you like, but for once, this isn't my fault."

Tink fluttered around the room twice and then pointed up at Joseph's room. Being here, hiding in Castle Grayskull, she didn't know what happened to Joseph.

I looked down and shook my head. "He didn't make it."

Tink buzzed 'round and around at speeds I'd never seen

her go before finally settling in on the turret of her home. The fairy was crying.

"Oh, Tink …" I started, but she turned away.

I took a step forward and she looked up at me as golden streams ran down her cheeks. Then she put her head on her knees again and her tiny shoulders started bobbing with wails of abandonment. I never knew silent cries could be so deafening.

"I'm sorry, Tink. I liked the guy a lot, too, and …"

But it was no use. TinkerBelle was too far in her own grief for me to reach her.

Confused and grief-stricken myself, I left the room and headed to the only place I knew that I could get any answers.

↔

I passed by Judith's room on the way up to Penemue. A pang of guilt and anger shot through me as I walked past the floor where Joseph once was, knowing that if I opened his door, all I'd find was an empty cavity. The box weighed heavy in my pocket.

"Jean," came my mother-in-law's shrill authoritative voice, "I was going to ask a favor from you."

"Sure," I said resignedly.

"Find that smiling asshole and kick him in the nuts for me."

"OK," I said with a weak smile. "Cross my heart."

I knocked on Astarte's door. She opened it, still in her teddy from earlier. She looked me up and down before saying, "Believe it or not, I'm not in the mood."

I didn't say anything, gesturing for her to follow me, and we went to Penemue's loft.

"First of all," I started, my voice dripping with sarcasm, "let me thank you for your help earlier. While I was getting my ass kicked downstairs, it was really comforting knowing that I had two demigods upstairs hiding."

"How," Astarte started, "do you know we did nothing?"

"Because while I was getting pounded down there, I didn't see a winged angel or a succubus in a teddy coming to my rescue. Would it have killed you to use a bit of time to help?"

Astarte rolled her eyes and I turned to face Penemue, who had his nose buried in some ancient leather-bound tome. "And what do you have to say for yourself?" I asked the angel.

Penemue put down the book on a stack. It had been some time since I was in his room and it was pretty much exactly as I remembered it. There was an angled roof, the peak running along the center of the room. It was only under the apex that Penemue could stand upright. At one end there was the straw bed that we'd made for him. It was literally a bale of hay held in an old, empty sandbox that we stole from an abandoned playground. An ad hoc solution for a bed, but how would you make a bed for an eight-foot-tall, four-hundred-pound angel? At the far end was the stoop where he flew in—when he wasn't too drunk to fly—and it had the same stained glass window that I installed four years ago. There was a bucket filled with half-empty bottles of Drambuie, and the rest of the room was filled with books stacked from floor to ceiling. Where he got them all, I didn't know, nor did I want to. I suspected there were several libraries in Paradise Lot with open windows and missing books.

Penemue took a swig of Drambuie. "If you remember," he said proudly, "I came down only to have the ex-werewolf throw something at me, presumably for me to whisk away. A task, mind you, I attempted before I was rudely pinned to the ground by burned time."

"You mean this?" I said, pulling out the box and throwing it to him.

"Yes," he hiccuped.

"What   is   it?"

Penemue put down the box and said, "There are other questions that need answering. Questions that I am currently researching."

"And pray tell," I said, exaggerating the vowels, "what does your research reveal?"

"That you are screwed," Astarte purred, grabbing my crotch. "And not in the good way."

I flinched and pulled her hand away. "What's going on here? Someone give me some answers. Who were those guys? No, scratch that … let's start from the beginning. Who—rather, *what* is … ahh, was Joseph?"

"The Unicorn. But you knew that already," Penemue said, slurring his words.

"Yes, but I thought unicorns were white horses with a single horn?"

"Oh, my poor misinformed mortal friend," Penemue said with an admonishing smile. "There is, was and will always be only one Unicorn. And now he is dead, he truly is a myth." Penemue put a hand over his heart.

"A legend," Astarte chimed in, a hand over her own heart.

"A fable," Penemue finished, taking a large swig of Drambuie.

Astarte walked over and put a hand on his shoulder, before taking the bottle from him and taking a drink herself.

Now it made sense why all the Others reacted to him the way they did. He was a singularity in their worlds and this one. Being truly unique, he belonged to no tradition or species other than his own. He didn't belong to some clan, have some historical beef or hold allegiance to any group over another. If anyone had a chance to unite all the different kinds of Others, it was him.

"And as for being a white horse," Astarte continued, "Joseph was whatever we needed him to be. Tell me, who did you see when you saw him? A friend? A parent? Perhaps a lover? You saw whoever you needed to see. Whoever brought you the most comfort. Perhaps if you saw him at another time in your life, he would have appeared as someone else."

An emotional chameleon, I thought. "Who did you see?" I asked.

"Light," Penemue said. "Just light." His eyes grew distant at the memory as a warm, content smile crept on his face. Even in death, Joseph still offered comfort to the fallen angel.

"And you?" I said to the succubus.

She gave me a sly little smile. "Wouldn't you like to know," she said as she pretended to zip up her lips with an erotic gesture of her fingers and a hint of tongue. Hellelujah, Jean—*focus.*

"OK," I said, "what about the Other who saved me? What is he?"

Astarte shot Penemue a look and said, "He is not an Other. He was a human."

"But he burned time," I said. "Humans can't do that."

"Hence the 'was,' " Penemue said. "Besides, some

124

humans can—rather *could*—possess magic. Harry Potter for one."

"Fiction," I said.

"Harry Dresden, for another."

"Again, fiction."

"I would have cried more for his death than my own … Both Harrys are very real, I assure you."

Dealing with Others hurt my head. "So, what? He's a ghost like Judith?"

"Something like that, but I fear it is a bit more complicated. You see, he is not a ghost, but rather *the* Ghost. As in the first human who chose not to 'shuffle off his mortal coil,' but to stick around."

"The Ghost?" I repeated, unable to keep out the skepticism in my voice.

"You're still not getting it, Jean. He was a human and now he is the Ghost. Before the gods left, he was the conduit between them and mortals. He is Isimud, Zaqar, Turms, Hermes and the Holy Ghost."

"The *what?*"

Penemue ignored me. "Tell me, Jean … Who do you think was responsible for telling the world that the gods left?"

↔

"So, what? That guy who saved us was also the guy responsible for the gods' broadcasting system to us? *This is GBS—this just in …* '" I said.

"You mock, but how did they communicate to you?" Penemue asked.

"I guess I never really thought about it before," I said, my head spinning with the meaning of it all.

OK, I get how the gods couldn't just broadcast their leaving on Facebook, but still, an actual living breathing conduit who was still on Earth? And what's more, at my hotel, saving my ass from some Fanatic? Hellelujah, this night could not get any weirder.

"So what do we know about him?" I said, looking from Penemue to Astarte. She was sitting on Penemue's bale of hay and even though she wore the same teddy from earlier, she somehow had an innocent-farm-girl look to her. All your fantasy needs in one neat little succubus's body.

"Nothing," Astarte said, jarring me from my thoughts. Who knew that standing up after sitting in hay could be so tantalizing? So many stray straws being drawn out of so many wondrous, mysterious places.

"Ahem … Except," Penemue said, "that the Unicorn engaged with this ex-human. And that he came to your aid with magic far more powerful than either of us have. And for the Unicorn to reveal himself means that he was on a mission of great import. And we know that whatever that mission was, it failed. No matter how important your quest may be, death has a way of ending things."

"OK, so what I'm gathering is that, although you know who Buzzcut is, you don't know what his involvement is in any of this. I don't suppose you know a bit more about that freak who killed Joseph …?"

"That is not for mortal knowledge," Astarte snapped with such a godly authority that I felt shame for wanting to know.

In her domain that would have ended the conversation. But down here, well, the tune of "I was once a goddess" was sung a lot in Paradise Lot.

"Don't give me that crap! He came in here and blew up my hotel. My home! *Our* home! He killed the most decent

Other that any of us has ever known. A totally unique, one-of-a-kind life extinguished by that asshole and you fall back on your 'It's not for mortal knowledge' crap. If you haven't noticed, we're all mortal now and if …" As I got into Astarte's face, there was a part of me that wanted to rip off her clothes and have the angriest sex ever known to mortal or Other. I started breathing hard, sweating as I came to. "GoneGodDamn succubus," I cried out.

I stepped back and caught my breath, immediately feeling more in control once I was a few feet away from her. I looked over at the sex-goddess and saw real fear in her eyes. But not of Grinner. She was afraid of me. And she was defending herself the only way she knew how. "OK," I said, forcing myself to take deep breaths, "OK … I'm sorry. But there are no more mortals and immortals. There's only us and we're all going to die. So please, tell me … what is he?"

Penemue grunted, throwing back his papers on the table. "Ahhh, how can one know what any of us really are?"

"Stop stalling. And none of your typical cryptic shit. What is he?" I demanded. "Tell me."

Penemue adjusted his armless glasses and flattened out his tweed vest before standing up straight and looking over at me.

"Don't …" Astarte started, but Penemue put up a hand.

"He is right, Astarte," Penemue interrupted, "the rules have changed. We are all mortal now."

Penemue crumpled up a piece of paper and dropped it. It fell like most things do—down. "When the gods made this world they needed to be able to communicate with certain immutable principles—the Laws of Nature, if you will. Whereas there are many laws that govern nature, there are only five Laws that are essential for life. They are known as the First Laws—Energy, Life, Death, Time and Gravity.

Each is necessary for this universe to possess life and they exist with or without gods. Energy is the force that allows motion, growth and change. Life and Death are the principles of renewal—they are the Laws that allow the world to keep evolving, ensuring each generation slightly improves on its predecessor. In theory, at least. Are you following me?"

I nodded.

"Then there is Time, through which all must make passage. Relative or not, Time moves us ever forward. Finally, there is Gravity. Gravity keeps the world together, it moves the Earth around the Sun. The Sun around the Milky Way. Our galaxy within the Universe. Gravity, some of us theorize, was the first of these Laws, for it is what originally paved the way for the existence of all. Without it, we would all be wandering atoms of motion, never attached, never together. Never alive.

"These five First Laws were needed to make all that is, and therefore the gods needed to negotiate with them in order to shape the world in the ways they wished. But how does one, even a god, communicate with a First Law?"

"Avatars," I said, the word catching in my throat. No wonder Astarte was frightened. Grinner was the Avatar of a friggin' First Law.

"Exactly," Penemue said. "You are astute … for a human that is."

"The gods created avatars for the First Laws so that they could speak to the principles and negotiate with them for certain concessions. They asked Life and Death to not touch the denizens, they asked Time to leave their dominions be, they asked Energy to imbue them with miraculous powers and they asked Gravity to allow their realms and this one to coexist, theirs invisible to this one."

"So it was because of Gravity that Heaven and Hell were invisible to humans?"

"Partly, yes. And partly for other reasons that even we," he pointed at Astarte, "are not privileged to know."

"So this Grinner guy is the Avatar of Gravity?"

"Indeed, Human Jean-Luc, he is."

↔

"Because gravity still works, Grinner doesn't burn through time like you guys do when you use your magic," I said, mulling through the logic of what it meant that your god was still around. Unlike Penemue and Astarte, whose gods abandoned them, gravity was still here. Otherwise we'd all be floating away to oblivion.

"Yes and no," Penemue said. "He is a creature like any other Other. But unlike myself or the succubus, he has so much power that he is as close to immortal as any of us could ever hope to be. Because his source of power still remains, there is a theory that he can renew himself, given enough time."

"You shouldn't have told him," Astarte said to Penemue. "There will be repercussions."

"Perhaps," Penemue said. "But, I have paid for giving humans knowledge in the past and I suspect I will again. But if he is to have a chance against his foe, he must know who his foe is."

"His only chance is to run. That is the only chance any of us have." She turned to me. "Run, foolish human. Run. Gravity does not have the ability to track you. Run, and pray that old age takes you before *he* does. That is what I plan to do." She lifted the hatch to leave.

"What does he want?" I asked.

Astarte turned from the hatch and said, "What do any of us want? Either for the world to return to what it once was or for it all to end." And with that, Astarte left.

"What's with her?" I said.

"After this night, things will have to change, yet again," Penemue sighed, speaking with a softness that he rarely displayed. "Change has come again. We are ancient beings used to the world being static. This constant revolution, it disturbs us."

Of course, I thought. Others spent eternities in one place, doing one thing. I'd met valkyrie who had stood guard duty at the halls of Valhalla on century-long shifts, fairies who'd hosted parties that lasted thousands of years and a giant who had slept for an entire eon, only to wake up, see the world was as it was and go right back to sleep. Dealing with change was not high on their set of life skills.

I nodded and pointed at the little box. "And that?" I asked.

He picked it up and looked at it closely. "A box," he said without a hint of irony.

"And …?" I pressed.

"And *nothing.* It is a plain wooden box."

"Grinner, ahh, I mean the Avatar of Gravity really wanted it. He almost killed me to get it. It must be magic or something."

Penemue snorted. It was an angel's version of belly-wrenching laugher, but to me it looked like he was sniffing in copious amounts of phlegm. "Magical item? What are we doing here? Playing *Dungeons & Dragons?* Items are not magic. They are only meaningful. Magic comes from you."

"Meaningful?" I asked, more confused than ever.

"When you possess something meaningful to you, truly meaningful to you, it will naturally accept magic with very limited amounts of time needed to be spent. Think of it like driving. Going uphill you will have to use a lot of gas, but downhill you will use very little. The same is with a meaningful object. They will do for you what you need with almost no time burned. The question is not, What can this box do? The question is, Why is this box meaningful? I suspect that once-upon-a-time, this box held something of great significance. Perhaps Joseph and—what did you call him?—Grinner wished to use its meaningful history so that it could hold something else of significance, but what do I know? Sadly, this box is meaningless to me."

"But if you knew its history, could you use it?"

"Perhaps. It depends on if it means anything to me." The angel adjusted his armless glasses and held the item closer to himself.

"Is there any way to find out?" I asked, hopeful.

"Of course, in time, perhaps I could figure it out," he said, pointing at his massive stack of books.

I smiled—it wasn't every day that the celestial librarian you need is living in your attic. "Hop to it."

Placing the box back on the table, Penemue walked over to the stack of books and picked up one that was lying on the very top. It started to glow. "Internet," he said, showing me his iPad. "Best place to start."

"But where did you get—"

"I stole it from Tommy Fisher, forty-two years old, married just before the GrandExodus and who made out with his bride-to-be's sister on their wedding night. Karma," he said, smiling as his taloned, oversized fingers surfed the Net, leaving me to realize that divine justice was also not a thing of the past.

"Fine," I said, "Internet, books, whatever. Also, one more thing—do your research somewhere else. I don't want you here in case he comes back."

The angel looked at me over the rim of his glasses. "I seriously doubt that—"

"Please," I said.

"Very well, I shall sit on the turret of the National Library," Penemue sighed. Then, lifting the iPad, he pointed at the Wi-Fi symbol and said, "I can get two bars from up there."

Chapter 15

The Question Is an Answer

After receiving the hodgepodge of *oh-so-not-confusing* information from Penemue and Astarte, I headed to the reception, hoping that there would be some other clues as to what was going on and what my next steps could be. Right now I was grasping at straws and was desperate for anything. Anything at all. I was fairly certain that this was the calm before the storm.

EightBall and the rest of HuMans would be off somewhere licking their wounds, probably more scared than ever. They'd be planning their next attack, and after last night, I was pretty sure that they'd rule out a head-on assault. A group like that lacked inspiration and, like everything else they did, stole their ideas from what was around them. I would bet my entire collection of G1 Transformers that they would probably be inspired by the explosion and that they were online looking up how to make homemade Molotov cocktails. That's exactly what I would be doing in their shoes.

Not that there was much of a hotel left to blow up. Still, there was no chance of them backing down. No way. Not after last night—not kids like them. If the hotel wasn't here, they'd hunt down whoever was, which meant that every Other they saw in the foyer was in danger. Penemue, Astarte, Judith, Sandy … Oh, *hell*. Whatever they were planning, it was coming and coming soon.

But still, that wasn't my real problem. I was equipped to handle punk kids. What I wasn't equipped to handle was a pissed-off archangel, and what I really, really wasn't equipped to handle was the anthropomorphic representation of

133

gravity. Hellelujah!

There was nothing downstairs that was of use. Turned-over chairs, blown-out windows, broken glass. Even my desk was splintered apart. Other than the super bell over my front door, the only thing that remained intact was my phone, which was in a plastic Evidence bag, thanks to an enthusiastic pixie officer. It blinked with a message. Somehow I suspected it wasn't someone calling to reserve the room.

Unwrapping it, I clicked checked my voicemail.

Beep. "Jean—are you OK? Michael came by and told me what happened to Joseph. The sanctimonious bastard even implied you had something to do with it. I know you didn't. I have faith in you. Bella had faith in you. The loss of Joseph will be felt throughout Paradise Lot. There will be a lot of grieving, angry Others. We'll have to handle this carefully, otherwise we will have a riot on our hands. I've called an emergency meeting with some of the locals. I think we can contain this, but we really need a miracle. I don't suppose they left any behind, do you? Call me. Or better yet, come by." *Beeeep.*

Ohh, frig, Miral was right. I hadn't even considered how Joseph's death would be taken by the Others. Shit—their Unicorn was gone, killed in a human-run hotel. Whatever she did, she'd have to handle the news of Joseph's death very carefully.

I had to go to Miral, but first I needed answers. Something, anything was better than turning up empty-handed. Maybe Penemue would figure out what the box was, or ... *Oh come on, Jean. When did you become so useless? What does your training tell you to do?*

My choices seemed simple enough. Go to bed or find this Ghost guy, and seeing how I didn't have a chance in

Hell of falling asleep with all this going on, I decided to look for the gods' broadcasting system.

I turned inside to get my stuff, when I saw Astarte standing at the entrance. She had a suitcase in hand. "I'm going to be staying with some ... ahh, friends for a while," she said. "Not that it matters. Seems like your dream of a haven for Others is dead anyway."

I nodded, looking over at Astarte as she headed for the door. The ship was sinking and she was doing the smart thing—getting off. "OK," I said. "Good luck."

She paused at the door and said, "You know the origin of 'Good luck'?"

I shook my head, not really in the mood for another Other lesson.

Astarte didn't take the hint. "The original expression was 'May God give you luck.' "

"Really?" I said, continuing my Sisyphean task of shuffling around the rubble.

"Yes—but the problem with that was that often the god's luck was more of a curse than a boon. So it evolved into 'May God give you good luck' and then to just 'Good Luck.' That was the last thing they said to us when they left. 'Good luck.' I think they were mocking us." Her eyes took on a distant look as she recalled some ancient memory. "I never liked the expression. It implies that you don't have control over your fate. That was the lie that the gods tried to convince mortals of ... that what happens to you is destiny, out of your hands, the will of the gods. But it was always in mortal hands. Always."

I nodded. I didn't know what to say.

"Having luck means you have no control. But you always have some control. Even if it is only to run or to fight." She looked over at me, her deep azure eyes locking

135

with mine.

A car pulled up to the front of the hotel and its passenger's side door opened. "Jean, I'm sorry. It's just that …" she started.

"Nothing to be sorry about," I interrupted.

She looked at me with mournful, sad, vulnerable eyes and for the first time since meeting her I think I actually got to see what she looked like. I mean, really looked like, when you took away all the yearning and lust—deep down she was just like everyone else. Then the veil was thrown back up as she threw back her head and laughed, shaking away all the vulnerability and bringing back the want of her with it. "Look at me, so serious … Really, Astarte, mortality has made you such a drag. Listen here, lover. If you survive this, you look me up. We'll have a drink or ten, and laugh about when the world almost ended for a second time."

"Sounds good to me, Astarte," I said. "Sounds really good to me."

"Yes," she said, getting into the car, "it really does, doesn't it?"

↔

With the slamming of the car door, Astarte—my only paying customer—was gone. Not that it mattered. However this was to end, it wouldn't be with the One Spire Hotel staying open for business. I went inside and saw that my desk had been turned right-side up and there was an envelope on it. Inside, a note read, *I'm not really the apocalyptic kind of gal. May you make your own good luck.* Damn—even her handwriting was sexy. I opened the envelope and a stack of hundreds fell out—easily a room's rent for a year. Hell, two years, even.

I know that seeing that money should have made me

happy. It was enough to pay off the landlord and keep all the other friggin' bills at bay for a while. But it really pissed me off. It pissed me off that there was a hole in my hotel. It pissed me off that after all I'd been through, I'd have to shut down and break my promise to Bella. And it pissed me off that the kind, sweet, literally one-of-a-kind Joseph was dead.

But what really pissed me off more than anything else, what really boiled my blood, turning my anger into pure unadulterated rage, was that the bastard responsible for all of it was still smiling.

Chapter 16

Everything Leaves Behind a Scent

After Bella died, I joined Special Forces for a couple years. Those were the darkest days of my life and I am not proud of anything I did while obeying orders. It took a while for me to wake up, but I did. I woke up in the middle of what would be my last mission when Headquarters thought I got burned to a crisp by dragon fire. They were wrong and that's when I went AWOL, leaving the killing and fighting behind. But I still had all the gear they sent with me. And because I was Special Forces, that was some pretty significant stuff. Stuff I'd dragged halfway across the world. Stuff that, if they knew I was still alive, they would have hunted me down years ago to get back. Stuff that was going to be useful now. Most of it I left in PopPop's cabin where I lived in the years between leaving the Army and coming back home, but I did bring a few things with me to Paradise Lot.

I still had the chest piece of my battle suit, an Army-issue flashlight, my Swiss Army knife and my hunting sword. The hunting sword wasn't Army-issue. I got it off of an Other I took down in a particularly bloody battle, and because I was the scourge of the OnceImmortals, the Army let me keep it. It was eighteen inches long and curved downwards, with the last third of the blade about twice the width of the rest of it. The single edge ended about four inches from the tip where it met another razor-sharp edge, turning the last four inches into a double-edge knife. As it was intended to be a one-handed weapon, the hilt was not quite long enough for both my hands to hold it. The blade was engraved with an intricately decorated mural, depicting an ancient hunt. I asked Penemue one night what the image was of, and he—drunk and face-down in his bale of hay—looked up long enough to say, "Young Human Jean, this is the Earl King's hunting sword. The one he carries with him on the Great Hunt. To possess it can only mean one thing. You are the one to have brought down the great King. Not bad for a social worker. He was a legend and an epic asshole. With the gods gone, he would have been hell-bent on taking over this world. Still, he did have his loyal minions …" Then he put his finger over his lips and pretended to zip it up.

I thought about that as I tied the scabbard around my waist and sheathed the sword. Then, placing my backpack on the driest section of pipe I could find, I took a deep breath and clambered out of the sewers.

↔

Tracking magic is easy. Hell, you could download novelty apps to your phone that work pretty well. All you have to do is find time.

Seems that magic not only speeds up one's biological clock, aging the user proportionally to the amount and strength of the magic, but it also screws with your watch. The faster the second hand spins, the closer you are to magic. Simple.

Since my cell phone was one of those flippy kinds from the previous century and completely un-app-able, I went to my toy shelf and pulled out my Mickey Mouse wristwatch. It would do just fine.

I left my room and checked the second hand. It was going slightly faster. I walked into Joseph's blown out room. The site was still as it was—pipes flattened and the far wall missing. The only difference was that Joseph's body had been taken to the morgue. I shook my head as renewed anger swelled up inside me. I looked at the watch again and saw it spin around at nearly double-speed.

Good. This would be easier than I'd thought.

↔

One last thing to do before I could begin the hunt. I knocked on Judith's door. Light seeped out from the crack beneath her door and although she had no feet, the base darkened. She didn't open the door.

"Judith," I said. "I'm going out and I don't want you here alone just in case that guy comes back. I think you should go. Home." There was a rustling and I heard a click from inside. The light went off. "I know you hate it there. I do, too. Too many things to remind you of Bella, but it's not safe here."

Even though a closed door was between us, I could still feel the awkward silence. "Look, I just want you to be safe. Astarte is gone. Penemue is drunk and ... Listen, I know you hate me. I know you think this is all my fault. That I've screwed up again. That's fine, but I promised Bella that I'd take care of you and ..."

The door clicked open and Judith floated in front me. She was wearing her Sunday hat and carrying a packed bag. She glided by me with hardly a look, but when she got to the top of the stairs, she stopped. "You're going after him, aren't you?"

I nodded. "Not directly, but I figure I can find out where he's staying or something about him. A weakness maybe. Anything that will help take him down."

"OK," she said. She started to move again and stopped. I could see that she was having a raging debate with herself, and the side that she wasn't rooting for just lost. She shook her head and with a sigh, looked at me and said, "I don't blame you. For Bella. I know you did everything you could to save her."

It was an old pain. A scene I've replayed over and over in my head. The attack, the confusion. Bella lying there, me locked out, too late to get to her. As kind and unexpected as Judith's words were, it didn't matter. I blamed myself. "I wasn't fast enough," I said.

Judith rolled her eyes. "Always looking to argue with me." Her voice lacked its usual ire. "No one would have been fast enough. I saw the footage. I know what you tried to do. And if I don't see you again, then I just want you to know that I don't blame you."

"Thank you," I said. Things were evolving between us. This might even have been a new chapter for us. Too bad it was likely to be a very, very short chapter for me.

"Now, what happened at this hotel and to Joseph," she said, the shrill quality of her voice returning. "I absolutely blame you for what happened here. Really, Jean. There's only one way to make this right. Kick that smiling bastard right in the teeth."

"Yes, ma'am," I said. "That's exactly what I plan on doing."

↔

Armed with my Mickey Mouse watch, I tapped on Castle Grayskull's front door and said, "Tink—it's time to go."

She came out in a flash and shook her head in protest.

"Don't worry," I said, "I'm not taking you with me."

She gave me a concerned look and cocked her hand like a pistol, mimicking a shootout.

"No, no—nothing like that. I'm not going guns blazing.

141

This is a recon mission, and that's all. No engagement." I didn't know what it was about talking to Tink, but my old military vocabulary always snuck out whenever I wanted to get her to do anything she wasn't interested in.

She gave me a skeptical look, to which I crossed my heart and said, "Swear to the GoneGods."

She nodded and buzzed around, seemingly convinced. That was the thing about Others—they took swears, oath, and promises very seriously. I guess in some ways we were pretty similar.

"But still," I said, "I don't want to just leave you behind in case he—or anyone else, for that matter—comes back. We need to hide you."

Tink fluttered around, a golden tail of dust following her. She buzzed around my head three times and, like a comet, shot into Castle Grayskull. She popped out a couple seconds later wearing Man-At-Arms's helmet and carrying He-Man's sword. She saluted me, buzzed around three more times and grabbed an old velvet pouch I used to hold my dice. She handed it to me, gesturing for me to put it around my neck.

"No, Tink. It could be dangerous. We've got to hide you. In the spot we talked about. The drainpipe of the church, and you climb to the top. When I'm back, I'll hit the pipe twice and you come down. Remember?"

She nodded and then tried to push through my fingers again.

"It's too dangerous."

She fluttered into my face and wagged a finger at me. I'd seen that look before. She was coming and that was that. Truth was, I was glad to have some company and swore to myself that I'd hide her before engaging anyone.

"OK." I softened. "OK, but first sign of trouble, we

hide the pouch and you with it. Agreed?"

She nodded once and dove into the pouch. I put it around my neck right next to my silver necklace with the plastic twisty-tie, and with a whoop the pouch went flat. I didn't know how she did it. Burned time, I suspected. When I asked, she insisted that she didn't, miming that there was a hole in my chest where my heart should be. Thanks, Tink, way to make me feel good about myself.

With Tink in tow, I dressed, opting to leave behind my collarless black jacket and put on my old leather jacket and jeans. I started to put on my old Army-issue, steel-tip boots and then thought better of it. Where I was going, it was better to wear my knee-high rubber boots.

I grabbed my old Army-issue canvas bag, prayed I wouldn't have to open it and headed out the door.

↔

I didn't want to take the risk of being seen, so I decided to use the one advantage I had in getting around this city. I had my own personal tour guide in the sewers below. I headed to the basement and lifted the drainage grill in the center of the floor. Being in frequent use, it lifted easily enough and I climbed down.

I made a lot of noise when entering CaCa's domain. The last time I came in here I scared the lumbering, gentle beast half to death, and with a knee-jerk reaction he employed one of his natural defenses. There was very little natural about it. Think of a skunk's spray, then imagine that it hung in the air like a squid's black ink cloud. Now replace both spray and ink with what CaCa was famous for. It crusted within seconds, simultaneously blinding, nauseating and encumbering me. There were not enough baths in the world to get that stuff off of you and I never, ever wanted to go through that again.

"Hi," I cried out in an exaggeratedly friendly tone. "It's me. Jean-Luc." I added, just in case, "From upstairs."

There was a clamoring as I looked down the man-sized sewage drain. I couldn't see anything and as for smell—well, there was only one thing I *could* smell. I turned on my flashlight and saw a river of human- and Other-waste that was thankfully only ankle-high.

I held my breath and spoke loudly again. "Hey, CaCa—are you down here?" He might be out, painting another one of his masterpieces from his vantage point below. But then my flashlight caught a stirring and I focused on where the movement came from. Perfectly blended with the sludgy browns and grays of the pipe behind him, two eyes opened, a piece of something yuk falling into the sludge below. A grunt was followed by a hand that removed itself from the background as CaCa breeched forth from where he had, quite literally, stuck himself. It looked like someone coming out of mud, if not for the smell.

CaCa separated himself from the wall and raised a hand in a sort of wave. From the way he did it, I knew that he was mimicking something he'd seen humans do. The wave was as unnatural to him as my presence here was to me. Still, not wanting to discourage him, I waved back. He smiled and as his lips parted, little bits of solid waste fell from them.

Hellelujah, we can only be what we are, I thought and wondered if I was as repulsive to him as he was to me. I don't think so, because even though he literally wore a shit-eating grin, I sensed he was genuinely happy to see me. He gestured for me to follow as he lumbered away from the cellar grate entrance.

↔

CaCa led me to a drier—and considerably less *fragrant*—open chamber adjacent to the pipe I had entered. It was large, about three times larger than the breakfast room that I used for the "Coping with Mortality" seminar. In it were two dozen erect easels, each with canvases on them. I walked around the room and saw Paradise Lot, not for what it was, but for what it could be. Pictures of humans and Others walking hand in hand, children playing in clean streets, vibrant businesses that catered to all species. Each was rendered to a level that would have made Norman Rockwell turn green with envy, for CaCa captured hope in ways that I doubted any mortal born could. These paintings were the end of one possible path we could all take. And even though I really wanted to share in CaCa's view of a brighter tomorrow, I knew all too well that there were darker, more likely futures for Paradise Lot.

"I love them," I said to a smiling, proud CaCa. He raised his hands up like an old man dismissing a compliment, as if he were saying, *These old things. A hobby, nothing more.*

Such humility. CaCa was the best among us and his reward was to be tucked away, forever below, all because of the way he looked—well, and *smelled.* And yet, despite that, he was still so hopeful. But not for himself—I noticed that no painting had him walking in the sunlight above—solely for his fellow Others and humans.

CaCa disappeared behind his latest painting. I started to go around, but he gestured for me to stay on the other side of the aisle. I guessed whatever he was working on was not quite ready.

"CaCa," I said, "I need your help."

He looked around from his painting with an inhumanly

wide smile on his face in an imitation of Grinner.

"Yes. I'm looking for him. He killed the Unicorn."

CaCa's smile immediately disappeared.

"I need to also find that man who fought that grinning Other. Can you help me?"

He shrugged.

"That's OK," I said, "I have this."

I showed him my watch, the second hand running slightly faster than normal. CaCa understood.

"I don't want to wander the streets above in case Grinner is out there. And besides, he's not who I'm looking for. I want to talk to that other guy. The one who saved me. I figure that if he burned time he'll be relatively easy to find." I pointed at my Mickey Mouse watch. "Can you take me around?"

Without hesitation, CaCa stepped out from behind his canvas, smoothing his rumpled chest with his hands. With an unnatural speed, he drew a crescent on his chest that reminded me of a knight's banner. It was of a unicorn and human standing on a crown. Apparently this was his way of saying that he was in.

Chapter 17
The Light at the End of the Tunnel of Shit

Using the sewers was a fast way to travel around Paradise Lot. We walked under the city, the second hand of my Mickey Mouse watch revving up bit by bit as we progressed through the tunnels. And then we found it, in the heart of the city—Mickey went crazy, his tiny arm spinning 'round and around with such a fury I thought he'd fall apart. From the sidewalk's drainage grate across the street, I could see the building where one of the most powerful Others the world has ever known was holding out.

There was only one thing to do. Watch and wait.

We were just on the outskirts of Paradise Lot and, although technically a human part of town, this area was still close enough to the center that most of the humans moved out. And it showed. The adjacent houses were falling apart with several of them boarded up or with broken windows. It was an old story. Once-upon-a-time, families lived in this neighborhood, their kids playing together as the community thrived. Then the wrong type of neighbors started showing up. Real estate prices dropped and crime rates rose until it was "Bye-bye families" … Only difference was now humans discriminated against Others, as in with a capital O, instead of just others.

All the buildings on the street showed neglect—all except one. It was an old brick building, three stories high and had two blooming rose bushes and an old sycamore tree in the front yard.

I watched for hours, boredom taking its toll. At one point, my chest started to stir as Tink poked her head out of her hiding place. "Don't," I whispered. "We're not alone."

147

But the fairy pushed out nonetheless, looking down the pipe where CaCa stood, enthralled as he drew his latest masterpiece. How he found the right materials and colors in the patch of sewer where we were standing, I don't know, nor did I want to. But you know what? It didn't matter, when I looked over at the mural CaCa had drawn using the raw materials common to sewers. Still, despite his tools, what he drew was beautiful. There was a park with children running, flying kites, playing ball. Their parents were there, picnickers laughing, drinking, being merry, each with CaCa's signature joy on their face. But they weren't just human picnickers, there were Others, too. Standing next to each other, happy, each tolerant of the other's ways. A perfect scene of serenity.

And then I saw him, on a hill watching over the serene scene: Joseph. Except not my Joseph, who reminded me of my PopPop, or Penemue's who looked like light—but a roly-poly man with a Buddha belly, smiling down on all of us.

"Holy shit," I said, turning to CaCa. "This is amazing."

The demigod put a hand over his chest with a shrug that said, *What? This old thing?*

"Yeah, this! So is that what he looks like to you? Joseph, I mean," I said, pointing to the happy man on the hill.

CaCa shook his head, making a hugging motion.

"Oh," I said with sudden comprehension, "that is how he looks to most people."

CaCa nodded.

So that was it—he didn't depict Joseph as his own personal comfort, but searched for a figure that gave comfort to the most number of beings, Other and human alike. And seeing that happy man on the hill, well, it worked for me. I could buy into this symbol of Joseph.

I don't know if it was seeing the picture of a future

denied us by the Unicorn's death or if it was simple boredom, but I just couldn't sit around and wait any longer. I walked over to a more remote part of the pipe and removed the old dice pouch around my neck, placing it on a bit of brick that jutted out. Tink put out her head and started to gesture that she was coming with me when I whispered, "You promised."

I turned to CaCa and said, "Thank you, I can take it from here." Then, as an afterthought, I said, "CaCa—if you don't see me back at the One Spire Hotel by tomorrow, I want you to come back here and take this pouch to Miral. Make sure she, and no one else, gets it."

He looked at the brick ledge and nodded. Then he began lumbering back down the pipe.

"Thank you," I whispered and looked up at the manhole that separated me from the world above.

↔

The grate slid open easier than I had expected and I popped out in the alleyway behind the little house without making a sound. Luckily for me, the grate was in-between a parked van and an old SUV. Unless someone was standing right there, no one would have seen me getting out of the sewers.

The back door was less than seven meters away and I used the sycamore tree as cover as I slunk up the stoop. Whether or not he lived there, someone did.

OK—remember the plan. Get in, see who's here, gather intelligence. Do not engage.

I looked up and down the street. Empty. OK, it was now or never. In the Army, one of the skills that I particularly excelled at was sneaking around. Not to beat my own drum, but I was uncannily light on my feet. Bella joked

149

that it was because I was part cat. After the Army, when I retreated to the mountain side, I used to practice this skill by taking down game with only my hunting sword, which meant I had to be less than two meters away before the animal saw me. How good was I? Let's put it this way: I never went vegetarian in those mountains.

I employed my best skills, taking the most care to get to that back door. Just as my hand touched its handle, it opened. What was worse, my phone started to ring at that exact moment, professing to the world that I had forgotten to put it on silent.

"Aren't you going to answer that, Jean-Luc Matthias?" the Ghost asked.

↔

I picked up the phone, and a frantic Penemue said, "I figured out what the box is. Where are you?"

I shot a quick glance up at the street sign, before returning my gaze to the Ghost. "Bread Street," I said. "I'm with him."

"Who?"

"You know … the Ghost." Then, still looking at him, I asked, "You are the Ghost, right?"

He smiled, waving a hand. "Please, of all the names I once had, the Ghost is the least inviting. Call me Hermes." And with that he opened the door wide, gesturing for me to enter.

"I gotta go," I said, hanging up before the angel could protest.

"You seem upset to see me," Hermes said, his smile touching the corners of his aged eyes. The person, or rather Ghost, who stood before me was an elderly man, well into his sixties, not the young man who saved me last night. But there was no mistaking him. He wore the same white shirt, black pants and buzz cut, which was now more gray than black. The elderly man shuffled into the room, taking strides that his body simply was no longer designed to take. He wasn't used to being old and still moved as he had in his youth. "Did I ruin your surprise?"

"I really put a lot of thought into coming here. You could have at least had the decency to pretend you were surprised to see me," I said.

He chuckled. "I do not believe that traveling through the sewers was for me."

"True," I nodded.

"That was wise. Thus the only wasted theatrics was your approaching my home like a thief in the night, instead of the welcome guest that you are."

He led me to his living room, a sparsely decorated room with two couches, a throw rug on wood-paneled flooring and an open liquor cabinet. Frameless photographs were taped to the walls—him fishing up north, him in a military uniform, him with some girl. All of them showed a young man that, as far as I knew, could have been photographed yesterday. Gardening gloves and a small hand rake sat on a coffee table, dirt still clinging to them. It was your typical bachelor pad, sparsely decorated, a halfhearted attempt at decoration, except for the candelabrum that sat in the corner. There must have been fifty candles of various sizes and shapes, all lit.

He examined the candles, relighting one that had extinguished, and went over to the liquor cabinet, pulling out two glasses and a bottle of wine. "Drink?"

"No thanks," I said. "How did you know it was me and not … you know, Gravity's rejected son?"

He gestured at the candelabrum. "I have my own ways of hiding from him. Now, an enterprising human … well, that is much harder to hide from." Hermes looked at me for a long, uncomfortable moment. "So you've figured out that you are up against a First Law," he said. He poured himself a glass and lifted it toward me before taking a sip. "The Fallen One told you?" It was more a statement than a question.

"We're all the fallen now," I said.

He took a seat a little too quickly. The youthful thump rather than the careful lowering that an old man would do caused him to groan. He took another sip and said, "Touché. We are, indeed. Fallen and blessed. Are you sure that you do not want a drink?"

I shook my head.

"Too bad. When you reach my age you learn to slow down and enjoy the finer things in life," he said, not masking his bitterness. "I do pray that Joseph was right about you and that my sacrifice was not in vain."

What do you say to someone who literally aged fifty years in an hour just to save your ass? Thank him? Skirt the issue? Offer to help him with the gardening? All I could do was lower my head and apologize. I looked at my hands and saw more blood on them.

"You don't remember me, do you?" he said.

"Have we met before?" I said, looking back up at him. I tried to imagine him without the liver spots or wrinkles. I tried to see him as he once was and remembered nothing.

"I don't expect you would. I was … in the background. But we have met. More than once. We never spoke though, even on that long, turbulent plane ride to Helsinki."

Helsinki? I had only been there once, as a guard for the Ambassador and Bella on one of their failed diplomatic missions. I had never liked flying and when the plane was tossed around like a leaf in a hurricane, I threw up more than once. I was convinced that some demigod once worshiped for weather was trying to kill us all. I was supposed to be the soldier. The one calm in the face of death, and yet I was falling apart. Like I said earlier, I want to see death coming, and falling out the sky in a metal cage didn't cut it.

And all the while Bella and the Ambassador had laughed at me, both cool as cucumbers. "What's the matter, Jean-Luc?" the Ambassador said. "Scared of a little wind?"

"Easy for you to say," I said. "You have wings."

"Ahh, yes—that is true. And moreover, should we fall from the sky, I am strong enough to save at least one of you. But only one. Tell me, Jean, who should I save? You, Bella or someone else?" He gestured to the half dozen or so fellow passengers.

"The one who has the most worth," I said without hesitation.

The Ambassador chuckled. "That is a soldier's answer. But we are diplomats now. Answer me as that. Who do I save?"

"I don't know," I said in between dry heaves.

The Ambassador opened the question to the floor. "Come on—someone must know the answer. Who do I save?"

A couple of people said, "Me, please," joking. One said, "If you save him, he'll barf on your shoes in thanks." Another laugh.

Then from the back of the plane a voice said, "No one. Not even yourself."

"Indeed," the Ambassador said, snapping his blunted fingers. "To save one over another is to value one life over another. And in this brave new world, no one life, no matter their species, role or purpose, should be more valuable than any other. That includes my own."

"So do nothing?" I snorted with derision.

"I never said that. But as a leader, it is incumbent on me to save everyone or die trying."

Lost in the memory, I refocused on Hermes and said, "It was you on the plane. The one that answered the Ambassador's question."

He nodded. "He was a great Other."

"Was he?" I asked.

He met my uncertainty with his own certainty and nodded. "He was. And so was your wife. Not a great Other, but a great creature—a great human being." He poured himself a second glass. "You do not have to drink, but you do have to join me in a toast. To Bella." He handed me the glass.

I could drink to her. We clinked. "You knew her?"

"Worked with her. She was such a special human," he said, taking another sip. I could have sworn when he started drinking it the glass was filled with white wine, but now it was a crimson red.

"And you're in town to meet Joseph?" I asked.

Hermes nodded.

"And the cynocephaly? Were they here for Joseph as well?"

"Guards that knew both the Ambassador and Bella," Hermes said. "They were to meet us in town and resume their role as guardians while we continued their work."

"And what was their work, exactly?"

"All in good time," Hermes said.

"All in good time? What the hell is that supposed to mean?"

"It means that I have yet to assess your character and deem you worthy to know."

I felt the rage within me rising. "My character," I said. "My character? You've got to be kidding me! *You're* the guy who comes into my town, destroys my hotel and *I'm* the one being judged?" Hermes met my gaze with an even demeanor, which only served to anger me more. "So Penemue guessed right. You are the messenger."

"The messenger," Hermes said absently. "Yes, I suppose you could call me that."

"So you're the guy responsible for that doozy of a message … What was it? 'Thank you for believing in us, but it is not enough. We're leaving. Good luck.' You couldn't have given us a little more, don't you think?"

Again he nodded, casual and relaxed, as if I was asking him if he was the one who cooked dinner or brought the dessert.

"Of all the arrogant Others I've met … Our world changed in an instant, thousands died and all you could give us were those three short sentences."

"What did you expect me to say?"

"An explanation. A reason. Some guidance."

"Really," he said. "And tell me, had I spoken page after page of instruction, would you have listened?" He pointed at me as he spoke.

"Maybe not *me*, but others might have."

"Really? And what would have happened when one group interpreted my words one way and another group understood them another way?" he said, bitterness rising in his voice. "I'll tell you: exactly what happened every time they gave me the task of sending you mortals a message. More misinterpretation. More war. More death. No matter what I said, no matter how I consoled you, tried to guide you, you humans have an incredible ability to hear exactly what you want to hear and then kill anyone who understands differently. Well, no more. If this was to be the last message I was to give the mortal realm, then let it be clear for once."

"And was it?"

Hermes shook with rage. "I don't know," he yelled, "you tell me. In all the fighting, all the killing, did any of it have to do with how the message was received? Or was it just human nature's unwillingness to share? You know, Joseph told me all about you ... about your desire to redeem yourself, your promise to Bella ... He told me about how you want to fix some of the things you broke. Clean some of the blood off your hands." Hermes drew in close, his face less than an inch from mine. "But you are not the only one with blood on your hands. Try eons fighting over misinterpreted messages, centuries of killing for words misheard, and then you will understand what it means to have blood on your hands."

Hermes stood up and poured himself a second drink. Taking a large gulp, he turned to me and said in a calm voice, "But we're really not here to talk about me. This meeting is about you and the girl whom you promised to love forever. In this life and the next."

↔

"How do you know those words?" I demanded. "That's what I said to her the night I proposed."

Hermes ignored me. "When the gods left and kicked out their denizens from their realms, it was like ..." He searched for the simile. "Like kicking out your family, turning off the lights and locking up the mansion."

"So?"

"Look, when the gods created humans and Others, they gave both of us immortality. For humans it was the afterlife. For Others it was endless life. And when they left they took that immortality away from everyone. And that was OK. At least by Bella's estimation. At least it was equal to all. But what wasn't fair was forcing us to all live together. For so much change ... But if the Void could be reopened, for both humans and Others, then we'd have more space. And what's more, it wouldn't be about Others coming to Earth, it would also be about humans going to the Void. Equal. Even.

"So, Bella was seeking a way to reopen the Void. She figured if we get into that space and start again—this time without the gods to control us—well then, we'd be masters of our own destinies. And with that, things would get better."

I was stunned. It was true that I knew she was working on a secret mission, but I always assumed it was diplomatic in nature. I figured it was something like trying to find a territory where the Others could make their own nation—I just never assumed that that nation would be on another plane of existence.

"Did she?" I asked, the words stumbling out of my lips. "Did she find a way back?"

"I was hoping you knew the answer to that."

I shook my head. "All I know is that my wife is dead because a bunch of Others tried to play God."

Hermes looked down, hope draining from him. "You are right, Human Jean-Luc. We did try to play God. I am sorry for your loss."

"Oh, you're sorry for my loss. OK, then. All is forgiven. Are you friggin' crazy?" I screamed. "You've got to give me more than that. What happened? Tell me something! Anything!"

His eyes softened. He said, "Yes. She failed and that failure came at the cost of her life. Still, she found something. A clue as to where the Void is and how to get there. That's why Joseph contacted me, but before we could meet, the Avatar of Gravity showed up." His voice was distant. "That's why I saved you. Because I hoped you knew something. But you don't and I lost all that time believing in something that doesn't matter anymore. The mission is over. Failed. Done. Their once-upon-a-time divine purpose lost. It simply doesn't matter anymore. We tried to right the world, fix what was broken, and we lost."

"What about the Avatar? He clearly thinks there's hope."

Hermes shook his head. "No, I don't think so. I believe he followed the Unicorn in town for the same reason I saved you. For the hope that the Void was found. Once he learns that such hope is false, he too will disappear."

"Not good enough," I said. "He killed Joseph. He hurt a lot of people. We can't just let this go."

Hermes laughed. "Why not? For justice? What justice is left in this world? Peace is all we can hope for. Leave him be and he will leave you be. Nothing matters anymore. Now go. Leave me to live what little time I have left to tend my garden."

I looked over at this supercharged Ghost and saw utter defeat in him. I'd seen it before, in the eyes of soldiers who, either from fear or exhaustion, believed that there was a bullet out there just for them. And like some sort of self-fulfilling prophecy, those guys never lasted very long. Then I thought of Bella and the mission she had been on. How damn important it was. How much she believed in Others and this Ambassador. How determined she was to help. I couldn't let this all fade away. If not for me, then for Bella.

Our eyes connected. Even though I was looking at a face that was sixty years old, his eyes were still those of a young man. They had yet to soften by years of experience and understanding, still holding the hardness of youth and determination. There I saw the glint of empathy. He knew Bella. He knew me. And he knew how much we loved each other. How I would end my life without a millisecond of hesitation if it meant she could breathe for another hour. That's what we meant to each other, and everyone who knew us knew that.

I stood to take my leave as the pain still burned inside me. I thought about telling him about my dreams. About Bella. And how Grinner knew about them. That might mean something. Then again it might not. I looked over at the old, defeated Ghost and knew it wouldn't make any difference. Like I said before, I'd seen that look. He was done—no point in adding to his anguish. Still, before leaving I wanted to let him know that although his fight was over, mine was not. "It does matter," I said, offering my hand to him. "It matters to me."

He didn't take my hand. Like I said—defeated. Fine, I'd leave him to his relative peace.

I headed for the door when the chandelier lights flickered. Shock painted his face and in haste he ran over to his candles. They were all still lit and yet, somehow Grinner had found us.

The old man's eyes darted around the room before he took a deep breath and, resigned that escape was not an option, said, "It will not matter to you for much longer."

Chapter 18

Betrayal Can Be Sweet

The lights flickered as Hermes stood too fast for his old, brittle bones to handle. "Damn," he winced as he lit more candles. "I don't understand. I just don't understand. The candles, they are not working."

"Just tell him what you told me," I said, drawing my sword. "That it doesn't matter anymore."

Hermes ignored me, still looking at his candles.

There were two points of entry into this room. Others were into "grand entrances" and, given the kind of personality Grinner had, I was pretty sure that he'd come through the front door. I stood next to it, readying my sword. If I could time it just right, I might be able to impale him before he even got in.

That plan went out the window when the building started to shake. He wasn't coming in the front door, or any door for that matter. He was going to simply use Hermes's house to crush us.

Struggling to keep my balance, I yelled over at the demigod, "Do something!"

He returned my gaze with bitter, frustrated eyes. "I have already wasted enough time on you."

The baseboards were beginning to crack. I looked out the window and saw Grinner standing in the middle of the street, looking as youthful as he did the day I first met him in the parking lot of St. Mercy's Hospital. Holy crap, this Other hardly aged at all, with only light wrinkles and a few strands of white hair to show for his epic battle with Hermes.

Grinner rose his hands up in the air and I was no longer looking at him from the first-floor window. I was looking *down* at him from the first-floor window. He was levitating the whole house. Grinner wrenched his hands apart, crumbling away the floor on which I stood. I grabbed onto the window ledge, my feet dangling beneath me as I hung from the floating home.

Hermes had been smarter or slower than me, because he didn't grab onto anything when the building lifted. He just sat on his wood panel floor, which did not, clutching onto those damn candles which were no longer lit. Meanwhile my flooring did move. A lot.

The building hovered about fifteen feet above the ground and I prepared to let go. My plan: fall into a roll and use that momentum to charge Grinner with sword in hand. If I timed it right, I'd be able to cut off his head before he did anything else.

That was the plan at least, but the best laid plans of mice and men often go awry. Grinner pushed down with the palm of his hand just when I was about to make my move, dropping the house flat and cracking open the ground—and Hermes and I were together swallowed by the Earth.

↔

We tumbled into the sinkhole Grinner had created and I gracefully hit my head on every loose piece of furniture, debris and floor as I fell, conveniently missing carpet and pillows on the way. Hey, at least I was being consistent. Above me, the low-hanging chandelier was compressed against the ceiling. Grinner had flattened the building on top of us. I tried to imagine what it looked like from the outside—a building perfectly flat, the rubble on the smooth flat surface a comical jigsaw puzzle of brick and mortar, roof tiling and chimney. To the unsuspecting pedestrian, it would have looked intentional.

Hermes sat in the corner, still kneeling by the candles, gathering them around him like some goblin hoarding gold even though he knew there was no escape. If only to hold onto them one more minute. He quickly put unlit candles in pockets, leaving behind the few that somehow managed to keep their flame. He held the candles in his hands, under his armpits, one in his mouth.

"Come on," I yelled, the words sending a jolt of pain in my head. I was looking around the collapsed room for an escape.

Hermes looked up at me, managing a smile despite the candle he bit into, and muffled, "Uh coming ..." But it was too late.

As the words came out of his mouth, a section of the ceiling crumbled before moving apart and Grinner slowly lowered himself inside, sealing the hole he made behind him.

↔

"How did you find us?" Hermes asked, still holding his candles.

I was less concerned with how he found us and more concerned with escape. I stood to face Grinner, with my head still spinning, when the room went heavy—as in the-opposite-of-being-on-the-Moon heavy—and I dropped to my knees.

Grinner hissed, "How else? The fallen angel betrayed you."

Penemue. That's why he was so insistent on knowing where I was.

Grinner turned to Hermes, and in an exaggerated show, blew out one of the candles that remained lit. Once completed, his smile widened, pushing his eyes out to the sides of his head making him look like a crazed deer. He said, "You almost made it. Almost escaped. But how can a OnceMortal defeat one such as I? Still, to be so close must make you bitter." Then, turning to me, he said, "What is the mortal expression? 'Close only counts in …' " Grinner snapped his fingers, gesturing for Hermes to complete his thought.

"Horseshoes and hand grenades," I muttered.

"That is correct. Horseshoes and hand grenades. You cannot blame me for not remembering. Despite all these years of being mortal, there are so many of your mundane objects I have yet to learn about." As he said the word *mortal* he brushed the arms of his black overcoat as one might try to clean dirt off one's self, and now he was holding the box —he must have taken it from Penemue. Grinner looked over at me. "But that is all about to change."

"How?" Hermes asked. "The Ambassador and Bella— they failed."

The Avatar of Gravity's smile widened further. "You are half right. The Ambassador did fail, but the human known as Bella … she did not," he said, tossing me Joseph's box. I grunted as I caught it—it felt as heavy as a bowling ball.

"What do you want from me?" I asked, my head hurting way too much to think of anything obnoxious to say.

Grinner chuckled. "A kiss and nothing more."

End of Part Two

Part Three

Second Interlude

There is this girl whom I love very much. I've only been back with her for less than a year when the Devil walks through our front door and offers Bella a job. These days, the Devil calls himself the Ambassador, because he has dedicated his life in this new GoneGod world to brokering peace between humans and Others. He's still too large, too red, too self-assured and too sulfurous-smelling for me—a stinking rose by another name.

Paradise Lot is doing well, the Ambassador says, but there are still many pockets of the world where the species fight. Even here, there are frequent attacks by Fanatics and by roving gangs of Other-haters. There is still much good to be done.

The Ambassador's plan is to travel the world and broker peace deals, acting as a conduit between the species. But he needs a human counterpart. "Bella—I need a human who loves Others and whom Others love back," he says, taking her hand in his massive red paws. "And yes, before you say anything, *He* was right. It is about love. Will you help?"

Before she can answer, I scream out, "You are the Devil!"

"Only by reputation," he smiles, "I assure you that when the gods left, I abandoned my wicked ways. After all, the Devil can only exist when there is a god to oppose."

That night, Bella and I fight over her decision to accept the Ambassador's offer. It starts the way all of our fights do—electrified silence revved so high that the slightest movement will ignite the room.

"It is a chance," she says. The spark.

"He's the Devil," I retort.

"Was the Devil. *Was!* People change. Others change.

"*You* did!" she yells.

Now I know she's wrong. I haven't changed. I've just chosen her over my nature. I am better because she wants me to be better. But make no mistake—no Bella and I'm back in the army, pointing my rifle at anyOther that looks at me funny. I don't say that to her. I don't say that because I don't want to tarnish myself in her eyes.

Instead, I say, "First of all, I'm human. Secondly, I haven't spent the last several thousand years hell-bent on corrupting the human soul. And thirdly, I'm not the friggin' Devil! He doesn't want to help, he wants to control, dominate. Rule. You must see that."

"No, he doesn't." Her arms are akimbo, a stance I've seen many times. She will spend the rest of the argument like that—a statue that no clever retort, no witty reply, no concrete argument will move. As soon as I see her in that position, I know I've lost.

But I don't care. I'm angry. I may not win this fight, but come hell or high water, I'm going to get my licks in before it's over. "How do you know?" I ask.

"Because I do. I have a feeling."

"A feeling? A feeling! Are you honestly telling me that you'll take it on faith that the Devil has changed?"

"Yes! I am. And do you know why? Because I have to! If we don't believe that we can change, that the Devil can change, then we're doomed. And I'd rather live in a world where I believe the Devil is good and be wrong, than not give him a chance and be right."

Bella is resolute. An insurmountable force that cannot be overcome by guns, bombs, philosophy or debate. I know when I've lost and give in.

"OK," I say, defeated. "But I'm going to be by your

side. Always."

What else can I do?

↔

The Ambassador takes Bella on mission after diplomatic mission. We hardly see each other and I am tired of baking cookies. I protest and as a reward for my complaints, I get a job—I am now Bella's official bodyguard. I spend my days either training or on guard duty, bored out of my skull. Still … I am with Bella.

Helsinki, Tokyo, Geneva, Rio—sometimes I think we spend more time on planes than on the ground.

I do my best to be a good husband. An understanding husband. But I want my wife back, and the few evenings we have together are spent fighting over the little things that don't really matter. By the GoneGods, I am so stupid. We should be spending this time making love, holding each other, cooking, cleaning or the thousand other mundane things that couples do just to be near each other.

She doesn't talk about her work, partly because it is top secret, partly because she knows I am jealous. Jealous of how important she is, and how useless I am. I am so stupid.

One day she comes home so excited that she can barely string her thoughts together. "There is a way," she tells me, "to make everything right again. We found it." She is buzzing with excitement.

"Found what?" I ask.

My words bring her to reality and she focuses on me for the first time since coming home to the underground Army barracks that is our latest base of operations. "It," she says, drawing me close. I can feel her breath on my cheek as she whispers that word, *"It."* Teeth tease my earlobe. Soft lips kiss my cheek. "It," she repeats in my ear as she undresses me. "It." She takes me on the cold, concrete floor between the gray, galvanized bunk beds.

It.

↔

My memories fast-forward.

Lights are flashing as the alarm relentlessly rings throughout the facility. My first thought is of Bella. Make sure she is safe.

The wall's warning lights blink crimson red from the light-shield rotating within the heavy-duty, military-grade casing. An engineer announces that the reactor is overheating.

"Damn Eastern European technology," complains another engineer, "I told them the reactor was too small to handle the power that dam produces."

The first one yells that the coolant system is down and he is unable to get it back online. The other curses and tells the first to warn the others. To get above and to run. Then he asks me to help twist the giant metal wheel in order to cut off as much hydro power as possible. That, he says, should slow the whole thing down and therefore give us a chance to escape.

"Escape?" I ask. "Why would we need to do that?"

"Because," he says with an expression far too calm for the sirens and chaos he speaks over, "the whole thing is going to blow. Now twist!"

That's all I need to hear. My hands latch onto the comically large metal wheel. I use every ounce of strength I have in me to get the wheel to turn. I need it to turn. I need the valve to close. I need more time. Time to save Bella. I breathe a sigh of relief when it finally moves. Inch by inch it turns, and when we manage to twist it twice around, the engineer says, "That should do it."

He heads upstairs and I yell after him, "Where are you going?"

"Out of here," he says, "and so should you."

But instead of listening, instead of running up, I run down.

Down toward Bella.

↔

She is at the bottom level. Why did they need to hold their meeting so deep? I curse as I run down stairwell after endless stairwell.

Down, down, down—I run until I get to the bunker. I look through the reinforced metal door, through the portal window a bit too small for a cat to pass. I see Bella, the Ambassador and several Others running about, gathering materials.

The door is locked. I pound on it. "Bella," I scream. "Bella!"

In the chaos, she looks up at me, our eyes locking, slowing down the world. That's what happens every time we look at each other. Everything slows down. Sounds are muted, backgrounds are blurred—all I can see is her. And despite the panic, that is what happens now.

She gives me her best *It's-going-to-be-OK* smile.

But that's my role. I'm here to save her. I gesture for her to open the door. To let me in. But she doesn't move. She just stands there, looking at me with that damn smile of hers.

"Hurry!" I scream.

She blows me a kiss as two cloaked Others that I've

never seen before grab her and throw her to the ground. She does not resist. One of them pulls out a long curved blade from dark, heavy robes. What are they? Monks? Priests? Satanist bastards? I don't care. I cry out, pounding on the door. I pull out my pistol and shoot at the window, but its reinforced glass does not shatter. I push at the door, praying, begging, pleading to every GoneGod to come back and let me in.

Save my Bella. Please. I'll do anything. Be anything. I forfeit my life for her. I give you my soul. Just save my Bella.

For a moment, I actually believe that the GoneGods hear my cry because the Ambassador approaches the two cloaked figures and stands by their side. He is a massive creature, twice the size of a minotaur and three times the weight of a baby elephant. He will be able to crush them under his heel. He is, after all, the once-upon-a-time Devil. But his hulking red body does nothing to help Bella. His horned head does not attack, nor do his cloven feet kick at them. Only his spiked tail swings—a dog excited for the coming meal.

One of the robed figures strikes down, piercing her body, the knife slamming down on her. As one carves, the other cloaked figure calmly puts his hand into her now-open belly and begins pulling out her innards and laying them by her side. He's neatly stacking them by her head, as the first takes out a smaller blade and with a smooth motion gouges out her eyes and places them on top of the pyramid of flesh and blood, organs and guts. They appear to be chanting as they do so.

"BASTARDS!" I cry out. But I am hollow. The same as my Bella.

A third figure draws in near and, judging from his appearance and the white coat he is wearing, I know that he is human. He lifts a giant glass decanter over Bella's body as another human in a lab coat focuses a light through the glass and onto her lifeless body. The scientists nod at each other and say something I cannot hear to the cloaked figures and the Ambassador.

The Ambassador nods then, looking up, notices me for the first time. His face softens and his shoulders hunch. *I am so sorry,* he mouths. *I am so sorry.*

I am slamming my hands on the door, but all I manage to do is cut my knuckles. *"I'll kill you!"* I scream through the blood-tinted window. *"I swear to the GoneGods, I will kill you!"*

Hands pull my shoulders away, too strong to be human, but when I turn, I see a human soldier. Before I can react, a needle pierces my neck and my body goes limp. Fading into unconsciousness, I feel the soldier hoist me on his shoulder. He runs up the stairs at an inhuman speed, where a helicopter is waiting for us. He throws my body in and slaps the helicopter's metal body with the palm of his hand. The metal bird takes off into the air and the last thing I see before passing out is the soldier running back inside as the dam begins to collapse.

There is a booming sound and, just as the engineer promised, the whole thing explodes.

Chapter 19
A Fight for Life and Life

I was pulled back to the present with Grinner's hiss: "A simple kiss is all I require …"

Things just went from weird to outright bizarre. Here I was, trapped with Hermes—as in the messenger demigod who, by the way, was also Mercury, Isimud, Zaqar, Turms and the friggin' Holy Ghost—because the Avatar of Gravity thought that he could reopen all the heavens and hells that were closed when the gods collectively got bored of us and left. In the process, this Avatar—who looked more like a zombie version of the Cheshire Cat—flattened a bunch of half-dogs, half-humans, destroyed my hotel and killed its most honored guest—who just so happened to be the one and only Unicorn in existence. And why did he do all that? Apparently because he wanted a kiss … from me!

When the gods left, I knew things would get weird, but really—come on!

"I'm flattered," I said, trying to let him down as gently as possible, "but you're really not my type."

Grinner threw back his head in laughter. "Not between you and me. No … I wish for you to embrace the one known as Bella."

OK, I guess I was wrong—things *can* get weirder. "You know Bella is dead," I said.

The Avatar took a seat on the half-decimated couch near Hermes. "Mortal poets have oft noted that sleep resembles death," Grinner said, picking up a miraculously unbroken wine glass and opening a fresh bottle he pulled from his jacket like a friggin' magician. He sniffed it before pouring himself a glass. With that same stupid smile of his, he looked over at me and said, "They have also observed that death may be undone by a kiss. Your fairy tales and lore speak of such wisdom."

"But the human Bella failed. She is no more," Hermes said.

"Ahhh. That was the mistake made by the self-named Ambassador. He failed to understand that death done must also be undone. Something that can be rectified by a kiss." He looked over at me. "To think, so much pain and so many dead, and all because you forgot to kiss your loved one goodnight."

A kiss? How could all this be about a kiss?

Penemue's words came back to me: *It is not about the box—it is the significance of the box that matters.* Perhaps the same would be true of certain mortal acts. Your first step, your first word. All milestones along the road that ultimately ends in death. And as for a kiss—that is the first clause in a contract forged between two people in love. *Or lust,* I could hear Astarte say. Whether it is a mother kissing a child, or a lovers' embrace—that simple act means so much to us. And our stories are filled with it: *Sleeping Beauty, Snow White, The Frog Prince, The Princess Bride*—all of their problems were solved by a kiss.

But there was one problem—there was no Bella.

"OK," I said, puckering my lips and making smacking noises, "there, I kissed Bella. Can we go now?"

Grinner laughed. Again. I swear to the GoneGods this guy was always in a good mood and I hated him for it. I much preferred those sulky doom-and-gloom villains.

He plucked the box from my weighted hands, replacing it with his empty wine glass, which I let fall to the floor with a satisfying crash.

"Tell me, Human Jean-Luc, when you meet Bella in your

dreams, can you touch?"

"I don't know what you are talking—"

The Avatar of Gravity lifted his hand and the world got very heavy, causing me to hunch over more. The sudden movement sent a shock of pain through my head. "You dream of her every night, do you not?" he said. "And when you do, can you touch?"

Hermes shot me a look. "What? Bella lives?" He stood up from where he knelt, against the gravity, shock on his face. "And you didn't think to tell me?"

"First of all," I said, sticking up three heavy fingers, "Bella is dead. I saw her heart plucked from her body. And yes, I do dream of her. Every night. But I'm pretty sure I'm crazy. To answer your second question, Hermes: you never asked. And I'd like to make one last point"—I lowered two of the three fingers, leaving the middle one at attention— "it's none of your damn business."

Hermes rolled his eyes and turned back to Grinner. "So it wasn't a failure?"

"What? You two know each other?" But before either could answer my question, I said, "Let me guess, you're both part of the same 'We Once Were Sort-Of Gods' club?"

They both ignored me, their gazes fixed on each other. "If the bridge worked, then we can restore the Void," Hermes said.

"We?" Grinner said, grinning (obviously). He looked over at Hermes and said, "Life and death—to think that only a breath divides them. I am afraid that I need those with more than a few breaths left to aid me."

Hermes grew angry at his words, but quickly looked down, the fight in him gone. Only a day ago Hermes was a man in his early twenties. But he had burned through so much time to save me that now he was little more than an old man, defeated and weak, too scared to do anything but pray for a peaceful death.

I forced myself to think. *I am under three stories of compressed brick and mortar and flattened furniture,* I told myself, *with an incredibly powerful freak who wants me to go to sleep and make out with the dream of my dead wife, in order to ...* What? Complete some ritual? My head throbbed and I was suffering from the worst hangover of my life. Man, I would have killed for an aspirin.

Still, I had to admit, I'd been in worse situations. At least this wasn't Christmas Day dinner with my mother-in-law. Thank the GoneGods for small miracles.

OK, so what could I do? I was in too much pain to fight, which left me with the only asset I had left: my affable personality.

"You're mortal, too," I said, giving Grinner my best *Don't-bullshit-a-bullshitter* look.

Grinner's smile faltered. If I pissed him off, maybe he'd make a mistake. He might just squash us like bugs, but given the stalemate we were in, that would be an improvement.

"Mortal, mortal, mortal, mortal," I sang to the melody of Adam West's *Batman* theme song.

"Don't call me that!" he said. He was no longer smiling. Moreover, his lips were pursed. Hellelujah! You know, with his mouth shut, he almost looked human. Hell, at that moment he might have been. But then that unnatural smile returned as he regained composure, putting him back firmly into the Other category. "The Earth's atmosphere is filled with little tiny spheres that bounce around but are still connected to one another. Atoms, I believe you call them. You mortals have even named them—carbon, nitrogen, oxygen, hydrogen. Tell me, what will happen when I push together the atoms called oxygen and hydrogen?"

As he spoke he waved one hand over the box and it disappeared—probably to the same place that wine glass had been. He then lifted his pinkie finger and the air around me became very wet. I couldn't breathe. This Fanatic was waterboarding me. In midair. Frig! Grinner lowered his pinkie and the water fell to the ground. "Are we done with your little game?"

"Mor-taaal," I sang, but before he could turn air into water, I yelped, "I'm done, I'm done. Promise."

Grinner nodded. "Now that the pleasantries are over, let us return to the subject at hand. Life and death are different stages of all mortals' lives. On and off. Alive and dead. But what can be turned off, can be turned on. What can die, can live again. Through me." His smile widened with those last words as Hermes shuddered under the weight of Grinner's gravitational push. "Human Jean, have you considered my request?"

"I would," I said, "but again. No body, no Bella, so—"

"No, Jean," Hermes said, his eyes wide with excitement, "Bella is alive. And in the Void. The Avatar plans on bringing the Void down to Earth and reuniting her with you."

Grinner clapped. "Indeed, I do!" he said, overjoyed.

"By the GoneGods, it worked," Hermes muttered to himself. Then looking up, he cried out, "It worked. I can't believe it. It worked!" Tears were streaming down his cheeks.

"What worked?" I asked.

"The experiment … Don't you see?" He dropped, kneeling, before me and taking my hands in his. His words tumbled out of him: "The experiment was to get back into the existing plane that once was Heaven. Get back inside and turn on the lights, so to speak. The only thing that could get back inside was a human soul. But when Bella died, we couldn't find any of the empty dimensions. That's why we thought it failed."

"I don't understand. If he can bring down the Void, then he should do it already. Why do you need me or Bella?"

"Hermes," Grinner said, sipping from a new wine glass—damn, this guy could open for David Copperfield. "Please enlighten the mortal."

"Others—creatures like us," he pointed at Grinner, "we can travel between planes of existence, but only if we are invited. Only souls, human souls, can get in uninvited. And once in, they could—potentially—invite the rest of us in." Hermes stood up, free of the Avatar's gravity, and raised his hands to the sky. "And it worked. Don't you see? She didn't fail. Her soul lives on. She lives. Bella lives!" Tears streamed from the messenger demigod's face as he spoke the words.

What? Bella was alive? All these years, all our nightly rendezvous, I had always believed I was just suffering from the happy hallucinations of a man who couldn't let go of the only person he truly loved. I was being told that there was nothing to let go of, that she'd just gone somewhere else. And this Grinner—this Fanatic who could will the powers of gravity like someone could command his legs to move or his eyes to open—was offering me a way back to her. So that we could be together again. It was damn tempting. We could find some place to call our own and live the life we were meant to live. Our own little version of Heaven.

Together.

Forever.

Hey, a guy can dream, can't he?

But I also knew that if it sounded too good to be true, it probably was. Grinner wanted to be a god, and by reopening the Void, he would succeed. But that was not Bella's vision—to put a guy like him back on the throne—and even though he was the only contender right now, I seriously doubted that the Avatar of Gravity was going to be one of those benevolent, validating gods. He was more of the touchy-feely, *I'm-going-to-hurt-you-if-you-don't-obey* type of gods.

No. Getting Bella back meant that the world would burn because of us. *For* us.

Still—with Bella in my arms ... would we feel those flames?

There was one more thing to consider. My promise. It wasn't made to the dream of her, like I had always thought. It was made to *her*—the real Bella. I promised to take care of Others, protect them and help them grow and be whole in this GodGone world.

Now, I know that it was ridiculous to be thinking about that when Bella was only a kiss away. I mean, come on, Jean-Luc—break your promise already. Be together. Be happy. I might have considered that when I believed that the promise was made to a figment of the imagination of a delusional, schizophrenic hotelier. But my promise was made to Bella's living soul and I could no more break a promise made to her than I could move to the Moon.

"What ... what do you get out of this?" I asked Grinner.

The creature's smile was so wide that the edges of his lips literally touched one another around the back of his skull. "Why, to help, of course. And be appropriately rewarded for such help."

"Rewarded? How?"

"How else? Godhood."

Just what I thought. I shook my head and said the hardest word I'd ever had to say.

"No."

If Heaven were to reopen, then it had to be done by

someone else. Someone like Miral or Michael. Hell, even CaCa would be a better candidate. And if they didn't have the power to do it, then they would find someone who did. Someone they trusted. Someone we knew wouldn't oppress the world for an ego trip.

At my refusal, I had expected Grinner to stop smiling, but instead his grin widened until the edges of his lip touched each other on the back of his head. Then he gestured at Hermes, as if his lips were stretched too far to explain himself. Maybe they were.

Hermes looked around nervously before whispering, "There are other ways. More painful ways. A kiss is best because it creates an emotional bridge between the two of you. But a less stable bridge could be created if he were to torture you in front of her, or ..." his voice trailed off.

"Or?" I said.

Hermes hesitated, casting a glance over at Grinner before continuing his line of thought, as if he didn't want to give the maniac any ideas. The expression on Grinner's face clearly said that he had considered everything.

Hermes finally said, "Or he could simply kill you in front of her. Seeing you die will stir enough emotion to create the bridge. It might not last, but he only needs a few minutes to bind the Void."

"Oh?" I said. So celibacy wasn't an option. "Wh ... where?" I managed, gripping my head and trying to keep my brains from rattling around in all that empty space.

Hermes had the same question, because he immediately asked, "Which existence is she in?"

"When the gods came together to create their realms, they made so many. Nirvana, Fólkvangr, Otherworld, Elysium ... Heaven," Grinner said. "And, in time, perhaps a hell or two."

179

Hermes's eyes widened and, taking my hand in his, he said, "Heaven … That is the largest of all realms." As he spoke, he handed me a bit of broken wax, careful not to let Grinner see. I quickly slid it in my jacket pocket, unsure how Hermes expected a little chunk of candle to help me.

Hermes said to me, "Bella was the best of us. That is why she was chosen."

"Chosen," I said. "You mean sacrificed."

Hermes gave me a guilty look as he stood. "Yes, sacrificed. And for that I am truly sorry. But don't you see? She *lives*. That is why this creature is here now. To find Bella. Things can be made right again."

"And when they are made right," Grinner's smile widened again as he gulped the last of the wine down, "I shall be the Alpha in a universe without an Omega. I shall be all and through me, all shall be."

"Indeed," Hermes said, his back to Grinner. "Jean-Luc. Would you be so kind as to do me a small favor?"

"Sure," I grunted.

"RUN!" he screamed as he turned and unleashed the hell-holy blue flames of Tartarus on the Avatar of Gravity.

Chapter 20
Run, Lola, Run

Flames of blue and red and orange and white consumed Grinner, encircling him in a hundred-thousand shades of heat. He lifted a hand and the flames rushed against an invisible force field, like water hitting glass. The fire no longer touched him.

But at least he was no longer smiling.

I wasn't a creature of magic, and being in that hot box was overwhelming—I now know how a turkey feels in an oven. I took a step back, searching for a way out. Directly above me was the compressed remains of the building. Three stories of rubble flattened to three inches thick. But a structure like this was never meant to be. There had to be a weak spot.

My hand ran over the ceiling and for the first time in my life I was actually annoyed not to get a splinter or paper cut. I thrust my hand at the scabbard on my hip, thanking the GoneGods that I hadn't lost it in the fall. Drawing my sword, I thrust it in the mulch, digging for something to pull at. Again and again I stabbed until, *clink*, the tip hit a piece of metal that was loose from the rest. Using my blade, I pried out a bit of chandelier and pulled.

I pulled, leveraging my weight and anger, and forced the unsure ceiling to collapse in on itself, and some of it, on me. There was a hole above. And what's more, enough debris that I could climb up.

I looked back at the battle that raged with the fury of Revelations, Ragnarök and Armageddon all wrapped in one, and marveled at how contained and focused it was, given the kinds of energy being thrown about. Perhaps if I waited,

Grinner would stumble just long enough for me to grab Hermes and the two of us could make a run for it. Besides, I enjoyed seeing Grinner sweat.

I noticed that Hermes also allowed himself to burn, the wax from his candles melting around him, forming a shield against the flames and Grinner's counter attacks. Hermes was a tank, the wax his steel shell, his flames the nozzle of his gun.

"Give him hell!" I screamed. I immediately regretted it because it made me feel like someone turned on a blender inside my head.

It did have a bit of an effect, because Grinner turned in my direction, momentarily lowering his shield, which in turn caused a bit of flame to get through and burn him. Grinner yelped and I put a notch in the "win" column for Hermes. Another part of me grimaced—although it had so far shown a resilience that defied, well, *gravity*, there was no way in Hell Joseph's box could survive this flaming deluge.

Just when I thought Hermes had Grinner on the ropes, the wannabe Alpha god threw his wine glass at Hermes's feet—a seemingly ineffectual, impotent gesture given the holy-fire fury that Hermes shot at the maniacal Avatar of Gravity. Shards of fine, wafer-thin glass landed at Hermes's feet and that was when I knew with increasing horror what he was about to do. Gravity ceased. No, not ceased ... *reversed.*

But because Hermes was covered with his magical wax, he was unaffected, leaving only the glass to shoot up. Tiny, razor-sharp pieces of glass flew up, slicing him up on the way. Then gravity restarted, cranked up so high that the same shards plummeted back down, cutting up the old man all the more. A thousand little lacerations smaller than paper cuts covered his body, each blooming with tiny crimson bubbles of blood.

Hermes healed himself in the light of the fire, his eyes widening as he realized the stakes at hand. It was a war of attrition—first one to burn out loses—and time was not on Hermes's side. The once–old man turned ancient as his hand remained outstretched, a heat hotter than the Sun engulfing Grinner.

I crouched and readied my sword. But it was too hot and I didn't have magic to protect me long enough to get close.

Hermes looked over and saw what I was thinking. Through gritted teeth, he grimaced, "Don't, you fool," redoubling his efforts as renewed magic flowed out of his outstretched hand. "Get out of here and find Bella. She'll know what to do." He was determined to hold Grinner at bay long enough for me to get away. This final sacrifice was going to kill him.

Frustrated, I sheathed my hunting sword and scampered up the hole, clinging to the fallen debris, using whatever my hands and feet could find as leverage.

As I scrambled out, I allowed myself a single second to look back. What I saw was Hermes's body frozen, his hand still out, held up as if by rigor mortis. And somehow, his magic persisted. Perhaps it was the remnants of his soul pushing forth, perhaps the will of his life continuing past death, I don't know. Whatever it was, his body deflated as he pushed out beyond life, until he was nothing more than bone. And still he fought on until that bone finally turned to dust.

It would be seconds before Grinner broke free.

I got through the rubble and outside. The sewer grate that I had climbed out of was still open. I jumped in, allowing human- and Other-refuse to break my fall. My head throbbed as I landed, the impact cracking several ribs. I wheezed and as I stood, my leg sent thunderbolts of agony through me. On top of the broken ribs, I had also twisted my ankle.

But none of that compared to the pain in my head. A haze of fireflies squirmed all over my vision, blinding me with pain and light.

Get up, Jean-Luc! Come on, I thought. Every time I tried to move, my head throbbed as if my skull were the leather surface of a bass drum.

So this is how it ends, I thought. *Not with a bang, but with a whimper of blinding pain.*

Damn it! I didn't mind going down, but I hated the idea that it was Joseph and Hermes's megalo-*I-wanna-be-a-god* maniacal killer who was responsible.

As these thoughts ran through my head, Bella blurred into sight. She reached out for me, her embrace stretching across the impossible expanse, and still she could not draw close enough. This was the end and she was too far away to comfort me. Then, as if the danger were over and everything were suddenly OK, she gave me her *You-were-worried-about-nothing-Silly* smile and a hand reached out for me and pulled.

I focused on my rescuer and saw a big, fecal-infested arm that smelled to high Heaven. I held onto an arm that felt like sun-baked waste and cried out, "CaCa! You're an angel!"

CaCa helped me up as TinkerBelle floated past by me. "Tink," I said. "You're not hid ..." but the thought was cut off by what felt like someone shoving a cattle prod through my ear and into my brain.

Tink shook her head. She understood what I wanted to say. But when she looked over at CaCa with empathetic, understanding eyes, I got it. Tink was hidden away from the world, just as much an exile as CaCa, but not because she was ugly, but because she was beauty incarnate. But unlike CaCa, who suffered scorn, the petty villagers chasing him away with their pitchforks, those very same petty villagers wanted to possess Tink. Own her. Enslave her.

CaCa and Tink exchanged glances, speaking some silent language, both nodding simultaneously. Then Tink pulled out her little wand and a puff of fairy dust floated past my nose. With a deep inhale, I sucked in the dust and in an instant, all the pain and dizziness went away. My head felt perfectly fine. Better than fine. Free and clear. Hell yeah! Fairy dust—Tylenol should patent the stuff! CaCa put his hand around my ankle, forming a cast made from GoneGods-knew-what. Not just any cast, but something that was warm and healing and comforting. Once you got passed the smell.

I looked over at the two Others that were putting themselves into harm's way for me, not only healing me, but giving me a second chance. A second chance that I swore not to throw away.

"Thank you," I said to both of them. "But you've done enough. More than enough. I need you both to hide. Now." But my words came too late—as I uttered them, the road above peeled back like the lid on a sardine can.

Standing not fifteen meters above us was Grinner. He had found us.

↔

CaCa immediately released his terra firma–squid attack on Grinner, which resulted in a cloud of very dark, pungent smoke filling the room. The cloud also got me and I started to curse CaCa until I saw what he was really doing. He was hiding Tink, who fluttered away and down the sewage pipes at an ungodly speed. Go CaCa! I was going to have to start paying him for his paintings.

Grinner's face convulsed as the smell reached him, his maddeningly wide smile turning into a frown of disgust and indignation. He pushed his hands together, forcing the cloud to compress into a sphere slightly bigger than a bowling ball, and dropped it. Right on CaCa's head.

But he didn't just drop it. He put a bit of force behind it and the ball fell like a comet of shit, hitting poor, gentle, kind CaCa square on the head. The globe of poo tore through him, obliterating his skull and spine as it hit the ground with a giant splat. All that remained were arms and legs with no body in the middle.

"No!" I screamed. I turned to face Grinner, who stood on the street above. His damned smile no longer touched his eyes, it actual went past them, pushing those soulless orbs in his skull inside and closer together.

My first instinct was to charge him. I still had my sword. My head no longer throbbed and even though my ankle was still busted, I had CaCa's cast of shit holding it in place. But my head no longer hurt. It was clear and I could think well enough to know that a head-on confrontation would only mean my death and much, much worse for Paradise Lot and the GoneGod world.

No—get away. Regroup. Plan. Lay a trap. Get a gun—a really, really big gun. Do whatever it takes to even the odds. CaCa's name would have to be added to what I owed the Avatar of Gravity, to settle at a later time of my choosing.

If there was a later. I ran down the pipe, but with every few meters of ground gained, he lifted more asphalt as he calmly walked on the street above. It must have been quite a scene, watching the asphalt peel back like that.

"Stop," he hissed.

"No," I said, turning around to give him my middle finger. Then I resumed my "Mortal, Mortal, Mortal" song, this time to the tune of the *Gummi Bears* theme song. I wondered why he didn't just stop me—push me down or take away gravity altogether. But he just kept peeling back the road as he followed me down the pipes.

I took a turn to the right, away from the chasm he was creating and down a pipe. I was trying to increase the distance between Grinner and me. It was working because it took him some time to get around the hole he had made and get to the other side. But still—he was on asphalt and I was literally sloshing through shit.

Then, as if my prayers molded reality, I saw hope. I saw salvation.

A city utility entrance stood before me, its door wide open.

Chapter 21

Revenge is a Dish Best Served as a Banquet

I ran into the utility entrance, closing the door behind me. From the door's porthole-sized window I saw the road above tear open. Judging from the angle at which the asphalt ripped away, I suspected that Grinner didn't know where I was. Still, he wasn't stupid, and even though I had managed to get away, it was only a matter of time until he found me.

I turned to survey the room. There were a few pressure gauges and a couple of turned-off computers, their black screens reflecting me in their emptiness. I looked like hell. Well, at least how I looked and felt were consistent. The room had a little metallic bridge under which the river of shit streamed by. There were several pipes with various labels on them, including one that read CITY WATER. There were also a few small turbines and a bunch of lab equipment, as well as a table with discarded beakers and vials.

I was in the city's access point, where officials measured the chemical levels of the sewer and water systems. That is, until Paradise Lot became overrun by Others and city officials decided that their tax dollars were best spent somewhere with a voting population. Now it was an abandoned building, used by really poor Others who resided rent (and utilities) free.

Above me were some of the roughest, ugliest residents of Paradise Lot, the kind that hated strangers almost as much as they hated humans they knew. Being both, I rated a special kind of ire. But they were all that stood between me and the outside, where, if I did make it out in one piece, the Avatar of Gravity was waiting to capture, torture and eventually kill me.

Fire, meet Frying Pan.

Frying Pan, meet fire.

Hellelujah!

↔

I opened the door leading upstairs. Whoever lived below was
watching the carnage above, but there were plenty of Others
that hung out in the darkened halls of Paradise Lot
Municipality. The One Spire Hotel was smack dab in the
middle of a slum—I have no illusions to the contrary—but
there was always a spark to it, a bit of life. The wino angels
sang, the pan-handling gargoyles thanked you as you passed
by. The poor and downtrodden may not have made eye
contact, but there was always a shift in their body language
that acknowledged your presence. But these Others were
something else altogether. They watched as I passed by, their
eyes filled with abandoned hate.

These were the Others who truly had nothing, the real
have-nots of the GoneGod world. They each seemed to just
sit around, counting the minutes as they waited for sweet
oblivion. I looked down the hall and wondered how many
lived here. A hundred? A thousand? How many of them had
lived full, happy lives before the GrandExodus? I'd seen
poor, and I'd seen desperate. But this was a whole new level
of destitute. And here I was, naïve and idealistic, believing
that I was living the worst of it, when there were many so
much worse off than me.

If I lived through this, I'd come back here and do
something. I didn't know what—but something.

Two valkyrie loitered by an open doorway. When they
saw me, their eyes lit up in surprise and one of them ducked
into the room. I knew if I walked down that hall, I'd be in

for trouble.

Best to find another exit, I thought, but before I could go back from where I came, the valkyrie came out, followed quickly by an uppity harpy.

"You!" the harpy shrilled. "What in Tartarus are *you* doing here?"

↔

I considered putting up a fight. Probably would have won, too. But given what was waiting for me outside, I thought I'd let this play out in here first.

The two valkyrie escorted me to a dim room that once-upon-a-time belonged to a middle-management employee and forced me to sit in a plush chair opposite an old office desk.

The harpy hopped onto the bureau and announced, "Hear ye, hear ye! Bow before the great Yara-Uno, Master of the Concrete River, Guardian of the Hallowed Halls of City Municipality."

Two candles were lit, illuminating a bulbous red creature whom I hadn't noticed in the chair opposite me. He was about three feet high, fire-engine red, bald, with two pencil-thin appendages that stuck out from where his ears should have been.

"Holy crap, you're a friggin' Yara-Ma-Yha-Who," I muttered as I stared at the Australian red vampire in awe. Unlike your typical vampire, this guy had no teeth—instead, he had many octopus-like suckers on the palms of his hands. Legend had it the Yara-Ma-Yha-Who gobbles up his victims, sucking on them like hard candy for a day or two before spitting them out whole and healthy, if not wet and somewhat traumatized. I'd seen all sorts of demons and monsters, but I'd never seen one of these before; I had been sure that, amongst the thousands of pages we were forced to study about all the different kinds of Others, the Yara-Ma-Yha-Who wasn't real. I mean, come on, he looked like a giant red thumb with limbs. "I thought you were just a legend."

The Yara-Ma-Yha-Who smiled. "I am a legend," he said in an Australian accent. "You the reason why the First Law is tearing up the streets above?"

I nodded.

"And he is here, why?"

"He thinks he can reopen Heaven." Why lie? They'd eventually find out. Hell, the way Grinner flapped his mouth, I was kind of surprised word hadn't gotten around yet.

The red devil shifted in his seat. "Which one?"

"Not sure," I answered. "He listed like five of them. And something about how he was the new 'god of gods' ..."

The Yara-Ma-Yha-Who nodded. "Doesn't matter," he grunted, opening a drawer, pulling out a piece of paper and tossing it over to me. "You him?"

I picked up the page and saw one of CaCa's drawing—a sketch of Joseph at the "Coping with Mortality" seminar. Miral was standing behind him and to his left was little old me, another pair of eyes watching Joseph as he spoke. From the overly optimistic smile I wore (not to mention the distinct smell of shit), this had to be CaCa's work.

I pointed at myself in the sketch.

"And you were there when he died?" the Yara-Ma-Yha-Who said, pulling out a metal knitting needle and brandishing it like a fencing sword.

I gulped, looking at the needle and imagining a death by a thousand pokes. I shook my head.

"Then you are a friend of the One Made from Refuse

and Archiver of the Lot. A friend of his is a friend of ours! I am Yara-Uno, the first of my kind and the last of my race."

May the GoneGod bless your soul, dear sweet CaCa, I silently prayed. *That's twice today that you've saved me!*

The little red thumb stood on his chair extending out his wafer-thin arm at me in an awkward handshake, a wide smile on his face revealing thousands of suckers in his gums. Then his expression went very grave and he said, "Tell me, the Unicorn killer—that him outside?"

I nodded, a gesture he imitated. Yara-Uno's nod turned into a swaying as he put the weight of his little body on each leg. The change in his demeanor seemed to act as a signal because without a word, the harpy leapt off the desk and left the room. Yara-Uno continued his odd oscillation for a few more seconds before fixing his eyes on mine and saying, "Thanks be to you, human, for you have brought our enemy to our home. This is a truly appreciated gift."

↔

Then things happened much faster than I thought possible. I mean, I'd been in the Army, I'd been in Special Forces, I was used to having to get ready for battle at a moment's notice—still, I'd never seen troops prepare as fast as they did. There must have been a hundred Others, all armed to the teeth: helmets made out of paint cans and buckets, body armor fashioned from sheet metal and chicken wire and weapons that were bats with nails, kitchen knives with door handles as hilts and a whole hodgepodge of common items taken to their deadly extreme. Hell, one gargoyle had an old Christmas stand as a shield and candle stick with fashioned razor blades as a mace. A valkyrie wielded a short sword, a minotaur a war hammer. There were Others who, given how deadly their equipment looked, I figured were once-upon-a-time warriors of Other worlds.

And within seconds a makeshift army of mythical creatures stood at the ready, Yara-Uno their commander.

By the GoneGods above and below—all this time I had arrogantly thought we won the war against the Others because they were too weak and incapable to stand up to human brutality. But seeing this makeshift army standing shoulder to shoulder, I suddenly understood that the only reason we "won" was because most of them did not want to fight.

But give them a cause—a true cause like avenging the death of the One and Only Unicorn—and you'd see a whole new kind of enemy. I only prayed that humans would never do anything to unify them against us, because if we did, we'd surely lose.

"Now," Yara-Uno said, "tell us about our enemy."

There was a chance to take down Grinner. So here I stood with my brothers- and sisters-in-arms—more like my brothers- and sisters-in-wings and -horns and –other appendages.

"OK people," I said, looking into the crowd. "Ahh, not people, but creatures." Not a good start to a pep talk. I cleared my throat and started again. "The thing outside killed the Unicorn." This drew a reaction from the crowd— dwarves punched the floor, valkyrie threw their heads back and shrieked, minotaurs snorted—every Other in the room jeered in their own special way. "That freak killed Joseph because he wants to be the new head honcho. Something Joseph died trying to stop. Something we're going to finish."

I told them about the gravity and air attacks I'd seen, his desire to rule Heaven and everything else I knew about Grinner. Once I was done, I waited with dramatic pause before throwing my hands up in the air and crying out, "For Joseph! For the Unicorn!"

The crowd erupted in snorts and cheers and cries. "Good speech," Yara-Uno said. "Not as good as mine … but good enough." He gestured to the troops of Others that were working themselves up into a battle frenzy.

A distraught pixie fluttered in and whispered something in Yara-Uno's ear. The red vampire listened, then lifted his scrawny arms in the air to silence the crowd. "He's outside and he suspects we hide the human."

"Took him long enough," I said, drawing my own sword.

Yara-Uno shook his head. "No. You stay here."

"What? This is as much my fight as yours," I said through gritted teeth.

"With that?" he said, pointing at my leg. He had a point. "Besides, your smell will distract me."

"Fine," I said, "but if you start to lose—"

"Lose?" he said, pulling out his knitting needle. "Yara-Uno never loses."

↔

"You killed the Unicorn," Yara-Uno said with an eerie calm as he walked out the front door. I watched from the third floor where I could fling rocks at Grinner from my balcony seat. From above, I could see the top of Grinner's head. He wore that wide-rimmed fedora of his and from this vantage, I could see that the top of his hat was unnaturally sucked in, tightly hugging his skull. "You spilled his blood and now he is no more," Yara-Uno announced in an even tone as he circled Grinner, forcing him to turn his back to the building. A solid tactic. Pretty good for a thumb.

Grinner didn't seem to notice or care about the Others watching. "I am here for the human." Grinner's gaze never left the Yara-Ma-Yha-Who.

"You … killed … the … Unicorn," Yara-Uno repeated in a slow and angry tone, each word carrying with it his full ire. "You spilled his blood and now he is no more."

"It was painful for me to kill one such as the Unicorn," Grinner said. "He was a good creature that would have served me well in my new kingdom. But he refused and therefore had to be crushed."

"Sure, sure," the red devil said. "He stood in your way, Yara-Uno understands. But myth says you crushed his innards. Fable says you tortured him. Legend says he died on his back!" This last point drew in some protest from the crowd. To most Others, dying on your feet was a noble death. One allowed a defeated foe to die standing up, or on the back of their horse. But a prone death—that was a coward's death, and to force one such as Joseph to lie there being tortured … that was an unacceptable insult.

Grinner shrugged. "Feet, back or knees. All will bow to me."

From the corner of my eye, I could see a ghoul and valkyrie flanking the Avatar of Gravity. Fairies fluttered about with staffs in hand. The crowd was near explosion. The minotaur snorted and with it the crowd erupted in jeers and taunts. For the first time Grinner seemed to notice the crowd. Turning around, he addressed them: "Servants of the OnceGods, serve me now and I shall return you all to the realms you once belonged to. I shall give you life anew. And all for the price of obedience. A fair exchange, think you not?"

"I serve no one," Yara-Uno said. "Not anymore."

"You will bow to me," Grinner said, turning to the red

devil, his hand lifting above his head. But before he could employ his gravity trick, Yara-Uno let out his war cry.

Dragons roar, centaurs stomp, banshees shriek—and each one of their battle cries strikes terror into the hearts of their enemies. But a Yara-Ma-Yha-Who's battle cry? It came out as a short "WAAN, WAAN, WAAN!" If I wasn't on Yara-Uno's side, I would have laughed. This was the creature that faced off against Grinner? Why couldn't it have been a wakwak or a hill giant? At least they had war cries I could respect.

Seems that my lack of fear was out of ignorance, because the crowd all backed away with terror. It was as if the Yara-Ma-Yha-Who's battle cry was akin to the kraken rising from the deep or an archangel's trumpet sounding the End of Days. Even Grinner's smile wavered.

With the *WAAN, WAAN, WAAN!*, the valkyrie lobbed his homemade arrows and the pixies shot their pool balls from their bra- and tensor bandage–slings. Grinner took the hits with a whoop, dropping down to his knees.

"Hell, yeah!" I shouted, throwing a cue ball at his head. "You're going down!"

"Ahh, Human Jean-Luc, how kind of you to join us," Grinner said as he turned off gravity. The pool balls and homemade arrows floated up in the air before they started to circle him. After that, nothing else got through, each new volley adding to the meteor belt that orbited around Grinner. Then the Avatar of Gravity fanned his fingers in the direction of the crowd, each gesture sending a torrent of shrapnel shooting back up at us like bullets fired from a cannon.

I gotta watch my mouth, I thought. I ducked into the building and away from Grinner's counterattack.

"You! Spilled! His! Blood!" I heard and chancing a look

outside, I saw the Yara-Ma-Yha-Who's gaping orifice of a mouth stretch open, as his tiny hair-thin legs propelled him forward at a supernatural speed. He dived into Grinner's zero-gravity, his arms stretched out like Superman's big red thumb. Yara-Uno's left hand held the needle and I thought he was trying to stab Grinner. Apparently Grinner thought the same thing, but only had time to put up a small gravity shield to block the attack. Like I said, the little bugger was fast. But Yara-Uno wasn't trying to stab him.

He wanted to slap him.

Yara-Uno's right hand flashed up and slapped Grinner's cheek. With a sharp smacking sound, his palm connected as he cried out, "You spilled his blood! And now I spill yours!"

Way to go, little guy!

In zero-gravity everything floats, even little red Australian vampires. As Yara-Uno floated up, his octopus-like suckers latched onto Grinner's cheek, making it look like Grinner was holding a big, red balloon with his teeth. Grinner shuddered as Yara-Uno's eyes brightened and his mouth widened. Don't get me wrong, Yara-Uno already had a big mouth, but it somehow fit his little red face. The smile that widened on his face was unnatural. He looked like ... Grinner. Apparently, when the Yara-Ma-Yha-Who sucked your blood, he got a little bit more of you than red and white cells.

He got Grinner's powers.

"You spilled his blood," Yara-Uno repeated.

"How can this be?" Grinner said as he, too, started floating.

The two of them floated up into the sky. They must have gotten a hundred feet up when Yara-Uno's face returned to normal. He was shutting off his new powers.

"And now I spill yours!" Yara-Uno shouted one last

time as they fell.

A valkyrie dove out the window and caught Yara-Uno as Grinner fell to the Earth with a shattering *BOOM!*, and I could see from Yara-Uno's approving look that he'd left the last bit of juice to increase gravity and give Grinner a big, crater-causing taste of his own medicine.

The minotaur and centaur didn't hesitate. They charged Grinner as the pixies slung more pool balls. The minotaur brought down his hammer and the centaur stomped Grinner with his hooves. They were winning, literally trampling him flat.

Then the Earth shook. Slabs of asphalt tore from the ground, slamming into the creatures over and over. The minotaur managed to roll out of the way, but the centaur was crushed.

The army of Others, seeing the death of their comrade, now seemed to understand what and who they were up against. They also knew that it was now or never. Everyone charged, each of them glowing, shining, a halo of rage encompassing them—they were all burning time. A lot of it.

But Grinner was no longer caught off-guard and he swatted them down like flies as he continued to hurl down debris. Bodies flew up only to be squished down again. Grinner was pulling no punches, and I suspected that mercy and forgiveness were quite low on his godly priorities. The road beneath me ran rainbow with blood as goblins bled green, orcs gray, pixies yellow and centaurs purple.

I couldn't just watch anymore as Grinner turned these poor creatures to mulch.

One of the things that made me good at killing Others was that I was good at using their physiological weaknesses against them. Angels were strong except where their wings met their bodies. Fairies were fast, but couldn't fly against the wind. Minotaurs were sturdy, but they were damn near blind. Grinner had to have a weakness. I remembered the way he smiled and how that friggin' grin of his would touch his eyes and move them. They always shifted left or right, never up or down. And given how good he was at countering ground attacks, I figured that his eyesight was excellent at scanning the horizon but not so great at seeing attacks from above. The harpy that had escorted me to the top floor shot her bow, missing yet again. In her latest attempt, the arrow flew straight up into the air, not getting anywhere close to Grinner. I whistled at the creature and pointed at the top of Grinner's head, miming the gist of my plan. Thank you, TinkerBelle, for all those years of practice!

The harpy swished into the air, grabbing me by the shoulders and moving to drop me on that damned Grinner's head. The minotaur saw what we were up to and charged with war hammer in hand, coordinating his attack with the drop.

This was going to hurt.

The harpy dropped me and, with sword in hand, I fell. Falling is easy. Timing my sword's swing while falling is not. I pulled back my arm, getting ready to strike at Grinner's head, just as the minotaur drew back his war hammer for a body smash. If we had hit, it would have been a synchronized slash and smash that would have divided Grinner in two.

But we didn't hit.

We weren't even close.

At the last minute, gravity ceased, stopping my fall right out of reach of Grinner's head, while it increased a thousand-fold for the minotaur. He collapsed to the ground, crippled under his own weight.

This was new. I'd seen Grinner do both, but never at

once. He looked up at me and, with an admonishing finger wag, said, "Tut, tut, tut—we can't have you falling and hurting that precious head of yours." Then the freak blew me a kiss, and, still looking up at me, grabbed the minotaur by his left horn.

As far as I could tell, it was out of malice more than any tactical gain that he crushed the minotaur's horn, turning it to dust that hung in the air. The minotaur howled. To the ancient Greek monster, losing a horn was the worst of all possible fates. When we would fight a troop of Others, we'd always try to find a minotaur in their midst and shoot at his horns. This would drive the beast into a berserking fury. Berserking meant not thinking. And not thinking, when up against a trained and coordinated Army, meant easy pickings for us. Like I said, I was good at what I did.

The minotaur swung wildly. There was nothing he could do and Grinner knew it. With a cackle, he propelled the mighty humanoid bull through the air and into the building across the way.

Grinner turned to me and said, "Now you."

The air got heavy and I dropped to the ground, pinned under tons of atmospheric pressure. I was a goner and knew it.

Then I heard a terrifyingly sweet voice from above. "Cease! Leave the human alone!"

Hellelujah! The archangel Michael had arrived.

Chapter 22

Life from Above

"Leave the Human Jean alone!" trumpeted Michael as he descended from the sky. The Billy Goats Gruff were also there, surrounding Grinner, each staying over thirty feet away.

"What concern is it of yours?" Grinner asked. He took a step toward the largest of the Gruffs, who in turn took a step back, keeping the distance between them equal. At first, I thought the distance was arbitrary, but then I looked around at the carnage that surrounded Grinner. Nothing really extended beyond those thirty feet, with the impact of his destruction lessening the farther away it got from him. I felt stupid—how had I not noticed that before?

"I have vowed to uphold the law on this plane of existence," Michael said.

"Human law," came Grinner's reply, with disdain on *human*.

Michael shook his head. "Mortal law."

"Why," Grinner pointed at the archangel, "do you insist on protecting a mistake? Does your god still command it or is it sentimentality that compels you?"

"It is neither," Michael said, but did not offer his reasons.

"Tell me, Archangel Michael, did He tell you He was leaving? Or did He just go, leaving you behind like so much unwanted garbage?"

Michael just stared at the Avatar of Gravity, his face betraying nothing.

"I see," said Grinner, then his eyes flickered as if he remembered something and he spoke in a language I did not understand. But to say this was a language would be incorrect, because human language has structure, cadence, and a flow to it. It is why we can distinguish the babbling of a baby from a language we do not speak—there is a certain rhythm to the words. There was no rhyme or reason to the sounds that Grinner uttered, but nonetheless Michael nodded and responded in the same alien language.

Tongues—the undecipherable language of the gods.

I watched in awe as two beings born at the dawn of time conferred in their shared non-language. Grinner nodded, then pointed to the sky and, again speaking in tongues, said something that shocked Michael. From his reaction, it was something he clearly did not want to hear, because the archangel trumpeted the command to attack and the Billy Goats Gruff began slinging stones at Grinner. The first few hit him before he could manipulate the gravity around him, but then he changed their trajectory, shooting the stones back at the Gruffs. The largest Gruff, Magnus, charged and Grinner sent him flying straight up. The other two Gruffs also attacked—and all the while Michael watched without comment or action.

With the Gruffs attacking Grinner, Gravity's Avatar was no longer paying attention to the fact that he was slowly crushing me to death. I had maybe five minutes before I passed out. Another ten minutes and I would never wake up again. And all the while Michael was doing nothing, letting the Gruffs continue their tactics that only served to keep Grinner's mind off of me and on them.

Then it hit me. Michael most likely knew that I was the key to Grinner's plan. From his reaction to their little chat, I was sure that Grinner explained all that happened, offering him the same deal he did Joseph and the Others that fought him before Michael arrived. *Serve me as you did your OnceGods*

202

and I will restore all. But Michael could not accept the ascension of another being besides his God. That was against his nature and what the first Fall was all about. But even though he wasn't powerful enough to stop Grinner, he still knew that without me, the bridge would be lost forever. Michael was a force of good and he could not outright kill me. But he could allow me to be killed, and that was exactly what he was doing now.

I've been told that close to the end you see your entire history flash before your eyes. Here, under that suffocating weight, I was as close to the end as I had ever been. I thought about what Hermes had done—his sacrifice. I thought about Bella and the Ambassador, and all those wasted years I had spent angry and distant. I thought about my promise to her.

But then the more mundane memories entered my mind. I thought about the One Spire Hotel and its collage of guests. I thought about Paradise Lot and its insane collection of shops and temples and restaurants. St. Mercy's Hospital and Miral's attempt to do good. I thought about mortal pain—hunger, lack of sleep, thirst and how bad Others were at being mortal and how abysmally terrible they were at filling out forms. What was that Once's name? I wrote it on that first form I filled out … Asal, the Ass of Kvasir? He was so grateful, said all I had to do was call out his name and he'd be there. Swore it. An Other's vow. And oh how seriously Others took their vows. Their promises. It was an unbreakable oath … almost magical in nature …

"Asal," I whispered.

Nothing happened.

"Asal!" I cried out.

Michael looked at me curiously, perhaps wondering why my last word would be that of a strange onocentaur whose name never made the history books.

"Asal!" I said once more.

"Yes," a voice brayed. "You called?"

↔

From friggin' nowhere, I heard the trot of hooves on asphalt as Asal appeared and said, "Human Jean, how shall I be of service?" He stood right outside Grinner's radius of effect.

"You big beautiful talking donkey! Get me out of here," I said.

Asal dug his hooves in the ground and said, "As you command!" He walked into my personal waterfall of gravity, the weight of the air pushing him down as he entered. His knees buckled, his back strained, but like any stubborn donkey built to shoulder heavy burdens, he stood strong and continued to walk. Step by step, he got closer until he was able to reach down, picking me up and putting me on his back. I worried that my added weight would bring him down, but he was too stubborn to fall. He took heavy step after heavy step until he got out of Grinner's sphere of influence. Outside and free, he trotted away.

As glad as I was to be pulled out of the fray, I really wished some Other with a bit more speed had come to my rescue. Asal's donkey legs carried on much like a donkey did—slow and stubborn.

I looked over at Michael and yelled out, "Your plan to do nothing didn't work. Now it's time to do something!"

Michael nodded at me, respect in his eyes. "You are resilient. Perhaps even worthy of the redemption you seek." Then he turned to Grinner who was dealing with the Gruffs' annoying distraction. Grinner was slowly winning, with only Hunter, the eldest of the Gruffs, still standing.

Michael spread out his wings, his primary wings spanned twice the length of a city bus. His two smaller sets of wings swathed his body, and with that done, he wrapped his primary set over his shoulders. It looked like he was clamping on armor . Enveloped by his own wings, he took the tips of the large wings and propped them under his chin. Then his hair made way for the layer of feathers that rested underneath, forming a helmet. No, to call what I saw a helmet would imply that they were somehow in the same league. This was more like a second skull. I didn't think there was a gun with a high enough caliber to scratch its surface.

Michael stepped into Grinner's radius. Step by step, the archangel drew closer, wading through that immense weight as if it were the shallow end of a pool. Grinner saw the archangel's approach and with a push, knocked the Steve Gruff down on his goat-tail.

He turned his full attention on Michael, straining as he called down more and more weight. But Michael still moved forward, an outstretched hand reaching for Grinner's neck. Grinner took a step backward, calling down even more weight. Michael faltered, and I thought for sure he'd go down. But then he stretched out his third, lower wings, and using them as crutches, and took another step forward.

Grinner hissed and said, "Have it your way!" putting his two hands together. This gesture caused the air to literally compress, and it hardened into a block of oxygen and hydrogen, nitrogen and every other gas in the atmosphere, turning them into a substance as hard as stone and as transparent as glass. It fell right on Michael's head and I thought for sure that the archangel would be crushed to a pulp ... but he wasn't.

He just stood in the impossibly dense solid air, surrounded by a halo of light apparently completely shielding

Michael from the pressure and the weight of being inside Grinner's crushing sphere. I could see the strain. There was no doubt that he was burning through time—a wildfire of years, stripping away what he had left.

The strain on Michael's face was palpable and for the first time in all the years of war and battle, all the encounters I'd had with angels of all hierarchies, I saw an angel sweat. I thought that wasn't possible, that somehow they were created without sweat glands. But he did. Little beads of sweat formed on his forehead which, in turn, became streams that ran down his face. It was somehow so humbling and terrifying to see the archangel Michael sweat. It made him look so weak. So mortal. So human.

Michael could die. But still, he was putting up some kind of fight, because Grinner's own face was strained as he concentrated on dealing with the archangel, all his attention on the sphere that he had conjured.

I had to do something. I had to help. "Quick, Asal, take me to the edge." Asal faithfully did as I asked and when we were close, I dismounted. Cautiously I took a step forward and came up against the hardened air. I felt around. Any structure that recklessly compacted would have a weakness, a point where the compression was uneven. I'd seen it with stones compressed for asphalt, with structures compressed by the deep sea—I'd even seen it with my over-baked cookies. It had worked with the ceiling. The pressure had to be uneven and there was no way Grinner was concentrating on that. All I had to do was find the weak spot and exploit it.

My hands ran across the transparent surface, smooth and solid. It was perfect. I guessed when you employed the entirety of gravity it would be even and—

My hand ran across a slight ripple. A scratch thinner than a hair that disrupted the smooth surface. It was hardly anything, but it would have to do. I pulled out my hunting sword and struck down on the fracture. Nothing. I hit again and my blade reverberated against the surface like an aluminum baseball bat hitting a giant gong. *No, no!* This wasn't working and I could see Michael starting to fail. His knees were shaking and the sweat was stained with particles of light. *Damn it!* No. I took my hunting sword and thrust it point first into the hairline crack and ... it stuck.

Hot GoneGodDamn! It stuck. I pushed, but it didn't budge. I doubled my efforts, crying out with all the strength I could summon, and although it moved forward a millimeter, it was still not enough. Then the minotaur with the now-destroyed horn came forth, dusting off bits of the building Grinner had thrown him into. "Master Human," he snorted. "Let us ... Together."

"Asal, take a step back," I said as I knelt to hold the blade steady and the one-horned minotaur readied himself to swing. He pulled back and rocketed forth his mighty war hammer, connecting perfectly with the end of the hilt. Once, twice, thrice, the bull struck. Four, five, six—it was working, but too slowly to be of use. "This is hopeless," I said looking over at Grinner, who still focused his power on containing the archangel.

"No, not hopeless. Let Yara-Uno be of assistance," said the Australian vampire.

In the hole that my blade created, Yara-Uno inserted the needle-sharp point of his fencing sword. He hung there, ineffectual and limp. I was about to pull it out and resume the attack with the sword when the minotaur put a hand on my shoulder. I looked up and he shook his head. Yara-Uno pulled out the needle and closed his eyes, lifting it in line with his nose. Then he began humming—not humming, so much as *vibrating*. The Earth beneath us shook and bits of rubble started lifting from the ground.

Without warning Yara-Uno opened his eyes, which were now two white disks, more headlights than eyes, and yelled, "I am Yara-Uno, the last of the great Ma-Yha-Who clan, and I summon the strength of all my ancestors and their ancestors before them. I summon my bloodline from the dawn of time and before. I summon all of them for one last strike!"

I swear to all that I know to be true, in whatever universe the GoneGods were, they felt this little guy's cry. Yara-Uno thrust his needle's tip into the hole and beyond, and with a whopping crackle, the atmosphere cracked.

And splintered.

With a burst of energy, the solid air shattered.

The minotaur must have sensed that the thing would fly apart because he shielded me and Yara-Uno from the blast as invisible shards of atmosphere pierced his back before turning into harmless, effervescent air. I could see the life leaving him—one more soul going nowhere—and as it did, I said the only words I knew to comfort him.

"You fought well. The angel is free."

The beast smiled as his eyes glazed over. Then his face took on the expressionless indifference of death.

Michael, now free, did not hesitate. He leaped forward with unearthly speed and grabbed Grinner by the throat. I thought he was about to snap the Other's neck or smash him against the ground. Punch him in the teeth, rip his head off. I could see that part of the archangel wished to do so, but another part of him, the part that made Michael *Michael*, hesitated. I could see him grimace from the battle that raged within him. Suddenly the archangel pulled Grinner's face in close and whispered something in his ear. Then he let the maniac go.

Grinner nodded, looked around and then disappeared.

"What's wrong with you?!" I screamed. "You had him, and you just let him go!"

"I swore an oath long ago that I should never harm a First Law. It was part of the covenant between the Highest Order of Angels and Nature," Michael said, surveying the carnage. All around us were hurt Others. Yara-Uno, ever the leader, was organizing the less hurt to tend to the mortally wounded.

And Michael let him go! Rage overcame me and now it was my turn to poke a finger at the archangel's chest. "The old oaths don't matter anymore!" I growled. "Not since they left."

The archangel dismissed me. He was an angel of the highest order and a little thing like his god abandoning him wasn't going to stop him from being who he was. I guess I understood. It was all he had left. It was all any of us really ever had. "I upheld my vow and will live with the consequences of doing so. What I have done is to grant us time to prepare and give you an opportunity to run."

"Run?! I will never—"

But before I could finish the sentence the great angel dropped to one knee and, breathing heavily, vomited a mixture of food and light. From where I stood, I could see the angel had several broken ribs. I felt my own chest: my insides felt so crunched together from my time in the sphere. I was sure there was some internal bleeding. I calmed down—the next steps could wait. He was right. We needed time to heal, to regroup.

I sat by the angel, happy to be resting, and said in a soft voice, "What did you say to him?"

"I asked him a question," Michael said and as he did, he regained a bit of his majesty.

"What, like a riddle?" I asked.

"In a way … I asked him to solve a mystery for me."

"A mystery." I couldn't help it. I burst out laughing. I mean, really, really laughing. I think I must have broken two more ribs as I keeled over and brayed. At first, Michael looked at me, confused. Then he joined in. Soldier to soldier, he understood. You laugh now because you might not get a chance tomorrow.

We must have been quite the sight—a human and an archangel sharing a joke no one else got. Eventually our laughter died down and I asked, "You sent that maniac away with a 'mystery,' whatever that means, and what happens when he solves it? Do you tell him a joke?"

Michael went solemn. "When he solves it, Human Jean, he will return and there is nothing I or anyOther can do," the archangel said.

Hellelujah! Way to kill the mood.

Chapter 23

Choices, Choices

When I was a kid, the circus came to town. Everyone gathered to watch the parade of clowns and jugglers, animals and trainers, daredevils and ringleaders march down the street. I was fascinated by all those exotic creatures marching down the road. Man oh man, I loved every minute of it. I was only ten at the time. Now, my mind went back to that day as we walked down the streets of Paradise Lot. We must have looked like a macabre version of that circus, a funeral procession of horns and hooves, humans and Others, misery and pain.

As we walked, Asal informed me that I was the second human to be carried by him. The first was Kvasir, the human responsible for brokering peace between the Aesir of Asgard and the Vanir. And the reward for his good deeds? He was tricked and killed by dwarves, his blood brewed into the Mead of Poetry.

"You know, Human Jean, if you too were to meet a similar fate, then that would mean that my carrying you now foreshadows your death. How poetic!" Asal was way too excited by the prospect of my death.

Yara-Uno looked over at me as we made our way down the street and in a downtrodden voice said, "I did not win this night."

"Hey, you're still breathing. That means you didn't lose, either," I said.

Yara-Uno shook his head. "I failed to avenge the Unicorn."

"I don't know about that," I said. "Maybe revenge isn't what the Unicorn would have wanted. Maybe he was after

211

something else altogether. He came to Paradise Lot to make things better for everyone. Maybe that's how you can honor him."

"As the one who was by his side as he died, tell me the truth. Is that truly what he would have wanted?"

"Yes," I said, thinking back to the brief moments I had spent with Joseph. He was all about peace. About feeling good and taking care of others. "Yes," I repeated.

Yara-Uno considered my words. "Then I shall honor the Unicorn as he wished to be honored. I shall make this place better for everyone." Looking over at me, he said in a triumphant voice, "And Yara-Uno never loses."

Our procession of doom and gloom eventually ended at St. Mercy's Hospital, where Miral divided the wounded that needed treatment from the dying that needed comfort.

Miral was Paradise Lot's true angel that night and for as long as I live, I will forever be grateful to her for all she did.

↔

The fairy receptionist took me to my own room, courtesy of Michael, who insisted that we have a private place to speak. The receptionist gave me some painkillers— finally!—and a towel, reminding me that I was still covered with now-dried sewage. "Try to flush the solid pieces down the toilet," she said, pointing at the shower.

Fine by me. I peeled off CaCa's cast, though my ankle immediately ached with the desire to get back into its warm embrace. I stripped off my clothes, setting my collarless jacket, with Hermes's parting gift of wax safe inside it, on the counter, and hopped in the shower. The warm water felt good. As it cascaded over me, I had time to clear my head and think.

This Grinner guy wasn't going down easily, if at all. Half of Paradise Lot attacked him with swords and magic, and they barely got any licks in.

"No more time," I said to tiles on the bathroom wall. "Burning time isn't going to kill him." Trouble, if a whole army burning time didn't hurt him, then what would? It was then I made a resolution that I wouldn't let another Other waste a minute of time on Grinner. Whatever the solution was going to be, it would have to be done without magic.

I was still in the shower when Miral burst in. "How long have you been dreaming of her?"

"Hey!" I screamed, "I'm naked!"

"Oh please, I've seen your kind naked before. Now answer me—how long?"

"Shouldn't you be taking care of the wounded?" I said, wrapping a towel around myself while trying to turn off the water.

"I have stabilized those who needed it, and there are nurses and other doctors. And don't change the subject!"

"How do you know about Bella?" I started, while I tried to shimmy my underwear under my towel.

"The Avatar of Gravity told me all," Michael said as he walked in. "Of all the humans to be crucial for the restarting of the world, I would never have thought—you? As for the end of the world ... *That* I would have whole-heartedly predicted." Michael smirked. He was making a joke, or at least trying to. Michael had many strengths. Humor was not one of them.

"How long?" Miral repeated, pacing the room.

"Six years," I said, managing to put on my pants. My shirt, however, was behind Miral. It would have to wait.

"And you never thought to tell me?" she asked.

"Tell you? Tell you! Why is everyone suddenly interested in my dreams? OK, yes, I've dreamt of her every night since I went AWOL. But I thought she was just a dream. My dream. A hallucination of someone barely holding it together. I thought I was crazy, but you know what, if being crazy meant seeing her, I just figured sanity was overrated. You know?"

"Human Jean-Luc, if you think that excuses—"

"I don't care! Bella is alive," I said, lifting my hand, "she's alive," the sound draining out of me as I said the words out loud. "That means that we can be together again." My heart contracted with every word, like it was trying to push out every drop of blood. *Bella is alive and we can be together again.*

Miral stopped pacing and gave me a look that would melt a puppy's heart. I swear, these angels and their expressions. But she said nothing, the words failing to leave her lips. We stared at each other for a long time before Michael finally broke the silence with words that came out uncharacteristically soft.

"I am afraid not. She is dead."

"But in the Void. She's alive in the Void."

"No, it is not her that lives, but her soul. Once the soul leaves the body …" He sighed, shaking his head. "Death is a one-way valve. Once you cross the threshold, there is no way back."

"But there has to be a way to bring her back."

"No, Human Jean, there is none."

"Then send me to her," I said, "… please."

Again the angels gave me that look of sympathy, only this time it was more like that of a mother trying to fix their child's first real boo-boo. *How do they do that?*

"No, Jean," Miral said, her voice infinitely soft. "When

214

the gods left, they took with them the path for souls to follow. Whereas death to Others means the ceasing of existence, death to your kind now means that your soul wanders aimlessly until the nothing of Beyond erases it. I am sorry, but your death will not reunite you with her."

"But …" I said, "there has to be a way."

"Perhaps," Miral said. "We would need time to consult other Others to find a way. But with the Avatar of Gravity desperate to have you, I fear that time is not on our side."

"That is why we must hide the human," Michael said to Miral, and I got the impression he was recalling a recent conversation of theirs. "While the Avatar is occupied, we must use this opportunity to run."

"Oh yeah," I said, looking up at the archangel, "why didn't you kill him? I mean, your hands were around his neck."

"I already told you—"

" 'I vowed never to harm a First Law,' " I said in a mocking baritone. "OK, fine—but what did you say to him to make him go away?"

My sarcasm was either missed or ignored, because Michael nodded with pride, walked over to the room's window and pulled back the curtains, revealing the night sky. Even with the light of the room and the lights of Paradise Lot, I could still see stars floating above. Michael looked out at them and said, "After God and the gods left, many of the stars' orbits changed. This galaxy does not follow the same paths as it once did."

This, I already knew. Hell, everyone knew it, with whole new sciences popping up to explain what happened. AstroMetaPhysics they called it, and some of humanity and Other's top minds were working on the reason why—and getting nowhere, I might add. I never much cared for the new science. What was the point? The oceans still had tides, the world still had seasons. So what if the stars didn't follow the same orbits they once did? In truth, the only practical effect this change had on my life was that the Sunday paper's *Astrology Fortune Telling* page no longer printed the typical "Fortune finds you," or "Ask and the answer will be yes," but rather essays on what the new GoneGod world had in store for me. And it was rarely good.

Michael sighed and continued. "I asked him to explain to me the Natural Law that would allow for such a difference. In other words, I bought us time."

"For what?"

"To hide you."

"Do you know how many Others died today because of that—that creature? I'm not hiding."

Michael leaned over, looking straight down at me, and said, "Yes, you are. Do you understand how many more are at risk because of you? He will level this city to find you. The only way to save Paradise Lot is for you to not be here. That, or ..." He drew a finger across his neck.

"There will be none of that," Miral cut in. "We will do what we have always done. Protect humans. Protect that human." She pointed at me.

Michael grunted, shrugging his shoulders. "Very well, then ... it is settled. You run. You hide," his voice drummed, giving me a look that, I swear, said, *Like all cowardly humans do.* But then again, I might have been over-sensitive.

I shook my head. "No."

"He will come for you again."

"Then keep sending him away with riddle after riddle. I bet you we could come up with thousands of them. What has four legs in the morning, two in the afternoon and three at night?"

"It doesn't work like that," Michael said calmly.

"Man. What is black and white and red all over?"

"I said—" Michael was speaking a bit more slowly now, pronouncing each word, "—it doesn't work like that."

"A newspaper … How about this one? Thirty white horses on a red hill: first they champ—"

"I *said!*"

"—then they stamp—"

"It *doesn't!*"

"—then they stand still."

"Work that way!" Michael bellowed. The room shook. Not in the metaphorical sense. It actually shook. "I am the archangel Michael, Captain of the Host, Guardian of the Faith and First amongst all angels. I am the Angel of Mercy and Bringer of Rain. I am the Slayer of Heretics and the Protector of Nations. And despite my lofty position in the angelic hierarchy, I am only allowed to formally request anything from a First Law once and only once."

I couldn't believe what I was hearing. "You mean to say, with all your power you can only speak to him once?"

"No, that is not what I said. I can only formally address them once, be it a request or a question. With Time, I asked him not to touch the divine. With Death, I requested that God and gods have dominion over souls. With Energy, I asked that she never cease to flourish in the celestial domains. But with Gravity, God spoke to Gravity directly and what He asked of the First Law, none of us know." Michael stood up and took a sip of his coffee, looked at the cup and grimaced. I guess they didn't have homebrew in Heaven. He looked down at me and said, "And I wasted the only question that Gravity's Avatar was divinely bound to answer, in order to save you. I would think that after such a sacrifice, you would owe me a little respect."

That did it—this angel thought that I owed him my life because he'd used up some once-upon-a-time favor for me. To Hell with that! He'd been willing to let me die to end this little problem. And now he wanted my gratitude? "Owe you? Owe you! I owe you nothing! You would have gladly let him kill me."

"A means to an end."

"A means to an end? A means to an end! Is that how the gods saw us? Little mortal pawns, a means to get what they wanted? And what exactly did they want from us? What? You don't know, do you? You were never privy to their private little plans ... Maybe, just maybe, if we were not treated like stepping stones to get to some unknown ends, we would have been more grateful and had a little bit more ... what was the word you used? Respect?"

I expected Michael to lose his temper, bellow at me in that mind-thumping voice of his or take me for another flight in the sky, but instead the archangel just nodded. "Yes," he said. "Truly, you have earned that from me." And with that he put a fist over his heart and took a step back.

I fought the urge to say *Now that's more like it,* opting for the less confrontational, "Even if I run, won't he level the city anyway, believing that I am hiding?"

"I will tell him you are gone," Michael said.

"So?" I asked, but I knew the answer. This celestial Boy Scout couldn't lie. If he told Grinner I'm gone, it would be because I'm gone. "Fine," I said, "but there has to be another way. He might leave Paradise Lot alone, but won't he just go from city to city, looking for me? Isn't running just transferring the problem to somewhere else?"

Miral nodded. "Indeed, Jean-Luc. But the alternative is worse. He must not find you. Have faith that we will hide you well, and pray that when the Avatar of Gravity tears this world apart to find you, he leaves enough of it intact for us to survive. That is the best any of us can hope for."

"That can't be the solution," I said. "There has to be another way!"

But even Miral's eyes were downcast, and I could see that two of the oldest and strongest creatures to walk this world agreed—the only hope for humanity and Others to survive was for me to run. Or die.

"Then kill me," I said. "Kill me and be done with it. Show my carcass to Grinner and he'll have to stop."

Michael and Miral exchanged a glance. "Yes," Michael agreed. "That would be a cleaner solution, and one we have considered. But Bella lives in the Void, which means there is a way back. To kill you now without—"

"Without trying to find it yourself," I hissed. "You're just as bad as he is."

"No, Human Jean-Luc," Miral said, coming to my side and taking my hand in hers. "No—we do not wish to become gods or God. We do not seek dominion over humanity or Others. We merely want life to be better for all. I want to fulfill Bella's destiny, save my friend and see her again. Imagine, Jean-Luc, if we could connect again with the Void, turn on the lights to our Father's mansion—then we would be whole again and the worlds would be safe. That is all we seek. I swear it on the very essence of my being. Michael and I only want to go home. And in going home, we wish to reunite you with Bella."

"Is ... is there a way back?"

Miral shook her head. "I don't know. We do not have the power—not at the level that Gravity's Avatar possesses. But there are beings out there whom we may consult, and other items that may be available to us ... We both have faith that, in time, a way home will be revealed."

"Faith." I shook my head. In the past, I never had much faith, but it was all I had right now.

"Here," Michael said, handing me the photo of Bella. "I took this from Evidence."

"But the case isn't closed yet," I said.

"We know who the murderer is. That is enough."

I looked at the picture. There I was again, looking down at Bella as she smiled and shook the hand of the Other that would betray her. I wondered if she had known his plan, if she would have told the Ambassador to fuck off. Probably not. Knowing Bella, she would have held out for some hope that he'd change his mind or that things would go differently. Or maybe she would have had faith that he would succeed. *Damn you, Bella. Your optimism is a real pain in my ass.*

I stepped to the counter and slipped the photo in my jacket pocket, the breast opposite the one holding the candle. Didn't want to get wax on my Bella.

"OK," I whispered. "OK. How long do I have?"

Michael stepped back to the window and looked to the heavens above. "He will need to observe the night sky for a full cycle to fully be able to answer my question. We have until dawn."

It was eight in the evening, which meant that I had roughly nine hours until sunrise. "Good," I said. "I have enough time."

"For what?"

"To say goodbye."

Chapter 24

Putting Affairs in Order

It took some convincing to get Miral and Michael to give me a few hours to get my affairs in order. What eventually won me my freedom was pointing out that a chief of police and a head of St. Mercy's Hospital would have to make a few phone calls before going on the lam. It was, after all, protocol. That was something that neither Michael nor Miral had considered. In Heaven, they only acted when under direct order by You-Know-Who. Here on Earth there were no direct commands, booming voices or divine inspiration, there were only protocols and rules.

Angels understand rules. They get order. But what they don't understand is bureaucracy. That is something uniquely human. There were papers to fill out, requests to be made, people to be informed before they could leave. And I, being a human hotel owner, would have similar, albeit less demanding, requirements. They saw the wisdom in that and, in the end, settled on meeting up three hours before dawn. The minimum amount of time necessary to get a head start on Grinner. And just enough time for all three of us to locate and fill out all the necessary paperwork.

↔

I could no longer protect my guests, but I could make things a little bit better, if only by a single degree.

First up—settle my debt with the fairies. At the "Coping with Mortality" seminar, I had asked them for a favor, which they'd agreed to do for the lofty price of seven vials of glitter and two bottles of Elmer's Glue. Since I had neither on me,

I asked Miral if I could raid the children's ward. Glue they had, but sadly no glitter—so eight clown noses and a rainbow afro wig later, the fairies agreed to my revised payment terms and handed me what they found.

Now on to the next thing … Fun, fun, fun!

↔

Over the arched door of the Palisade hung a crudely-drawn picture of a creature with pointy ears and dull fangs. The face had an X over it and in poor, nearly illegible letters read, *No Others Allowed.*

From the phone booth across the street I called the arcade.

"Whaaat?" answered a vile voice that I recognized as the HuMan kid that had hit me with the baseball bat.

OK, Jean-Luc, it was now or never. In an uneven, gruff voice I said, "EightBall. Now!"

"Yeah, who the hell is this?" BallSack asked.

"This is the shit-kicker that's gonna make an example out of you if you don't get me that shit-ball leader of yours on the phone. *Now!*" The words flowed awkwardly out of me and I finally understood what it felt like to be Steve from the Billy Goats Gruff. Difference was, I got my tough-guy vernacular from *CSI*, whereas he got his from old *Dick Tracy* comics. I vowed that if I survived this, I'd buy him all the seasons of *CSI*.

My gambit must have worked, because BallSack's voice faltered before he said, "Ahh … ahh … Ahh'm gettin' him. Hold on." From the receiver I could hear some scrambling before another voice came on.

"Ah, hello?"

In my best sultry accent I said, "Hi there, lover …" I

sprinkled a bit of Parisian for good measure.

"Who is this?"

"Oh, come on … You know who this is. I'm that Other who makes dreams come true."

"Why, you little—"

"Hold on, lover. You can act tough for them. And maybe you act tough for me later. I'm a bad, bad girl and I need a spanking from a big, tough guy who will set me straight." My cheeks were red with embarrassment. This would not be one of those stories I planned on telling anyone. Ever. "Will you set me straight? Huh, will you, lover?" I said for good measure.

"Well, ahhh, damn right, I will!" he said. I got to hand it to the kid, given how little blood was flowing to that tiny brain of his, he was doing OK. Just when I thought I had him, he asked, "Why?" his tone carrying with it more mental power than a hopped-up horny teenager should have.

"Protection," I said without hesitation. "My gifts, for you making sure your friends leave me alone."

"Oh yeah?" he said, "How often?"

"As many times as you want it for as long as you want it. It is a straight-up deal. My body for your muscle. Simple."

There was a silence as he contemplated it for a while. Then there was a heavy swallow on the other end before he said, "Fine. Where?"

"Good," I said. "The hotel."

"I'll be there in twenty minutes," he said and hung up.

↔

Given how the conversation went, I gave it 50/50 that he'd come out alone. He was too calm, too collected and for a moment I thought that he really hated Others enough to turn down a succubus. Not a simple feat—I should know.

But then he popped out alone and I knew teenage hormones had won the day. He probably figured he could have his cake and eat it—quite literally—by having an unbelievable night, followed by some Other-bashing.

He looked down the street and before he could get his bearings, I put a pillowcase over his head. I then took out a piece of lead pipe and pressed it hard against his back, hoping the cool metal feel would give him the impression I had a gun.

"I just want to talk," I said. "Ten minutes, then I'll let you go."

"Screw you, man!" he hissed.

"Look, don't make me gag you." I dug the lead pipe in to his back and, twisting his arm, forced him to walk forward.

Asal trotted forward pulling a rickshaw.

I smiled. "Asal, my friend, if you would be so kind."

↔

It took Asal nearly half an hour to trot over to where we were going. That's a long time to sit next to someone handcuffed and blindfolded. Not exactly ideal for facilitating conversation, but I think we did well, all things considered. He swore at me and I ignored him. I've known marriages less civil.

Once we got to where we were going, I pulled EightBall out. He resisted, tried to make a break for it, but the blind can only make it so far before running into something hard, like a wall.

"Come on," I said, helping him up and opening the front door of the abandoned building, "this way."

I led EightBall upstairs and into a burned-up room. The moonlight streamed through a hole in the roof. With the darkness hiding the details of destruction, the husk of a room was actually quite beautiful. I let him go. Again he tried to run, this time tripping over some rubble before falling to the ground with a whoop. I pulled off his hood.

"You son of a bitch, I'm going to …" He started looking around, but as soon as he recognized the place we were in, he stopped. With confused eyes, he asked, "Why the hell did you take me here?"

"Astarte told me to give you what you really want and since she's older than sin, and a damn-near goddess of desire, I figured her advice was pretty sound. But what does someone like you want?"

I stepped behind EightBall and pulled at the chain linking the handcuffs. He resisted, but from the angle, the strain on his wrists got him on his feet pretty damn quick.

"I tried to think what a punk kid like you would want. I mean, really want," I said. "What does someone who grew up on the streets want? Peace? A vacation? Nah, that's not it. Maybe a brand new gun or knife. If I asked you, you'd probably say something macho like a minute alone with me in a locked room."

"That's exactly what I want," he growled, crooking his neck back to meet my gaze. His eyes burned with a fresh fury and I knew if I released him, he'd go at me with everything he had.

"Maybe," I said, pretending that his hate didn't bother me. "I have no doubt that you desire my blood, but I don't think it's what you really want, deep down."

I sat him down on a chair and sat facing him on another. A coffee table was all that stood between us. "I struggled for a while with an answer. For a long time I couldn't come up with anything. Until, that is, I realized that you are exactly like me."

"I'm nothing like you! Other-lover," he spat.

"Both of our parents were killed by Others. Both of us have hated them for a long, long time. I had all the lines down pat. 'They don't belong here. This is our home, not theirs!' And 'Why should I care that they were evicted from their home without so much as a warning? Too bad for them! Screw 'em, right?' "

EightBall nodded, smiling at the thought.

"Only difference is, I was wrong," I said. "Something I realized about six years ago. And given our age difference, it'll be something you'll realize in about eleven years, but by then you will have caused a lot of hurt. And not just to them." I put down a book on the table. "Believe it or not, I'm trying to help you, kid."

"What's that?"

"A book," I said. "It was inspired by something that Penemue told me about."

"That pigeon?"

"Yeah, that *pigeon*," I said. I took off my collarless jacket and placed it on the back of my chair. Then I unlocked his handcuffs. As expected, he immediately went for me, so I kicked the back of his knee, forcing him to sit back down on the chair. I put a heavy hand on his shoulder and said, "You see, I know what I really, deep down in my core, want. I want to belong. To somewhere. To someone. And I figure that's what you want, too. This book is where you belong. Take a look inside and if you still want to stab me, I won't stop you. Not this time." I removed my hand from his shoulder and took a step back.

"So, I look at your stupid book and then I get my free shot. That's the deal, right?"

"If you still want it, then yeah, kid, that's the deal."

EightBall picked up the photo album, each page displaying a single picture. It was skillfully rendered with elegant calligraphy ordaining the book's margins. I gotta give the fairies their due credit—they were not well-equipped to live in the GoneGod world, but they sure knew design. The book was beautiful.

He thumbed through it. Fast at first, skipping over the photos he didn't recognize, but then he slowed down when he got to a picture of a young girl, no older than eight. She still had her whole life in front of her, but looked enough like who she would become that EightBall recognized her. He slowed, his hands gently touching the surface of her face. The next image was of the girl's father, the two of them at the local grocery store in what was now Paradise Lot's downtown. The young father owned the place and his daughter, no older than ten in this picture, proudly helped him stack the shelves, a smile on both their faces. The next was of the same bright-eyed little girl, now twelve, dancing ballet, her grace unhindered by the black and white gloss of the photograph. Next she was playing the piano, then she was standing on stage, having won second place in a father-daughter foot race. Then of proud parents, standing by a young lady who wore a blue graduation dress and a proud, glowing smile. The young woman at Christmas, sitting by her aging father, who wore an oxygen tank but still managed to smile, happy to be surrounded by his family.

EightBall wiped away a tear as he turned the page to that same young woman, walking down the aisle, an old man in a wheelchair clapping in the front. Then her hand was out as a nervous young man put a ring on his new wife's hand. Then the same woman, older now, holding her protruding belly. Page after page of the young couple preparing the baby's room, getting ready for the new addition to the family, until the pictures showed the proud mother holding her newborn in her arms. More tears of joy as she held the fragile little creature.

The last picture in the book was of a young EightBall—Newton—standing with his mother and father, holding a plaque of his own: first place in the piano recital. He smiled, two front teeth missing, as proud parents each put a hand on his shoulders. And then, abruptly, the book ended, several blank pages remaining to be filled.

Tears streamed down his face as he looked up at me and asked, "How … how did you get this?"

"Fairies. They dug through this wreckage and found the photos and put it together. Not bad for a bunch of talking gnats. Man, I will say one thing about those guys—they will do just about anything for glitter."

I waited to see if his tears would turn to rage—after all, I made a deal with the kid—but there was no fight left in him. He sat there leafing through the book, turning to the earlier pages he had skipped over.

"Newton," I said, "I know that you blame them for your loss, but even you have to see how they no more wanted to hurt your family than come to Paradise Lot in the first place. They're outcasts, just like you and me, without a home, most of them without their families." I put my collarless jacket back on. "I have to go. I can't protect them anymore. And I know that the book doesn't go very far for returning what you've lost, but maybe it will go far enough for you to let go of your hate for them."

And with that, I left him to his tears and confusion, praying that those pictures were enough.

Chapter 25

On the Road Again

I had no idea if my little conversation with EightBall would work. All I could do was hope. Hell, seems like hope and faith was all I got. Funny that I found both after the gods left. So after leaving EightBall, I asked Asal to drop me off at my last destination before I had to leave.

I asked him to take me home.

↔

The little bell over my front door rang as I walked in for what would probably be the last time. I climbed the stairs of the One Spire Hotel and opened the loft door above. In the corner sat Penemue, books thrown about, his hay bed in tatters and a bottle of Drambuie in his hand. He was crying, cuddling his bottle as he tried to coax comfort from its hallowed contents.

When he saw me, his eyes glistened, lit by angelic tears. "I was so afraid. I always believed that I would face my death with bravery, honor even, but in the end I was so very, very afraid. I am sorry for betraying you, Human Jean-Luc," he said with a drunken hiccup. "But I am most sorry for breaking my promise."

"You never promised me anything."

"No, no—not to you, dear Human Jean. You are not the only one who makes sacred promises. I broke a promise I made to myself before the Earth was formed and when the sky still burned red. When He cast me into the pits of fire and brimstone, I swore that I would never ask Him for anything. Never again." Penemue tried to stand, but drunk as

229

he was, all he managed to do was fall on his back. His wings spread out and contracted, like he was trying to fly. He looked like an overturned turtle. I offered him my hand and as I righted him, he said, "But today, Jean, I prayed. I begged. I pleaded with Him to let you live, and here you are. He listened. He heard me."

"I don't know about that," I said, pulling with all my weight to get the angel to sit up. He managed to get himself half-erect and with my help he was able to rest his back on the wall. From the corner of the room, I took the pitcher of water and poured him a glass of water. "Here, drink this."

"You live. He must have listened."

"Actually, I think it is Michael you have to thank. Michael tricked Grinner into leaving me alone. For a little while, anyway. I don't know if that was His work." With the last phrase, I pointed up.

Penemue's face went grave. "Of course that is. He sent His emissary. An asshole, yes, but His emissary nonetheless!"

I shrugged. "Maybe, but that doesn't matter anymore. The box? Did you figure out what it was? Not that it matters anymore."

Penemue perked up, not hearing my last remark. "What is it *not?*" he exclaimed, hands and wings both outstretched in excitement. The tips of his wings hit the room and bits of drywall flaked off. He lowered his wings and, controlling his volume, picked up a discarded Drambuie bottle and cradled it like it was the box—man, this was one *drunk* angel. "I have never, ever, ever, *ever* held anything with so much history before. Truly unique! Singular in the significance imbued within its making—"

"And?" I interrupted.

Gesturing for me to draw closer, he whispered, "It is Pandora's Box! I know, I know, shocked me, too." He nodded in mock, drunken surprise.

"Pandora's Box? As in the container from which all sin sprang forth—"

"Its contents emptied, leaving behind only Hope. Yes, the very same. But it is not only that ... It is also the Ark of the Covenant, and Pharaoh's Vial, and the Wineskin that once held the Blood of Kvasir, otherwise known as the Mead of—"

"Poetry?"

"You know it?"

"I'm familiar with the legend," I sighed.

"In days gone by, it was the last cup from which Jesus drank, the first goblet which ever held Ambrosia and the bowl from which an asp bit Cleopatra's hand as she reached for a fig in its basin! It is all those things and more. Whoever constructed the box itself, and I suspect that it was Joseph, did so by taking little pieces from all those items and putting it together into one place."

"Why?" I asked.

"Why else! To contain something of extreme significance."

"But it's so small," I said, holding up my hands with enough space to hold a Rubik's Cube.

"Bahhh!" the angel dismissed me. "Mortals always think in size, size, size. 'Bigger is better.' A thousand angels once danced on the head of a pin. How do you think we did that? By getting a really, really big pin? NO! Size, cosmically speaking, doesn't matter. Only space. And even the smallest of spaces can hold the vastest of universes. That box, with all the significance it possesses, can hold a thousand universes and still have room to spare."

"Big enough for a heaven?" I asked.

"Heavens," Penemue retorted, "and hells and

purgatories and a thousand other dimensions that your kind have yet to perceive."

"I see," I said. So that was Joseph's plan. And that was why Grinner needed it. And considering what it was, now I suspected it would take a lot more than a little Hermes-fire to destroy it, which meant Grinner was still in the game. Now all he had left to do was fill the box, which was exactly where Bella and I came into play.

So I told the twice-fallen angel about Grinner, Hermes and the fight in Paradise Lot. About Michael and Miral. And about Bella. My dreams and how my wife existed in another realm. And about the kiss, and how it creeped me out.

"Bella's soul is not lost," Penemue said to himself. "A bit of joy can be found in every terrible situation."

"Yes … Yes, it can."

"Human Jean-Luc. The only way the Avatar of Gravity will be able to make the connection between Heaven and Earth tangible is by extracting it from you."

"I don't understand," I said.

"Our magic works by making abstract concepts real. Gravity is a Law, so the gods created an avatar with whom they could negotiate. Turning the abstract into the real. Your connection with Bella—your dreams—that is an abstract bridge built by your love. Grinner wishes to make that real. He wants to rip your connection to her out of you and turn it into a bridge that Others can use."

"And if he does, what will happen to my connection to her? To my dreams?"

"They will no longer be a part of you."

"You mean, I'll stop loving her?"

"No, that is beyond our magic. What I mean is that your love will no longer be enough for you both to find each other, to speak across worlds." Penemue drew heavily on the

Drambuie. "Without it, she will truly be lost to you."

I looked at the angel, who stared back at me with heavy, swollen eyes that glistened with the light of trapped tears. This twice-fallen angel had lived in the One Spire Hotel for six years and in that time he had been a colossal pain in the butt, but he was always my friend. What I had to do next would be the hardest thing I'd ever done.

"Do you know why I fell the first time?" he asked.

I had heard the story before, but before I could answer Penemue said, "Enoch, the judge of the Fallen, wrote that my sin was that I taught humans how to read and write ..." His eyes went distant as he recalled the judgment against him. "You see, by his estimation, humans weren't supposed to have that knowledge because ... well, because you guys weren't smart enough. The fear was that you'll write down a false idea and, like the Golden Calf, worship it. An idea is far more dangerous than a statue, no matter how big or golden it is.

"But I didn't think so little of humans. I thought that if they could only have a chance to record their thoughts and learn from their ancestors that in time their ideas would evolve into something worthy. That's why I taught you how to read and write, how to make paper and brew ink."

The angel sighed, drawing heavily on his bottle before continuing. "I knew I would be punished, but I did not believe I would be cast from Heaven. I thought my sin was great enough that He would grant me death—true death. And despite believing that, I did it anyway, because I thought I was doing the right thing."

"Penemue, you're punishing yourself when there is no need," I started.

The Fallen lifted a hand asking me to let him finish. "I was willing to die for what I believed. I was willing to face the abyss for the knowledge I granted you. But when I was asked to lay my life down for what really matters, for my friend, my resolve faded away into nothing and I told him all. I am a coward, Human Jean-Luc. A worthless, pathetic coward."

"Enough," I said. "You got scared. You chose to live over dying. I will never, ever hold that against you."

Penemue's eye cracked open and he looked at me confused. "Dear Human Jean, I tell you this, not because I am seeking your forgiveness, but because I want you to understand who it is you fight for. I was once willing to die for my cause, but for a friend, I betrayed you the first chance I got. I do not deserve your protection or your care. None of us do. You need to understand that in the days to come. We are not worth it. None of us are. So, should the Avatar of Gravity extract the connection from you and make the bridge real, then let him win. This world and its paltry occupants are not worth you losing Bella again." From behind a stack of books, he pulled out another bottle of Drambuie and opened it with a twist of his pointy fingers.

"Maybe, but then again maybe your second chance isn't up yet. None of ours is. And maybe if I give this world a bit more time, then they will be worth saving," I said.

"Jean-Luc the optimist. When did this happen?" Penemue said, handing me the bottle.

"It was always there, just buried deep. Really deep." I sighed, taking the bottle. "Look, I have to go, but before I do there's one last favor I need from you."

"Of course," he roared with a sudden excitement, "I owe you for my betrayal and am eager to work off the debt."

"For all the years I helped you stand when you fell—yes, you owe me. For all the times I saved you from that mouth of yours—yes, you owe me. But for saving yourself from

Grinner—for that, you owe me nothing. Understand? I free you of that debt."

The angel nodded. "Very well, then. A favor for a friend."

"Yes, a favor for a friend," I said, a lump catching in my throat. I handed him two envelopes.

Penemue sat up, his massive shoulders hunched over in defeat as he took the paper from my hand. "What are these?" he asked.

"One is instructions to you, the other is for someone else."

Penemue read the notes and looked up at me. His voice trembled as he spoke. "But … but this is suicide."

"Maybe, but we're all going to die one day. Might as well die for something worthwhile." I raised the bottle of Drambuie and said, "This is it, old friend. Time to say goodbye. What do you say—one more for the road?"

↔

Penemue and I downed a shot of Drambuie, and I left the big guy alone in his sorrow and headed down to my room. It always amazed me how the world might be ending and yet your room would look exactly as you'd left it. You'd think that it would have faced the same whirlwind that you did, but my things all just sat there unmoved and untouched. I hung up my collarless black jacket on the coat rack.

My junktiques sat on their shelves and Castle Grayskull sat empty on my chest of drawers.

Damn.

I had hoped that Tink would have made it back by now. I was sure she escaped; I saw her light flutter down the tunnel. Where was she? My only hope was that she was too scared to come home, afraid that Grinner would be here. But there was a big difference between knowing and hoping.

The part of me that lived with and cared for Tink for the last six years had to believe that she was alive and well, hiding somewhere safe. That she wasn't crushed by some random rock or lost in tunnels filled with Others that would like nothing more than to own a true myth. To believe anything else would be too much for me to bear after a day of so much loss.

And it was hope that led me to leave behind a bit of the candle that Hermes gave me. I figured a creature as old and unique as Tink would know what to do with it, and if I couldn't keep her safe, well, at least I could give her something to help.

I also left a recording on my old Dictaphone, telling her that I probably wasn't coming back and that if she needed sanctuary, it was Miral whom I trusted above everyone else. It was up to Tink if she was going to entrust herself to another guardian or not. I couldn't make that decision for her.

"I'm sorry, Tink," I said, "but I can't keep you safe. Not anymore," and as I spoke those last words, warm tears fell down my cheeks.

I closed the little drawbridge on Castle Grayskull and headed out the door.

↔

The clock on the dashboard flashed two a.m. Good, that meant three hours and change before dawn, just enough time for me to get on the road.

Convincing Michael to let me go had been quite the feat. He wanted to get on the run right away. I had to swear on every GoneGod and living soul I knew, vow up and down, and absolutely promise to come back at least three hours before dawn, and even then he let me go with great protest. The thing about oaths and Others is that they are always making these grand gestures, spoken in archaic chant, that are absolutely binding. Before the GrandExodus, to break an oath meant death. "Cross my heart and hope to die" was quite literal. Magic, karma, chutzpah—call it what you will— but the Universe always got even with them, and as a result, making and keeping a promise was very serious business, indeed. I get that. Really I do.

Unfortunately for Michael, my promise was made with my fingers crossed behind my back. I don't know how that cosmically works and I doubted that pre-GrandExodus, you could get out of it that easily, but still—that's what I did. Didn't make me feel any better, but I couldn't keep my promise to him when it went against another, higher promise I made earlier. To Bella.

You see, Michael was right. Miral was right. Hell, even Tink was right. There was no hope in fighting an enemy like Grinner. I had to run.

But they were wrong about one thing—it wasn't Bella's dream to reopen the Void and send the Others packing. She wanted us all to live together. Here on Earth and in Heaven. That's why she helped the Ambassador. She believed he was the key to peace in this life and the next.

I knew that Michael and Miral meant well and that they wanted to help. But after a while, even they would be tempted. There would be some shaman or prophet or Other that had a key or chalice or talisman that would find Bella and Heaven. And then what? Another experiment, another grand scheme, another maniacal wannabe god. If the road to Hell is paved with good intentions, then what's the road to

Heaven paved with?

And even if they did find a way back to their Heaven, I don't think it would solve anything. I'd gotten to know their kind and, well, they don't play well with Others. Reopening the Void would lead to a war between Others, which meant more rainbow blood painting the roads. No, I couldn't let that happen. That wasn't what Bella wanted.

Besides, I had other plans in mind. I might not be able to beat Grinner in a fight, but there was more than one way to skin that proverbial cat. I had an ace up my sleeve—a long shot, but far more tempting than spending a life on the run with Michael and Miral. As much as I hated not keeping my word, this was something I needed to do on my own. They were adults a couple of thousand times over—they'd get over it.

As for the other detail … well, like I'd said to Penemue, this was it—one last favor.

I turned my PopPop's old 1969 Plymouth RoadRunner ignition and took to the road. It felt good to be in the driver's seat. Soon the city was out of view and highway lights were exchanged for stars. I looked at the clock—just an hour to go before dawn. Right about now, Penemue was delivering a map to Grinner with a big X and the words "Come and get me," scrawled in red.

End of Part Three

Part Four

Third Interlude

There is this girl whom I love very much. She is killed, and I go on a rampage of hate and destruction, accepting every mission they hand me. As long as I get to kill Others, I don't care where I am, who I kill. My grief chases me, but as long as I am slaying Others I am able to outrun it. For a while, at least. But I am in a losing race and I will soon learn that there is no one in this world—or any other—that is fast enough to outrun grief.

Mine will catch me while doing an extermination mission on a remote island in northern Scotland. Recon says that there are Fanatics planning a suicide mission. Doesn't matter to me. We get to the island and I glance at my watch. The minute hand is spinning, the second hand is moving so fast it's invisible. Magic. On a hillside there's a cave and an Other is burning time to hide. I point and we get into position. We don't know what we're up against. We should investigate. Plan. Prepare.

Instead I throw in a grenade.

What comes out isn't a terrorist cell or group of Fanatics, but a single golden dragon. It always amazes me that no matter what kind of face an Other has—humanoid, elongated, animalistic—you can always tell when they're scared. This dragon is terrified.

It charges from the mouth of the cave, a breath of flame climbing ahead as claws strike out. It manages to take out half of my team before it takes to the sky. It's trying to get away.

Without hesitation I aim my rifle at the scale right over its heart—a dragon's weak spot—and from this distance I have a one-in-a-thousand chance to hit. Today must be my birthday, because a moment after my rifle thunders, the dragon drops. What's left of my team rushes at it and I note that the titanium-reinforced bullet has ripped through its hardened scales at exactly the right place. Or wrong place, depending on where you stand.

My bullet broke through its golden scales, but didn't reach its heart. The hurt dragon is far from dead. Its eyes glow as it attacks with a blazing speed that is amplified by burned time. It swipes down, sending me and two other soldiers flying, as it bites down on a fourth. A thistle bush breaks my fall, my armor saving me from an evening of pulling out needles. As for my two comrades, they aren't as lucky, both of their bodies splattering against unforgiving rock. The dragon turns to run away.

My team is dead. I am alone on the island with a pissed-off injured dragon. I know I should call for backup. For evac. But it can't fly, which means that I can track it down. Find it. Kill it. I put down my rifle and leave behind some bulky high-powered equipment, taking only my hunting sword with me. Today will be a good day to die.

I track it to some rocks by the sea where it is cleaning its wound, trying to remove the bullet so that it can burn some time and heal itself. When I walk onto the beach it looks at me, surprised, clearly not expecting me to have pursued it. It eyes me, then scans the empty hillside, glances back at me and my sword, shakes its head and turns back to the sea to continue cleaning its wound.

I charge and it looks at me with more genuine surprise. I slash down on its reinforced scales, but my sword bounces off them without effect. That's fine. That's what I want. It turns too late to swipe and I roll, swinging again. The dragon snorts, assuming I cannot hurt it and, no longer on high alert, swipes again, leaving an opening for me to tumble past its front claws and thrust my hunting sword into the hole left by my bullet. I know my blade is long enough to pierce its heart. I push and in the second I have before it turns to crush me, I manage to nick the chamber wall of its heart.

It rears up with a roar, throwing me nearly ten meters away, where this time there are no bushes to break my fall. I must have hit my head because for the first time since she died, I see her.

Bella. Standing there on the beach, hand outstretched.

"Silly Jean," she says, as if I have simply fallen and scraped my knee, "You should be helping, not hunting."

Behind her I can see the dragon getting up. Sure, it's dying, but dying isn't dead. All it needs to do is stomp on me or bite my head off.

Kill your killer—not a bad end for a warrior.

"Bella," I say, reaching my hand out to her. "I've missed you."

"Jean, why are you doing this?" she asks.

"Because they hurt you," I say.

"The dragon did not hurt me," she scolds.

"No, but other Others—"

"Other Others are not that Other," she says, pointing at the dragon. "Stop punishing them for something they did not do. And stop punishing yourself."

The dragon is stumbling over to me, determined to enact its revenge by dining on my guts.

Bella looks over her shoulder.

"Jean, I need something from you."

"Anything," I find myself saying. *Anything.*

"Promise me that if you live, you'll help them. Promise."

"But …" I start to say, but Bella holds up a hand.

"Promise me," she repeats, tears streaming from her eyes.

242

And I know that, dream or not, real or not, I cannot deny her anything. I nod.

"Say it," she says.

The dragon is on me, its massive skull eclipsing Bella's body—this is it.

"Say it!"

"I ... I promise," I say.

What does it matter? I am about to die. Here and now.

A light shines off the dragon's eyes and it opens its mouth, ready to breathe out its last bit of hate on me, when Bella turns around so suddenly that the dragon takes a step back.

It sees her, I think. How?

I can't hear what she says; all I know is that they are discussing my fate. Eventually the dragon nods and walks away, making it about fifty meters before it collapses from its wounds.

What happens next is darkness.

↔

It is the dark of night when I regain consciousness. A soft flicker of light catches my eye and in the distance, I see the body of the dragon illuminated by the star-filled night. It is dead.

The dragon never came over, never spoke with Bella. It must have been a dream, I think.

A soft glow of gold sits on the dragon's neck. Walking over, I see, for the first time, Tinkerbelle, sitting there, crying. When I approach, Tink does not run or hide, she just sits there, hugging the dragon with an abandoned grief.

Seeing Tink there, her grief, the dream of Bella ... it all just washes over me. Tink will later tell me that the dragon's fury and fear was not for itself, but for the little fairy it once protected. But now, all I see is a crying little golden myth. I am stunned and shamed by her misery—it is so pure, so perfect, so complete.

I think back to all my time with Bella, all her hopes and dreams. I have not honored Bella with who I have become, and for the first time since she died, I let myself feel her loss. At first only gentle tears come but soon they give way to pain far more powerful, until my grief pours out of me in such a violent torrent that I actually think it will suffocate me. I don't just cry. I scream. I bellow. I wrench off my armor.

After what seems to be an eternity, I eventually gain enough composure to stand. The radio clicks. HQ wants to know what's happening. I throw it to the ground and then stomp on it. Let them think we're all dead. Everyone else is—what's one more dead soldier going to change?

That's when I go AWOL, hiding in my PopPop's old cabin. It takes a year, but eventually an uneasy peace is brokered between humans and Others.

That's when I return to Paradise Lot in order to fulfill Bella's dream.

Chapter 26

Memories

The road to the cabin was winding and to get onto the property you needed to climb a steep hill. The old RoadRunner struggled and I had to push the accelerator all the way down to get her old wheels over the crescent.

This would be the same hill Grinner would have to climb when he came, assuming he didn't fly. Since I'd never seen his feet leave the ground—at least not by his own will—I guessed flying wasn't high on his modes of transport. That and because he was the Avatar of Gravity, I figured he was a feet-on-the-ground kind of guy. I supposed he could make his way through the thick tree line or cross the lake, but I doubted that, too. The forest was too dirty for his clean pleated trousers and the lake required hiring a boat or walking on water. Gravity could do a lot, but that trick required a different kind of magic. But the biggest proof I had that he'd use the main path was that he wasn't afraid of me. This soon-to-be god saw my defiance as an annoyance that had to be dealt with, not a problem with the potential to undo him. Everything I knew about Grinner told me he'd be coming through the front door. As I climbed over the hill's zenith, I made a mental note to put some sensors in the brush. I'd know when he passed this point, at least.

The cabin was at still there, standing alone on the hill's plain. It was a lone structure, one story high and completely made of pinewood. There were two bedrooms—one on each side of the cabin—no electricity, a kitchenette with a gas stove and running water that was installed about thirty years ago when PopPop fitted a pump from the lake. As for a bathroom—well, that was what the trees were for.

I parked by the old wood shed and walked up the steps, opening the unlocked door. What was the point of locking it? Someone could spend all day kicking down the door without a soul to stop them. Inside I noted that, either by luck or because the cabin was so far off the beaten path, no one had found it since I last visited it all those years back. I walked onto its old, uneven floor. A green two-seat sofa sat in front of the fireplace. The floor creaked as I pulled back the sofa and threw aside the tatty orange rug that it rested on. Beneath it was a false floor that I had built. It opened with a *pop*, dust flying up into the air, and I stuck my arm down the hole, feeling for the old gray-green canvas sack.

It was right where I'd left it. With a strained pull, I lifted out my old military bag from its hiding place. It was heavy, about as long as a ski bag and eight times the width. I pulled back on its heavy-duty zipper, opening its mouth as wide as it would go. And there it all was. All my old military stuff that I had stashed in the cabin when I naïvely believed I would never need it again. Weapons specifically designed to kill Others. They felt familiar in my hands, muscle memory taking over as I held them. Old friends.

Old addictions.

I checked my rifle and went through my bag of tricks. *Once more into the fray ... into the last good fight I'll ever know,* I thought as I inventoried the content.

The way Grinner burned through time, he believed it was infinite, so the plan was simple: rain holy Hell on him and wear him out. Of course, my plan also required me not getting flattened in the meantime. No plan was perfect and besides, it was a good day to die.

I grabbed my bag and started distributing its contents in the cottage and surrounding lands. When the fight started, the more options I had, the better off I'd be. Then I sheathed my hunting sword and pulled out my trusted rifle, preparing myself for the next part of my plan. I had to get more information and there was only one person I knew who could tell me what I wanted to know.

I needed to take a nap.

Chapter 27

Dream a Little Dream of Me

The darkness came for me the way it always did, its tendrils reaching out like some gruesome, undefined monster. I wanted to run, to run like I had every night for the last six years, but tonight I let the darkness envelop me.

It hit me like a rush of air from a fan suddenly turned on and then I was in it, completely consumed by its nothingness. For a moment I was alone, until she came for me like she did every night—a light in the endless Void, an angel floating down from nowhere, her presence chasing away both darkness and fear.

"Hi Jean-Luc," she said, her tone soft and careful, "I suspect you have a few questions for me."

"Yeah," I said, looking up at her blinding light, "a couple. But I think I've figured out a lot of it already."

"Fine. But first, where would you like to be?"

"Excuse me?"

She rolled her eyes, tempering the gesture with a playful smile. "Oh come, Jean-Luc. We're about to have a fight." She stood arms akimbo as she gave me her mocking, *It's-time-to-get-serious* look. It was the look she always gave me when trying to lighten the mood before we were about to have a hard conversation. "Jean-Luc, we might as well do it somewhere beautiful. Where would you like to go?"

I looked at her blankly, still not sure what she meant.

She swallowed hard, as if pushing back her frustration, and in a controlled even tone she said, "Do you remember where we met? Just outside that diner you used to work?" In the darkness a glass-and-steel door appeared with a neon yellow sign above it that read: JACK'S DINER.

"Jim's Diner," I corrected, "not Jack's."

"Ahhh, that's right, Jim's Diner." The sign above the door morphed from JACK to JIM, keeping the same neon-yellow shine. "You were a busboy, weren't you? My mom took me out to dinner as a treat for getting a perfect report card or winning a spelling bee or whatever it was. Even then, she hated the way you looked at me." Bella flattened her dress, nervously pressing out wrinkles in the fabric. "We could go there. Or we could go to our first apartment. That hole-in-the-wall just off of—"

"Where I proposed," I interrupted. "I want to go there."

"But we went there last night," she protested, but I held resolute.

"So what?" I said. "You asked me where I wanted to go and I want to go there."

"OK, fine. You were always such a creature of habit."

Then from the darkness, mists bloomed from a thousand flower buds that I did not know were there. Maybe the unblossomed pods were hidden in the darkness, or maybe they were never there and Bella somehow, magically, made them appear. Whatever it was, wisps of smoke billowed out as the Void filled around us with a translucent smoke. Then we were standing on a cloud, cool fog shifting in an effervescent dance beneath our feet. The haze had a pleasant smell that I couldn't quite place. Something safe and pure, like when PopPop used to bake apple pie, or the strong leather smell of his car. Perhaps it was one of those. Perhaps both.

Slowly the smell changed, bringing with it tinges of salt and water and … I smelled the ocean. More than that—I could hear the waves lapping against the shore just in front of me. More out of instinct than anything else, I took a step forward, forgetting that I was suspended in the darkness, floating in nothing. I was surprised when my feet caught onto earth. I shuffled them. It felt like I was standing on sand. I looked down, expecting to see cool white wisps still dancing around my feet, but instead what I saw was hardened vapor that congealed into a white, sandy beach.

A light that was not there before shined above me and I looked up, blinded by the sudden appearance of the Sun. As my eyes adjusted, I looked around and saw that we were on the beach and Bella was no longer haloed by light. She was wearing her white sundress, the one with lilies. There were so many little details that were different from how I remembered them. The boats off the shore. The tree line behind us. A tiny shell that dug into my knee when I bent down to propose to her. And why not? It was fourteen years since we last stood on this beach. In real life, that is. In my dreams, we visited this place often. Still, it had been so long since either of us had been here, our memories of this place were bound to be a bit off. Trouble was, the beach we were standing on wasn't the recollection of my imperfect memory, it was hers.

All this time when she took me to places to have our nightly chats, I'd believed that they were my memories that took us there. She was my dream, after all, so it made sense that we would go to places I remembered and loved. But we never went anywhere from my memories. We were always going to the places she knew, in the way she remembered them.

As if sensing my realization, she said, "Before I learned how to do that, I thought we had failed. After all, I was meant to be in Heaven, but instead I was lost in a place that transcended emptiness." She chuckled at the thought.

"But you didn't fail, did you?"

She shook her head. "I remember what the Ambassador told me. Why did the angels rebel?"

"Pride?"

"Envy. They envied our free will. It was a power that they wished to have for themselves. But what is free will? After all, didn't the angels rebel? How could they have done that without free will? It got me thinking … and I realized that free will isn't just the ability to do whatever we want, it is also the ability to shape the world around us. Mold it into what we want it to be. That's a lot more literal in a place like this."

She lifted her hand and from it sprung forth the twisty-tie I had used to propose. I felt around my neck—my own twisty-tie was still coiled around the chain. She smiled, tossing it to me. In the palm of my hand, I looked closely at the tiny piece of plastic that my seventeen-year-old self used in lieu of an engagement ring. At the time, I thought it proved me insurmountably romantic to propose with such a thing. Bella came over and showed me her own ring finger. She still wore her twisty-tie. Then she touched the thin band in my hand and it almost felt like her finger pressed on my palm. But like all my dreams, we never actually touched. I guess that was just another rule of this place. She rolled the twisty-tie on the palm of my hand and turned it into a silver ring, which she put on her own finger alongside her own twisty-tie.

"In this life and the next," she said, looking at the two rings.

Bella sighed and turned her attention to the sky above. "I think that is why they took all the human souls with them when they left. Because they knew that any human soul in

Heaven or Hell would understand that and would bend the Void to their will."

"I … I don't understand," I said, shaking my head, drawing in closer to her.

"When the gods created the world, they gave everyone immortality. Others were granted endless life and humans were imbued with souls. In other words, we were all given essentially the same thing—eternal life. But the two kinds of immortalities drew on different wells of power. When the gods left, they effectively turned off the lights for all the other planes. Others, despite all their abilities, did not possess the right kind of power to turn the lights back on. But a human soul, that is a different thing altogether."

I nodded, slowly understanding what Bella was saying. "Souls are the on' switch to this place?"

"Not just the on' switch. They're like a million nuclear power stations all running at full capacity. Watch!"

She flicked her hand and in an instant, the beach turned into our apartment where we first lived, then PopPop's cabin, the airplane on which we rode with the Ambassador, the hard concrete floor where we made love the night before she died. She was cycling through all the places that, once-upon-a-time, meant something to us.

"They are all our memories," I said.

She nodded. "And not just memories," she said. "Watch!"

With a wave of her hand, she brought forth a light show that made *Fantasia* seem like a child playing with flashlights. Meteors shot up as swirls of rainbow-colored imagery shone bright in the sky. The spectacular illuminations danced around us as she transformed the empty Void into her canvas, filled by her imagination. I giggled at the sight.

"And it's not just lights. I can make things, too. Imagine playing with these!"

Optimus Prime, Voltron and an army of Smurfs manifested before me. Each was life-size and looked so real that I thought they were standing in front of me. And it wasn't some 3D animation like what we got in the movies. These beings had a realism to them that made those renditions seem like a child's drawing. Whatever she was doing, she wasn't drawing or sculpting these creatures. She was creating them. All that was left was to breathe life into their husks.

"This is what the Others must do when they burn time. Except here—time is infinite," she said and as the words left her lips, her creations faded away. I looked over at my Bella, who breathed heavily from the exertion of creating. "I'm still learning to hold the creations. Right now I can form them, but I can't keep them. Perhaps in time I will be able to keep them around longer—or forever. But for now, the only things I seem to be able to manifest with any permanence are the constructs that I make from memories. The easiest ones to build are the memories that mattered most. The times I was most happy and in love," she took me to the PopPop's cabin, "or happiest." Suddenly we were in our first apartment, standing in front of the couch we used to cuddle on while watching TV.

I rolled my eyes. "Seriously? I thought you hated that couch."

She laughed, her eyes brightening. "I know, I know! But I loved being near you. And it was our love that allowed me to be tethered enough to the mortal realm to find you. It was our love that allowed me to eventually find you in your dreams. And perhaps it will be our love that will find a way for us to be together again."

"So, am I here?" I asked. She had stopped the memories outside Jim's Diner and I bent down to touch the ground, expecting concrete from the road, but my hand went through the ground, touching nothing.

"No," she said.

"Are you here?" I asked, trying to comprehend what this place was. She no longer wore her sundress—the one with lilies—but wore jeans and the V-neck sweater I bought her for her birthday.

"Yes, this place is as real as anywhere I've ever been. You are as real to me as ever before," she said.

My tears welled up within me. All these years believing she was not real, believing that it was my guilt and pain that caused my nightly dream of her. So much wasted time. "Why didn't you tell me any of this before?" I asked, knowing I should be angry, but unable to. I was so happy. Bella still existed.

"Oh Jean, I am so sorry for not telling you about any of this. I thought I was doing what was best for you. You were doing so well, you even seemed happy at times. I thought this was my role—to be your guardian angel, helping you through all the hardships you faced. Telling you would have only caused you more pain and it would have stopped you from doing all the good you have done. I didn't want you to spend years looking for a way to me, when you could have spent that time doing good that matters."

"But this matters," I said.

She shot me her best *You-know-what-I-mean* look and said with a smile, "I did what I thought was right, just like you've done so many times in the past. And I am sorry that my decisions have caused you pain. Cause you pain, still. I love you, Jean, in this life and the next."

I did know what she meant. I really did. After all, it was our love that got us through the really hard times, it was our love that allowed us to find each other even when we were worlds apart and it was our love that Grinner wished to capture in order to reopen Heaven. "In this life and the next," I said, "I love you, too."

She smiled, closing her eyes, the pressure from the closed lids causing a single tear to escape and fall on my outstretched hand. I could have sworn I felt it.

"Jean, we don't have much time. He is coming and whatever happens next, you cannot let him find me."

"But we could be together."

"In a world that would be in flames."

"And would that be so bad?"

"Yes," she said, her face drained of all joy. "Yes, it would be."

"So what do we do?"

"I don't know," she said, her voice flat. "What do we do every time we have a fight?"

I shrugged. "We go for a walk. Cool off … but it's not like there's anywhere we can go here."

"Oh," Bella said as her lips curled up, "but that's where you are wrong."

↔

Bella snapped her fingers and the world transformed around us. We were in the cabin, then in her childhood bedroom. Next my house, followed by the downtown bakery where we'd go and get ice cream after school. Over the next couple of hours, we visited a past filled by us. I could not begin to understand the emotions that stirred within me. Joy, anger, hate, elation, contentment, chaos—they all swirled around as she took me on a tour of her personal Heaven. A heaven that was only filled with memories of us. The one emotion that tempered all that I felt, that kept them from boiling over and wasting the little time we had left, was love.

Still, there was one memory we did not visit. One that held more pain in it than I have ever known before. I knew that if I were to win against Grinner, I needed to know as much as I could. I had to understand what happened the night she died. I wanted to visit that place as much as I wanted a threesome with Judith and the Devil, but I had to know everything if I was going to live through the night.

"What happened that day?" I asked.

"Do you really want to know?"

Her intangible hand on my cheek.

"I have to," I said.

Withdrawing her wraith hand from my face, Bella gave me her *You-asked-for-it* look. With downcast eyes, she took us to the room where it all happened. The room where Bella was killed.

↔

What she showed me next happened too fast to be natural—like watching a movie in fast-forward. But more than being too fast, she was showing me a memory. A memory that felt as ever-present as anything I had recalled for myself.

Every gesture happened at a supernatural speed, every movement finished as quickly as it started. My eyes struggled to catch it all. And just like my dreams, everything that happened felt as though it were happening *now*.

↔

We are in a room where several human scientists are analyzing data on a computer screen. They are excited, pointing to spikes on the screen. The Ambassador is standing by a large black orb. At first I think it is a three-dimensional hologram of some distant solar system, but the machinery that complements the high-tech computers and sensors is far too low-tech to have been built in this century, or the ten before it. Out-of-date apparatus is intermingled with modern tech. Ancient gears feed data into tablet computers. Vintage pulleys suspend a mixture of cauldrons and high-grade beakers. Supercomputers sit on workbenches made from timeworn oak tables.

There is some mumbling and I see Bella, my beautiful Bella, walk into the room. The Ambassador is pointing at the black spot on a large monitor. He is smiling and silent lips mouth, "There it is." Bella returns his smile.

Two hooded figures draw in close. They are the two bastard Others that ripped Bella apart. That *will* rip her apart. They are in the room. Everyone is calm.

The Ambassador stretches out his red palm into the darkness, fanning his fingers. He closes his eyes, and his facial features and neck muscles strain as if he is trying to lift something very heavy. Little specks of gray salt his goatee and his lush black hair recedes, if only a millimeter. He is burning time. Lots of it.

↔

"Da Vinci's laboratory," Bella said, pausing the memory. "His laboratory held a lot of significance and therefore power. We gathered a lot of his equipment and set it up to complement more modern equipment. It took years for the Ambassador and his team to figure out how to get it all to work together, but once they did, we were able to use it to find this place. To find Heaven." Before I could say anything in response, Bella turned the memory back on.

↔

The Ambassador is smiling, proud of his achievement. His find. The black sphere rotates then stops, a tiny gray speck of dust in its center. He points and everyone starts clapping, cheering and hugging. Even Bella wraps her arms around the Ambassador's big red devilish neck. They have found it. They have found Heaven.

The two hooded figures nod at each other, seemingly pleased as well. But before celebrations can turn into the next phase of work, the room shakes. Waterfalls of dirt and cement are shaken loose from the explosion above. Red lights start flashing and even though this memory is silent, I remember the sound of the sirens.

An argument breaks out between several of the scientists and the Ambassador. The two hooded figures are pointing at the Devil, obviously insisting on something. They point at one of the scientists, who shakes his head, fear painted on his face. There is more yelling as another explosion rips through the complex, causing all the lights to shut off. There is a flicker and the lights return. Everyone is visibly relieved that the sphere is still there.

There is more discussion and Bella raises her hand, silencing the room. Everyone is quiet, looking at her with a mixture of horror and admiration. The Ambassador mouths, "Are you sure?" Bella nods. The Ambassador's shoulders slump as he addresses the two hooded Others. Everyone bustles into motion, gathering materials.

And this is the moment when Bella turns and sees me standing at the door, desperately trying to open it. This is when she gives me that smile that says that it will be OK. This is when she blows me our final kiss.

And this is when the two hooded figures descend on her, ripping her apart with their sacred blades.

↔

"Enough," I cried out. "Enough."

Bella froze the image before the blade penetrated her skin. "There was no time. The explosions threatened to shut the whole thing down and if we lost Heaven it would be over forever. That is why I volunteered—"

"Volunteered?" I cut in, staring at her through tear-filled eyes.

"Yes," she nodded. "It was now or lose Heaven forever. I didn't have time to think—"

"You left me!" I screamed in anger, in hurt and in the thousand nameless emotions that ran through me.

"I had to. Don't you see what was at stake? We could have fixed everything. Made it better. Imagine a world where everyone was free to come and go to Heaven as they pleased. But someone had to get in there. Someone had to volunteer to turns the lights back on."

"But why did it have to be you?" I asked, my heart pounding so hard in my chest, it felt as though it were beating itself to death.

The look she gave me told me her answer. It had to be her because she was the only one who cared enough to sacrifice herself for the hope of making the lives of Others better. It had to be her because she believed that a brighter future came because of those who fought for it. It had to be her because she was the only one brave enough to take the leap of faith.

I looked back at the frozen image of Bella the moment before she died. Instinctively I reached for the blade but my hand went through it. I was just as helpless now as I was then. But I could see a detail that had escaped me every time I replayed that night in my head.

Reflected in the blade was an unmistakable grin.

Oh, Bella …

Chapter 28

Thanks for Making Me a Fighter

There is this girl whom I love very much and I once left her for four years while I fought a war against lost creatures who no longer had any place they could call home. Years were lost to my hate and fear and anger. When I returned, that girl took me back without hesitation or judgment, and I learned how powerful true love could be. And when I lost her again, I gave into that same hate and fear and anger, until she found a way back from the Void to save my soul once again.

I could have been angry that she volunteered to leave me. I could have spent the last few hours before that bastard Grinner showed up, yelling, sulking, accusing and crying. I would have, except a long, long time ago I promised to love her in this life and the next. Well, we were standing in the next and I planned to keep my promise.

Besides, too much time had been lost already.

↔

I wished I could have held Bella that night, but instead all we could do was stare at each other, standing dangerously close, but never actually touching. I never knew so much joy could also hurt so badly. How does one heart have room for both?

Unsure how to fill the little time we had left, I settled for telling her my plan. If we were to be together, it meant surviving this night. Perhaps if we talked it through, some insight would surface that could make all the difference. And once I got rid of Grinner, we could be together, if only in my dreams. As I spoke, neither of us noticed that the once-blue sky was starting to fill with clouds.

She listened, a frown on her face, and said, "It is a good plan. As good as any, I suppose."

"What," I asked, "you don't think it can work?"

"I didn't say that. I have faith in you, Jean. I always have." A single raindrop fell on my face. She looked up. "He's coming."

I nodded, looking up with her and watching as gray, heavy clouds grew in the sky. "I'm ready."

Beep.

"Jean," Bella said, raising her voice over the wind. "Be careful."

I shot her my best *I'm-too-good-to-fail* look and said, "In this life and the next …"

Beep. Beep.

"I will love you forever."

Beep. Beep.

"See you soon."

↔

Beep, beep, beep …

I woke up with a jolt, my alarm ringing. The clock read midnight and I thought how fitting that he should breach the perimeter at that exact moment.

Hellelujah! Grinner was here.

↔

"Human Jean-Luc!" a voice called from outside. "Come out and play."

My heart raced as I stood up. Before this moment, I had been ready to die to take this guy down, but now, knowing that Bella was truly alive and that there was a hope for us to be together, I wasn't so sure.

I picked up the remote control and stepped outside, expecting the same serene surroundings I had always known. Instead, I was greeted by something else entirely.

In front of my cabin, the forest hung in the air, a hundred trees suspended to make a wall of wood and earth. Grinner took a step forward and the wall followed him. Thirty feet, I thought. So he had me trapped, because either I charged forward and tried to break through a wall of wood, or I jumped in a lake. Literally. Maybe that's where the expression came from.

Wherever it came from didn't change the fact that Grinner was boxing me in. That was fine. I wasn't planning to run anyway.

The bastard stood in the foreground, his maniacal smile pushing out his eyes. "It is funny how the old ways still matter. When Michael asked me his question, I had to answer it. It was, after all, ordained that I must. There was so much ordained when the gods were here. So many protocols, so many rules. But that is all changing now." He pointed to the ground, then at me, and said, "By now you are aware that I can only influence the environment immediately around me. That, too, was ordained. A … precaution the gods put in place when creating me. They always made sure that when I spoke to them I was always at least five fathoms away. It was so much less threatening that way. I may only influence so far, but Gravity is so much more than fifty feet. I am not the embodiment of a principle in which all the Universe is connected as so many think. I am its shadow bound by rules that are slowly eroding. Just like the orbit of the stars that the archangel asked me to map out, so too are the rules that confine us all."

"Blah, blah, blah …" I interrupted. "Brave new GoneGod world, everything has changed. Boo-hoo. What's your point?"

Scorn colored his face. "Indeed, everything has changed. But what has been done can be undone. By now you must know that my words are no lie. Bella lives and I am the path back to her. I am also the path back to the Void. To things returning to what they once were." He pointed to the sky. "And all I need is a kiss between two mortals deeply in love. Let me draw Heaven in close. Once it is here, you will be able to touch your beloved. Embrace her so that I might be able to find the Heaven in which she now resides." He pulled a plain-looking box from his pocket.

"You killed her!" I said, reliving the memory of his dagger piercing her chest.

He nodded. "A necessity. Only a human soul can enter Heaven uninvited. And only Bella was brave enough to try."

"That's my Bella," I said.

"Come, embrace her. And by doing so, embrace the new world I offer."

It was tempting. I could have Bella back. But the cost of having someOther like him in charge was simply too high a price. Bella and I might not have seen eye to eye on many things, but we both agreed on this … Now that the gods were gone, it was up to us mortals to find our way. They might have left behind a mess of lost creatures to find *their* way, but it was our mess and I wasn't about to take the easy way out by letting the whole charade of gods and mortals start again.

"No," I said, pushing the big red button on my remote control.

↔

My two sentry guns had been set high enough in the tree line so that he couldn't affect them. They flared to life, and their shots rang out like a thousand thunderclaps, each clap sending out a bullet flying at supersonic speed. But not a single bullet touched him. Not one. I knew his gravitational power could cause the bullets to fly off course, but it was the way he blocked the bullets that was unnerving. He was picking up tiny stones, pebbles and rocks, causing them to orbit around him like some twisted version of Saturn's rings. Bullets ricocheted off the stones before joining their twisted orbit, except that the bullets were imbued with so much kinetic energy that they looped around him several times faster than the other debris.

The son of a bitch was showing off.

And that was OK—I wasn't trying to kill him with a bullet. That would have been too easy. My tactics were a bit blunter. The ferocity of the sentry guns forced him to move just a few feet farther down the path and by varying the intensity of each gun, I was able to maneuver him to where I wanted. Just another step and … there! You see, the way I figured it was that Grinner was prepared for a sideways attack and even one from above. But from below …

I hit another button, setting off several mines I had buried beneath the spot he now stood. The earth shattered upward, sweeping Grinner off his feet. He fell with a whoop, flat on his back. The thing about *these* land mines is that they explode upward, leaving the ground on which they rested virtually untouched. That meant that there could be several layers of them and it was a good way to lure an invading army into believing they were safe. Let their sweepers destroy the top row, only to have them walk on the field and set off the second row. That was dirty tactics, and that was exactly what I did.

The second row of mines went off, tearing at Grinner's back as bullets from the sentry guns managed to get through his defenses. He was literally being torn apart, piece by piece. I tore at him, bits of him flopping away, only to get further shredded by mines and bullets. And still he moved.

Explosions rang from all around us as I rained holy Hell on the bastard's head. I was going to tear him apart, if that was what it took. I was going to …

Suddenly everything went silent. And I don't mean quiet. I mean sound ceased to exist. Even the vibrations of the guns and mines stopped and at that moment the world went completely still. At first I thought that Grinner had removed all the gravity like he had done at the One Spire Hotel, but a quick look around proved that was not the case. The guns still rattled, empty shells falling to the side, dirt still went up in the air with each mine explosion and I was still able to move about normally.

With each bullet that ripped through Grinner's body, bits of blood fell about. Unlike most Others that bled different colors, Grinner bled in the same crimson red as humans; it made the scene all the more sickening to watch. I was thankful for the lack of sound. Somehow watching all this on Mute made it more bearable. I prepared my next few tricks, expecting Grinner to do something, anything, but he did not.

The last layer of mines exploded as the sentry guns ran through their final thread of bullets. Grinner lay literally in pieces, bits of him strewn throughout the field. Judith had asked me to kick him in the balls, but I guessed this would have to do.

I noticed that his hand rested not ten feet away from me, ripped away by a mine blast. Grinner was dead. I had won. After all that power and magic, in the end all it took was the brute, blunt force of a whole lot of land mines to take down the Avatar of Gravity.

And still the world was silent.

If living in a mute world was the price to pay for having rid it of this evil false god, then so be it. Bella and I would just have to learn sign language.

I put down the remote control and the other weapons that I had thankfully not needed, and withdrew my hunting sword from its sheath. I wanted a piece of his heart, assuming that he had a heart and that I could find it in this mess.

The first time he did this, back in the hotel, I had no idea what was happening, but I'd had some time to think about it. Grinner was so powerful that even sound could not escape his pull—just like a black hole—and that was why I needed to stop him. A force such as his did not nourish, it did not enlighten—it pulled at you, never letting you go, never letting you become what you were destined to be.

Then I heard a crackle. "Good show," Grinner said. "I knew you were a worthy opponent."

"GoneGodDamn it!" I said, looking for the source of the voice.

In the center of the mess was a single black sphere, no larger than marble. It shot up. Bits of Grinner started to float up, orbiting the tiny ball. Bits of flesh and blood, bone and nail all circled that center point. I even noticed a few of Grinner's abnormally large teeth joining the orbit.

The voice spoke again. "What is it you humans say? Earth to earth …"

Droplets of blood formed larger bodies, joining together to form larger parts of him. Organs were spawning—lungs, stomach, heart. And around them the skeleton began to form.

"Ashes to ashes …"

A thin filament of skin gathered around the organs and bones, like a jigsaw puzzle being constructed in 3D.

"Dust to dust."

Damn it, I thought, piercing his hand that still rested by me with the tip of my hunting sword. I held it up and looked at it. He might be piecing himself together from the tiny shreds I reduced his body to, but by the GoneGods, I was keeping his hand. Petty, I know.

Within moments Grinner was fully formed, only his hand missing. He smiled. I could feel him using a bit of his magic, but I was too far away to be affected.

"You and I are not that different," he said, pointing his stump at me.

I looked at the speared hand and grunted. "I am nothing like you." I backed away slowly. I needed to get back to my porch and use my last trick.

"Yes, you are. There is a piece within all of us that holds us together. For me, it is my core. For you, it is Bella."

"Don't say her name!" I spat out, still backing away. Letting him think I was afraid. Just a few more steps and …

"I picked her precisely because she was your core. I knew that if we lost her, you would always be the map back to her. In a way, her ascension happened because of you."

"Bastard!" I said, the back of my foot touching the base of the cabin's stairs. I turned and started up them. There were only five steps and I could clear them in two strides. I just had to be faster than him and make sure I stayed out of the thirty foot radius.

Grinner's hand moved on the tip of my sword. "Shit," I cried out and threw the blade down to the ground. "Come on, you got to be kidding me."

But it was too late—the hand freed itself from the sword pulled me off the stoop, somehow holding me down. Apparently, a First Law's hand didn't need to be attached to a body to work.

So. Totally. Unfair.

Grinner stepped closer. I was being pinned down by his force again and this time he wasn't messing around. He crushed my ankle, bones compressed by tons of pressure, until all that was left was a sack of purple skin filled with powdered bone. I screamed in pain.

"It is because of you that we are here," Grinner said. "Yes, she loved you. Loves you still. But what you felt for her was so beyond love. It was an attraction that could traverse solar systems. A connection that could defy even Time. Truly, amongst the human race, you are one of a kind."

"Screw you," I grunted.

"There is something I need of you."

"Let me guess ... a kiss?"

Grinner laughed. "A kiss, a touch—they are all the same. What I need is the attraction that you have for the human called Bella. Don't you see? You are a magnet which can draw close only one person."

"What? You don't like my affable personality?" I couldn't get up, but maybe I could move sideways. I inched forward, my fingers stretching to my felled blade. Just a few more inches. "And if I refuse?" I said, trying to buy myself some more time.

"By now you know that a kiss is just a ... how do you mortals put it ... a formality. All I need is for you both to join in emotion. Her witnessing your death is enough. But I do not wish to make a martyr out of you. Don't you understand? It is you whom she loves ..." His voice trailed off and he began swaying, as if dancing to music that only he could hear. His eyes closed and he hugged himself dearly. "And she loves you so, so much. No matter what comes next, you can take comfort in that certainty, Jean-Luc." His disembodied hand pointed a finger at me, so close it could poke my eye out. Then he pointed another finger to the sky, twirling it as one might when selecting a song from a jukebox—and all the while he swayed, entranced by the soundless music. "Yes ... there. I feel it. She worries for you. Worries that you have failed and are now dead. Somewhere beyond, your love cries in fear for you," he said, drifting off again, his arms outstretched to the sky—and the hand pinning me down zoomed up and reattached itself to his stump. I tried moving, but by now his gravity was weighing me down.

"Hey, Cheshire Cat," I said, but he didn't hear me. It was more than that—the way he swayed, he was so deeply concentrating that I sincerely doubted anything short of a nuclear bomb would break his trance. Since I didn't have one of those on hand, I looked around for another weapon. All I had left was my hunting sword that lay a few feet away. In agony, I began inching toward it again.

Inch by inch, I drew closer to my sword. Finally the tips of my fingers touched its hilt. Just a bit farther and ...

"It requires a lot of energy to summon Heaven. A lot of time must be burned. To search for the Void without knowing where it is would be suicide. But with you here ... Ah, yes!" Grinner said, his finger fixated on a specific point in the sky. "There you are!"

Then something happened that I'd never seen before. The sky got darker. I don't mean that it became overcast and the lights of fewer stars were reaching Earth. I mean the sky literally started to blot out. First the Moon disappeared, then the light from bright stars, then the most distant stars extinguished.

Gemini's brightest, as well as Castor and Pollux, were reduced from being reflective diamonds in the sky to pinpricks in a heavy wool blanket, until they disappeared altogether. The stars of Hydra and Leo flickered out like dying bulbs.

One by one, I watched the night sky disappear until all that remained were Mercury, Venus, Mars, Saturn and Jupiter, shining in a belt across the sky. Grinner left those four planets in the night sky, and they were the only real sources of light left.

"The doorway to the Void requires a ladder," he hummed as he swayed in his trance, "but for a ladder to exist, it must be hinged both above and below."

He pointed up to the four planets and then with a violent gesture, pulled down, falling to his knees as he touched the ground with his hands. The four stars ceased being spots of light in the sky, morphing into beams of illumination. Hell, not beams—that conjures up images of lasers and Buck Rogers. I'm talking more like columns of light that extended from their source in the Heavens all the way down to the cleared-out field in front of PopPop's cabin. Hellelujah—if I lived to be ten thousand years old, I seriously doubted I'd ever see anything as beautiful as this again.

"Don't you see?" Grinner panted, and suddenly I could see him aging. Back in Paradise Lot, he seemed like he had an inexhaustible amount of energy, but now—now he was out of breath. I guess bringing down Heaven can really take its toll on a guy. "I do this to give us all a chance at a new beginning."

He grinned. The columns of light moved across the Earth and gathered closer to Grinner—not like the planets' beams were twisting in his direction, but as if the planets were actually being *pulled* closer together across lightyears of space—as he exerted his gravitational will with a growing ferocity. I could see bits of gray appearing, adding texture to his jet-black hair as shallow but noticeable wrinkles began to crawl out from the corners of his eyes.

The four columns converged onto Grinner, four spotlights that entered him, turning his body into a transparent shell—now I could see what the inner workings of true magic looked like. It was a universe within a universe, a thousand galaxies orbiting his heart. But unlike the heart of our Milky Way, his was black and void, a force of absence. The stars from our night sky ran into that black heart, losing their effervescence as soon as they touched it.

And Grinner grew.

The stars themselves nourished him, and he grew.

First, he grew to twice the size of a human.

Then he was a hill giant, then a stone giant.

A dragon.

And still he grew, and all the while I watched it unfold far too fast to be natural—an odd scene viewed through the lens of a camera that only filmed in fast-forward.

"Truly, Human Jean, you must now understand that no matter how hard you resist me, the new world will *be*," Grinner bellowed, pulling out Joseph's box from his pocket.

The air got thick and every breath felt as though I were sucking in honey, and still I crawled forward, toward my final trick.

Grinner looked to the sky, now filled with a darkness that was not the absence of light, but an entity in and of itself. "Look there," he said, pointing up, "that is where your Bella is. Just one embrace. One connection and the bridge will be established and I will be able to hold it here forever and for everyone."

And from the Void that hung in the air like a black balloon, I could see Bella's face against its cusp. She looked down on me, less than a hundred feet away, anguish in her eyes. When we saw each other, my heart lurched and I could feel something being drawn out of me like slowly letting out a long breath. Thin gray wisps of smoke were filtering out of my chest and when I looked up at Bella, I saw the same wisps emanating from her and toward Joseph's box.

"You see?" Grinner cackled. "The connection wants to be free. Embrace her, let it go and save the world!"

"It's now or never," I muttered to myself, getting on my one good foot. The sack that was once my right foot wiggled from my ankle, each swing sending blinding pain through my body. I screamed. Taking deep breaths, I hopped up the cabin's steps, each jump agony, and managed to collapse just in front of the door where my ace card waited for me.

I pulled out a .50 caliber Beowulf that I had rubbed with the candle wax Hermes had given me. I remembered how the candles protected him, hiding his magic from the world around him. I had been mulling that over in my mind ever since. Why else would he have thought to give me one? If the wax could shield one from magic, maybe it negated magic altogether. It was a gamble, but it was all I had.

I loaded the bullet into the magazine and slid the bolt home. Then I prepared to shoot, figuring that the heat of the shot would melt the wax and burn its power long enough and strong enough that Grinner would not be able to block it with his gravitational tricks. Taking aim, I said a silent prayer to the GoneGods.

You left us here with so many problems. Let this bullet put an end to one of them.

I pulled the trigger.

Chapter 29

The Deepening

What happened next took less than a second and yet I was able to perceive it as if in slow motion. The shot rang through the silence with a rippling sound and pierced the gravitational bubble surrounding Grinner with a thud. He must have felt his sphere being breached, because he looked in my direction. I saw him fan out his fingers, seeking to stop the bullet, but just as I hoped, the wax shielded the lead missile from his powers. Understanding what was happening, he tried to lift a stone to block the bullet's approach. A good plan … if only he had thought of it a millisecond earlier.

The bullet ripped into Grinner, shredding apart a body that was created to be Gravity incarnate. From the wound a torrent of darkness billowed out, like black air rushing out of a pierced balloon. I tried to dodge the Void but I was too slow. It enveloped me, wisps grabbing at me with relentless power, and suddenly I was no longer at my cabin in the woods. I was no longer on Earth.

I was no longer here.

I was nowhere.

↔

What happened next came in degrees. First the chaos of the darkness's approach immediately ceased and I found myself standing at a crossroad, a single light hanging overhead. The gloom was so heavy I could not see more than ten feet away, four paths leading away from me into the eternity beyond. I was in the Void and Bella did not come to save me. I was alone. Slowly, inch by inch, the ten feet of visibility became nine, then eight, until the emptiness was less than five feet away. I couldn't stand it, the claustrophobic approach, like being boxed in a room that was shrinking. And with every inch that was taken away, I was closer to the Void's embrace.

Screw that! If I was going to die, I wanted to have a hand in it, not wait for it to take me away slowly but surely. I took a step forward, down the path that was straight ahead. Then another, until finally I stepped into the darkness itself.

What I felt is damn near impossible to describe. It was a sensation I had never felt before and pray I will never feel again. I entered heavy air, a lukewarm aura—like walking into a wall of water—and then all at once it was like being a thousand feet underwater, the pressure of being so deep crushing me under its immense weight. I was floating in the Void and I suddenly had the thought that I was back in my mother's womb, the amniotic fluid hugging me tight, suspending me in the darkness where up and down, left and right, no longer mattered. All that did matter was simply being. I even found myself curling up into the fetal position. I was suspended in nothing.

And that is exactly where I was. In nothing. I don't mean peace or tranquility or any other kind of Zen bullshit. I mean *nothing*. A complete and total, all-consuming emptiness. Darkness, sure. But this was more than darkness, because even if you stood in a pitch-black room with a blindfold, you still wouldn't come close to what I mean. And the silence—I can only say for sure that it did not come from the absence of sound, because that would imply that sound exists somewhere else. No sound existed here. It never had and it never would.

In the Void, I wasn't floating—that would imply that I was some kind of corporeal form. I was not there. Rather, my body was not there. Only my consciousness and that, I've learned, was not enough to negate the *nothing*.

I felt that if I stayed in this place too long I would die, not out of hunger or thirst, but because my body would eventually be absorbed by the nothing, my heart's vibrations syncing with my new surroundings, joining the perfect harmony of the Void. I could feel that already happening, my mind losing so many memories.

This was not like the Void I had been in with Bella in my dreams. There, I suspected, I was just a visitor. Like being in a movie, except I could walk around the set, watch what was going on, but not actually be able to touch anything. Certainly this was true every time I tried to embrace Bella, draw her in close. We were together, but not. And although she wasn't a hallucination, she was a hologram of herself. Where I was with Bella had felt like a dream.

This place felt real.

And I was suddenly gripped with a suffocating terror that I was dead and this was all that was left. Lonely, empty, lost—these words don't even come close to how I felt. It was as if there was absolutely nothing in the Universe but my consciousness, and it felt awful. Already I could feel the utter lack of anything pierce my mind, crushing me under its overwhelming absence.

But then ... well, remember how this all started. Me running from the darkness and her saving me. Perhaps we had come full circle, because from the emptiness of nothing, she came. And without doing or saying anything, by the simple act of being there, she saved me from a broken mind and lost soul.

Some things never change.

From out of the darkness Bella appeared. Not in my dreams, not a hallucination, but Bella made of flesh and blood. Bella, my wife, my best friend, my lover. My soul mate.

Bella, oh how I would have died a thousand times for you.

The joy of seeing her there and being overwhelmed by the nothingness of this place made me forget everything. Grinner, Earth, the Others, the GoneGods. But no emptiness could ever make me forget Bella. "Oh my love," I said, "I am so happy to see you."

↔

"You have to go back," she said, denying me as I approached her.

I was so desperate to be in her arms. "I don't want to go back," I said. "I want to be here with you."

She shook her head. "That is this place talking. It was how I felt when I first arrived. But you are not dead. Not like me." Her voice was soothing, calm.

"No," I said, "but this time I don't have to wake up. We can be together forever here."

Bella gave me her *You-know-that's-not-true* look and said, "Jean, don't you remember what's happening?"

"Remember?" I said, the word slapping me as I spoke it. Remember what? What else was there to remember? But like the opposite of waking up from a dream and it slowly fading away into oblivion, her words brought it back. Vague images, until all I saw were Joseph and Penemue, Tink and CaCa, the destruction of the One Spire Hotel and the devastation of Paradise Lot. All of it was slowly trickling back into my consciousness. It was terrifying. I was seeking the embrace of the one who had soothed my nightmares a thousand times before, but with each new memory, a chasm grew between us.

"Am I dead?" I asked.

"No," Bella said, "not yet. But the longer you stay here, the harder it will be for your soul to find its way back."

"Would that be so bad?" I reached out my hand, determined to hold her before the divide grew too far. "We'd be together."

Bella didn't reach out for me. She did not take my hand in hers, instead rejecting me with a look of pain in her eyes. A single tear running down her cheek. She shook her head and said, "Look, the darkness is already changing. You have to go back."

"I don't want to leave you here alone."

"Remember the beach, the mountainside, your toys that I brought to life?"

I nodded.

"I'm not alone. They're memories, but they are also real. I will learn to make those constructs more permanent. I'm getting better at filling the Void. And as I get better, I'm going to fill this place with things that remind me of you. Of us. Jean-Luc, I may be alone, but I am not lonely. This world is my canvas and already I have made so many wondrous paintings."

"I won't leave you."

"You're not leaving me," she said, giving me her *I-love-you-forever* look. "You can't." She looked down through the portal and at Grinner, who continued to hold onto Heaven. "He's weaker than he has ever been. He needs to build the bridge and enter this realm before he can be whole again. If there was ever a chance, now is it."

"Maybe … but he's so strong and I've run out of tricks."

"You have. But I haven't."

She pulled off the silver ring that she had made in our dream and threw it to me. I caught it—and unlike all the times before, I actually felt the hard, cool metal in my hand.

"Remember your promise, Jean-Luc. And remember how much I love you."

And from beyond the chasm, she blew me a kiss that hit me like a physical force, jarring me to life in the world beyond the Void. With a gasp, I was back at the cabin, on Earth and without Bella.

↔

Bella's kiss blew me back into the world. I looked up and saw the window from where Bella threw me out of Heaven. It was a shimmering, black glossy hole that looked like someone had ripped open the sky. Bella's face appeared at the threshold and her hand slammed against the inside of the portal, her palms flush against its barrier as if she were pressing against glass. She could not cross over. Like Michael said, "Death is the only one-way valve from which there is no return." Well, Bella had made that journey already and the path to Heaven was closed. Even death would not reunite us. Not anymore.

Still, there was one hope. We knew that Joseph's box was powerful enough to hold the connection. Hell, it had already drawn it out of us. With it, I could get back to Bella. So, new plan. Get Joseph's box and kill Grinner, and not necessarily in that order.

Simple. I mean, how hard could it be to kill a god?

↔

"Oath-Breaker!" Grinner screamed, drawing my attention away from Heaven's window. I looked behind me to see Penemue flapping directly above Grinner, exactly thirty feet away.

The cavalry had arrived and from the way he flopped about in the sky, I was pretty sure the cavalry was drunk.

"Hellelujah!" I cried out.

"Tell me, Fallen," Grinner said, "have you come to repent for your sins, or are you here to witness the ascension of your new god?"

The angel grinned, removing those rimless glasses of his and tucking them into the small pocket in his tweed vest. "In Hell, I was a hero," he said. "For my sin gave humans the capacity to sin from eternity to eternity. Why corrupt a single soul when you can damn them all? Perfect strategy, don't you think?

"In Hell, Belial built me a vast library and Mulciber a palace. They showered me with gifts and riches, praise and accolades. Even the Morning Star consulted me when contemplating the more subtle aspects of sin. All the while I nodded and imparted my knowledge, because if any of them were to suspect that I taught humans wisdom not out of malice but out of admiration, and, dare I say it, love, they would cast me out—and then where would I go? Better to survive in Hell than wither elsewhere, I thought. Well, I am tired of surviving."

Penemue cast a glance at me. "What was it you said? 'We're all going to die. Might as well die for something worthwhile.' Very well then."

From out of nowhere two daggers appeared, their hilts attached to a chain that bubbled out of his skin and wrapped around his forearms. He threw them down at Grinner, both piercing his back as the fallen angel yanked on the chains and

281

pulled upward. Grinner lifted up, wriggling like a fish caught on a hook. All this time I thought of Penemue as a celestial librarian, never once imagining that he had a few tricks literally up his sleeve. GoneGodDamn! Penemue was a badass!

Penemue took to the sky and I noted that his chains were over thirty feet long. He was keeping his distance. The angel pulled up, but Grinner quickly anchored himself to the ground. Penemue's arms and wings struggled to get enough power to pull him up.

He yanked again, rope-thick veins straining to provide enough blood to his massive muscles, but the huge Grinner did not move. I doubt he even burned time to hold himself to the ground, his newly-made massive body enough to anchor him down. But he was in pain. I could tell from the way his smile faltered.

Grinner reached for the blades, but Penemue had planned his shot well. There was no way a body of human design could reach those meat hooks stuck in its own back.

"I see that a leopard does not change its spots, just as a Fallen cannot do anything but fall!"

With this last word, Grinner spread apart his hands and tried to force Penemue down. The angel was outside of Grinner's thirty-foot sphere of influence and Grinner couldn't get a hold on him. But Grinner wasn't trying to pull down the fallen angel—he was focusing his powers on the chains from which he hung. Penemue must have anticipated this because he was flapping his wings for all his worth, the air beneath him stirring up the earth and ground below. Leaves and loose twigs were to be expected, but the torrent of his wings was pulling up the roots of full grown trees, their tendril roots popping up from beneath the ground. Man, oh man, I'd seen jet engines throw less air around.

Penemue fought Grinner, his strength slowly failing him. But he wasn't the only one who suffered from exhaustion. Grinner was also sweating, his face straining, skin thickening as he struggled to hold the Void while fighting the angel. He was burning too much time dealing with Penemue while trying to maintain his grip on Heaven.

The monster was aging, which meant that he could be killed, too.

But just when I thought we had a chance, Grinner pulled down Penemue. The angel hit the ground with a splat, his wings still sprawled out before him. Crap.

I stood, expecting to feel like Hell, but instead I felt whole, strong. My foot was still a sack of powdered bone, but I didn't care. I couldn't feel it. I was ... young. No—that wasn't the right word for it. I was more. I felt like I was going to live, if not forever, damn near close to it. Thousands upon thousands of years pulsed through my body and I knew that whatever Bella packed into that kiss, she threw in a whole truck load of time with it, too. I was— for this moment, at least—like an Other.

Bella's words ran through my mind: *Imagine playing with these!* Well, that's exactly what I did.

Summoning the well of time that was within me, I conjured Optimus, Star Scream and every Dinobot ever made. I brought forth Voltron, G.I. Joe and an army of Smurfs. And each one of my creations was three stories high and just as heavy. I summoned a squadron of Robotech's Veritech fighters. They were all at least thirty feet tall, and the ground shook as each one took a step.

And then, my army of giant 1980s toys opened up a can of whoop-ass on Grinner.

Grinner fought them off just as he had done with the Others in Paradise Lot, but unlike before when he fought a bunch of Others that did their best to coordinate their attacks, he now fought dozens of creatures that were one mind. When he swatted down Megatron, Snakes Eyes was right there to slash him with his sword. When he tossed away He-Man, WilyKat scratched him with his claws. I even threw in a Care Bear Stare for good measure.

And each of his counter attacks aged him. His shaggy dark hair was shot with gray, had receded back to his ears and kept pulling back. He simply could not fight so many while holding on to Heaven. And what was worse—for him at least—was every time he destroyed one of my toys, I made two more.

I had never burned time before so I really wasn't prepared for what it felt like. All I can say is that it was like emptying air out of your lungs. After a while, there wasn't any air left to blow out. Whatever Bella gave me was temporary. But it was enough.

When the last second of the extra time given to me burned out, I looked over at a Grinner who now panted heavy with exertion, sweat dripping from his brow. He dropped to one knee and I knew he was nearly beat. All that was needed was to push him over the edge.

I hopped over to Penemue, who slowly rose from the crater his body had made from his fall. "Those hooks," I said, "do they detach?"

Penemue nodded, threaded out one of his chains and handed it to me. I pulled out my hunting sword and, taking his grappling hook, I hopped closer to Grinner. He tried to turn, but before he could I threw the hook into him, its jagged edge connecting with his back. Then I pulled with all my worth. It had the desired effect—I was on him. Let him remove or increase gravity, I was attached now.

284

I pulled back my sword arm and stabbed, piercing my sword's three-foot blade into where Grinner's heart would be. He whimpered, but as soon as I withdrew my sword, he healed his wound. I had fought a lot of Others and, unlike the legends, you didn't need a silver bullet to kill a werewolf or garlic to end a vampire. Sure, those things helped, but at the end of the day, they were made of flesh and blood. Sometimes all you need to kill a monster is brute force. I stabbed and stabbed and stabbed, and with each chunk I carved out of him, Grinner healed, burning a bit of time as he did. He countered by crushing me with gravity. It felt like my chest was being constricted under the force of a powerful python, but I didn't care. I just wanted this guy dead. I fought through the pain, striking him again and again with my blade.

What was healing a slash worth? A minute? What about cutting off a finger, or slitting a throat? An hour? Maybe a day? What was my plan, anyway? To force him to burn through a hundred million years one stab wound at a time? This was the very definition of insanity, but if I stopped, he would heal himself and we would be right back where we started, a First Law with a god-complex seeking to oppress the world. I couldn't let that happen.

But he was burning more than an hour of life. He was going through thousands of years in the blink of an eye, such was the energy required to hold the Void. Even so, this would take hours and I was so very tired and my body so constricted. My muscles would fail me long before his time burned out.

"You fool!" he cried out. "I give you the chance to be reunited with her! Your one true love!"

"No," I said, continuing to press my advantage. "Not like this!"

Already I was failing. I wanted desperately to see Grinner falter even just the slightest, but exhaustion was overwhelming me. My arms were burning, each swing weaker than the last. I couldn't win.

Then I saw her, staring from the window, her hand on the glass that separated us. She gave me that same smile she did the day she died. The one that said *It will all be OK.*

No, it won't. I can't.

She smiled, her lips curled into an uneven line of both joy and fear. *Do it*, she mouthed. *Please.*

"No," I said. Then, summoning six years of frustration and anger, loss and anguish, I screamed it. "NO!"

But I had made a promise. To protect them and to love her. In this life and the next.

I knew what I had to do.

I spun around and grabbed at the box that still rested in his hands, bringing down my good foot in an arching swoop. As I did so, I took a moment to look up one last time at the Void, saw Bella's distant soul smile with pride.

I smashed down the box that once contained the bridge between Bella and I, and with more ease than should have been possible, I destroyed Pandora's Box.

↔

The little plain wooden cube splintered into a thousand pieces, tearing apart far too easily for something that would change my life forever. But then again, what did I expect? Sometimes it is the simplest acts that have the most profound effects.

With Joseph's box destroyed, I let go, a new kind of darkness coming over me. It was neither the Void nor one of Grinner's tricks, nor was it my dreams.

I was dying.

I looked up and saw Bella there, the window from where she watched slowly fading away.

"The Void, it is closing. Without the box, I can no longer hold on to it," Grinner said, now white-haired and grizzled. He was still burning time, but what he was doing I was not sure. Truth be told, I did not care. Heaven was closed and no amount of time or power could get it back. Bella was gone. If he used his time to crush me, so be it. I was alone and it hurt me to know that I would never see her again. Death sounded pretty good.

"I …" he muttered, wrinkling and stooping more with every syllable he uttered. "I … was created to speak to the gods. I gave them permission to exist, I opened their realms. I am the reason why all that is, *is*. And they left me here to die at Time's hand."

"Join the club," I said, my vision blurring all the more.

He looked at me as tributaries of wrinkles poured from the sides of his eyes like dry tears, the eyes themselves bursting red with capillaries. "Mortality—how do you bear it?"

How do I bear it? How does one bear the march of time, knowing that each moment spent will never return? How do you accept that the breath just breathed takes you one step closer to the Void? How do you accept that an end is coming and no amount of power or wealth or talent will ever save you from it? How do you live knowing you are going to die?

I had no idea, and my ignorance suddenly felt very funny to me. A laugh escaped me and my sides split in agonizing pain at the effort. "One day at a time," I said. "One day at a time."

I coughed and noticed that the blood that trickled from my mouth flowed slowly, which meant that my heart no longer pumped hard enough for my blood to reach my head. That or I simply ran out of blood. I guess that's what you get when someone cracks your ribs. I was getting cold. As my vision faded I knew that my last breath quickly approached.

I looked up one last time and said in a weak voice, "In this life and the next." I think I stretched out my arm, my hand reaching for her, but I can't be sure. The world was fast disappearing.

Grinner nodded at my words and said, "One day at a time," his nose and stubbled chin growing prominent, his body withering as he spoke. I noticed that he was getting smaller, too. "One hour at a time," he said, his eyes widening as if he finally got the punchline to the esoteric joke that was life. "One minute at a time."

Angels say that your soul leaves your body like a waft of smoke floating away from a recently extinguished candle, but that is not true. Like the tearing of fabric or the sheering of skin, your soul rips away from you. It is solid and hard and unmistakable. There is no confusion, no questioning. When you die, you know it. And on that day, just outside my PopPop's cabin in the woods, I died; my soul, although it did not possess eyes with which to see or ears with which to hear, ascended to Heaven and to Bella. I guess I didn't need the box after all.

I could sense Bella drawing close to me as I was carried up in the mists and toward the Void. She was only a few feet away. Only a little farther and I would be with her. *Soon*, my soul screamed, *soon!*

But before I could be with her again, I was drawn back into my body like dust being sucked into the mouth of a vacuum. I was no longer separate, but one with my corporeal self, and the window—oh, the window—it was all but gone.

I looked at the fading portal where Bella watched, staring down at me, her smile widening until it touched her eyes. *Live well,* she mouthed as she touched the barrier between our worlds one last time.

And then she was gone.

"What? What did you do?" I said to Grinner, whose hand rested on my body, knowing that it was him who brought me back—the scorpion's strike taking its final revenge.

But Grinner's eyes held no malice. No hate. With a calm voice told from straight lips, he said, "At the dawn of time, the gods spoke to me once, requesting only one thing from me. Do you know what it was?"

I shook my head, pain reverberating through my body.

" 'When it ends, keep them all together.' I wonder if they knew the weight of the burden they bestowed upon me."

"Oh," I said, because I could think of nothing else to say.

"Human Jean-Luc, my brothers and sisters … they are coming, and they are far worse than I," Grinner said. Then with a raspy chuckle, his maniacal, now toothless grin returned. "Now it is for you to keep them all together." His body started to shrink faster, all parts of him being pulled into the core that was his center. Gravity was imploding, and like a balloon being deflated, he withered, his features flattening and contracting, becoming less human, then less alive. Then less of anything.

All that remained was a tiny effervescent sphere, no larger than a marble, on the ground next to me.

As my body convulsed and quivered, I did not have time to contemplate what his final words meant. Exhaustion and the weight of grief for having truly lost Bella overcame me.

"In this life and the next," I said one last time as my own darkness flowed over me and I faded away into an oblivion of my own.

Epilogue

True pain is so much worse than death. True pain is the destruction of all that you are and the belief that no matter how much time passes, no matter how many pills are consumed, Band-Aids applied, counseling sessions attended, nothing will make you completely *you* again. True pain is living without hope. And the night Bella did not save me in my dreams was the night I learned what true pain truly was.

I would have died after that. Just shut down. Refused to think, to feel, because to do either would be to think of Bella. To feel Bella. I would have died after that. A passive death that can only be achieved from not moving, not eating, not sleeping. The slow suicide of a broken heart. I would have died after that. And I would have been happy.

But I didn't because of the damned angel who never left my side, forcing me to eat and to drink. Taking care of me every waking minute of every waking day as my mind slowly restarted. I have vague memories of strong hands gently spoon feeding me soup and water trickling down my throat. Of being lifted and cleaned, of being put to bed, of being woken up. Oh how I hated the angel who would not let me die.

↔

I don't know how long that went on for. Days, perhaps weeks. But it was some time later—much later—when the Sun shone through my cabin window and onto my face that I finally woke from my catatonic spell. My first words were an echo of what my soul demanded. My voice came out hoarse and dry, weak from lack of use.

"I want to die."

Penemue grunted as he looked up from his book. He had been reading to me. Then, as if he hadn't heard me, he continued reading, his voice coming out slow and deep:

"O Progeny of Heav'n, Empyreal Thrones,
With reason hath deep silence and demurr
Seis'd us, though undismaid: long is the way
And hard, that out of Hell leads up to light."

Milton in baritone. Looking up from the text, Penemue said in a soft tone, his voice lost in some distant memory, "Surprisingly accurate for one who has never lost as we have."

And with those words I understood. He saw us as one and the same. I may not have fallen, but like the angel who now nursed me back to health, I had also rejected Heaven and lost everything.

Not that any of that mattered.

"I said, I want to die." I spoke with more force now, my body slowly waking up. I knew what I was saying was filled with self-pity, but I didn't care. I wanted to die and, by the GoneGods, I was in a sharing mood.

Penemue, having returned to the epic poem, did not look up, merely countering in a low voice, "We all want to die when the light that once warmed us is taken away. Now, do you mind?" His words lacked sympathy, while at the same time expressed a depth of empathy beyond anything I had felt before.

Penemue continued reading.

↔

On the fifth morning since my first words, I tried to stand, careful to hop on my good foot. That was when I first noticed that the ball of powdered bone that once was my right foot was whole and filled out. But I had seen Grinner flatten it, had hopped with it, had felt the pain, even after he brought me back. I looked up at Penemue, who sat there smirking, Drambuie in one hand, book in the other.

"Did you …" I started.

"Indeed, Human Jean-Luc, I couldn't have my charge continue the rest of his miserable life as a hobbled wretch of a man. Misery, I find, is so much better spent when you can pace."

I put my foot down to test it and it hurt like the blue blazes of Tartarus as it touched the ground.

"I conserved some time by healing you up to the point where your own biology could do the rest. I recommend ice, elevation and rest."

"This doesn't change anything," I said.

"All I do is waste time." Penemue put down his book, leaning forward in the chair. "After the Fall, I spent all my time reading and brooding, barely a sober moment in between. Since the GrandExodus, I have spent all my time reading and brooding, barely a sober moment in between. And now, I wait for you to heal so that we can return to Paradise Lot, where I may continue to spend my time reading and brooding, with barely a sober moment in between."

"What's your point?"

The fallen angel rolled his eyes. "My point, dear Human Jean-Luc, is that you are wasting my time by not letting me read and brood. Now, if you don't mind," Penemue said, taking a long drag of his Drambuie. "Besides, you have a promise to keep."

My promise. By the GoneGods, why did that matter anymore? Why did anything matter anymore? I would never see my Bella again. I would never dream of her or touch her, share a secret or joke. I would never see her again, and it was all my choice. My promise was made to a woman just as gone as the gods. It wasn't like any of the Others kept their once-sacred covenants. Why should I be held to higher standards?

"I'll never see her again," I said, hoping the fallen angel was smart enough to connect the dots.

"Probably not," Penemue agreed. "But then again, it has been my experience that there is rarely only one way to get to a destination. After all, one could walk, run or fly." He gave his wings a little flap at the last word. "Bella is still there."

I gave him a blank look, to which Penemue sighed with a false patience. "My point, dear Human Jean-Luc, is that she got there using an entirely different method than the First Law did. My point is that if there are two ways to Heaven, then perhaps there is a third. My point is that if there is a will, there is a way."

He showed me the book he was reading: *An Advanced Understanding of Quantum Physics.*

"But really, my point is that if I am ever going to find a way back into Heaven before my body is old and brittle, I must have time to concentrate."

Penemue, like everyone else, was looking for Heaven. Why? To be a god? To get his immortality back? To help me? Why? *Why?*

"Why?" I asked him.

"Why *what?*" he said, looking at me from his book.

"Why are you searching for Heaven?"

He must have sensed my cynicism and, dismissing it with a gesture, said, "We're all going to die. Might as well die doing something worthwhile."

↔

A few more weeks passed and everyday Penemue read aloud, refusing to leave my side. Every night I dreamed of Bella. But unlike before, these dreams were empty, a poor conjuring of a lonely man. And then, one night I did not dream of her at all. She was fading away and all that was left was my promise.

My promise. My godless damned promise … Why did that matter anymore? Why did any of it matter?

But it did. And all the time in the world to wallow in self-pity wasn't going to change that. What was it the angel said? "We're all going to die. Might as well die doing something worthwhile."

And there is this girl whom I love very much …

↔

We packed up the cabin, forgetting to lock it as I had done so many times before. My foot still ached, so Penemue offered to drive, his massive body only fitting in the driver's seat because he stuck one wing tip out the window, the other encroaching onto the passenger's side.

Angels are not very good drivers. The car lurched forward as his massive foot hit both the clutch and brake at once. He grinded the gears and as he did, my heart thumped. He'd burn out the clutch if he wasn't careful. Hell, he might even blow out the whole transmission.

"Stop," I said, opening my door. "I'll drive." As we switched seats I could have sworn I saw the bastard smirk.

I hobbled into the driver's seat and revved the engine with my good foot. It felt good to be behind the wheel. *Fine,* I thought, *I'll get us home.* Perhaps being a dead man pretending to be alive didn't have to be all bad.

↔

We drove all the way to the One Spire Hotel. The building was still in tatters, police tape still on the outside. What did I expect? After all, we were in Paradise Lot. It's not like the place ceased being a slum because I killed one Fanatical wannabe god.

Penemue sighed, stretched out his wings and said in his baritone voice, "I have been sober far too long. If memory serves me right, there is a fresh bottle of Drambuie in the hay."

But before leaving, he walked over to me and handed me an effervescent sphere the size of a marble.

The once-great Avatar of Gravity.

"A trophy for you," he said, and took to the sky.

↔

I walked in and found the broom. This mess of a room was my front door; even though I didn't have a hotel anymore, I still had my pride. I'd clean this place up. Start rebuilding it one brick at a time and see what would happen. We all have to pick the hills we're willing to die on, and this hill was better than most.

The bell above the door rang. I turned to see Newton, a.k.a. EightBall, leader of a gang of HuMans that got their kicks from terrorizing Others.

"If you're here to cause problems ..." I started, but judging by the sheepish way he looked around the place, I doubted he was here to start a fight. His clothes were torn and he looked like he'd just spent the last few nights on the streets. He had bruises and cuts that were a few days old and dry blood was splattered down the front of his shirt.

"This place really had a number done on it," he said.

"Yeah." I was exhausted from the drive up and not in the mood for chitchat.

"Do you think you'll be up and running soon?"

"Given that it's city ordinance that rented rooms have four walls, I seriously doubt it."

"Too bad," he said, not moving from where he stood. He reminded me of, well, *me*, when I wanted something from PopPop, but was too proud to bring it up.

I stopped sweeping and looked at him for who he was. A kid. Before, he at least had his anger, and that anger gave him purpose. But now ... he looked lost. "What happened?" I asked.

"Me and the gang had us a ... falling out over our Other policy, and now that I'm freelance I was thinking maybe you got a job for me."

"Kid—do I look like I have a hotel, let alone a job for you?"

EightBall didn't say anything. Just kept staring at me with wanting eyes.

"Fine," I said, handing him the broom. "You can start by helping clean up. I can't pay you, but you can sleep in one of the rooms upstairs for free."

EightBall took the broom with a little too much attitude and started at the floor. He stopped mid-sweep and looked up at me. "Fine, but I don't do windows," he said, trying to save face.

"What windows?"

He looked at the broken glass that was all around us, shrugged and got to sweeping.

↔

Walking into my bedroom filled me with dread. Although it had survived the chaos of the previous days relatively untouched, it also carried with it the memories of a life now lost. My vintage toys still sat on the shelves, unmoved. Tink's castle was still empty; the note and candle wax I had left for her were exactly where I had left them. I don't know why, but I placed what was left of Grinner in the hollowed-out eye of Castle Grayskull, using Hermes's wax to hold it in place. I figured it was as good a resting place as any. I also put the picture of Bella that Michael gave me on the shelf— my little shrine to remind me how I lost her for a second time.

But the worst part of my intact room was my unmade bed. That was where I used to dream of Bella. It being exactly where I left it and my knowing that she would not be there to greet me filled my heart with a deep, restless sorrow. I wished, with every fiber of my being, that my room had been destroyed and with it some of the memories that haunted me now.

Looking around, I tried to find any change and noted one difference. Someone had been in my room and taken one single item—my black collarless jacket. I was sure I had hung it up before leaving, but the coat hanger was empty.

Frustrated, I looked around the room for it. Truth was, I was mad. It was my connection to the One Spire Hotel, the symbol of my promise. And I looked really good in it. By the GoneGods, I loved that jacket!

I lumbered about my room looking for it. Maybe under the bed? Or in the bathroom?

There was a knock at my door. I opened it to see Astarte standing there, wearing a tight red leather.

"Hello, lover," she said with that subtle Parisian accent. "Aren't you going to invite an old friend in?"

I opened the door wide.

She surveyed the room like one might look around their childhood home years later. "I like what you've done with the place," she said.

"It's exactly the same as it was when you saw it last." I walked over to my chair, noticing that my foot still ached. "How did you know I was back?"

"Do you honestly think that a god-killer could come back into Paradise Lot without everyone talking about it? You are somewhat of a celebrity now."

"So, what?" I said, pouring two whiskys. Penemue wasn't the only one who had a stash. "Are you moving back in?"

"Oh, honey," she said, the words trickling off her tongue. "I am not moving in. You are moving out."

↔

It took some persuading on Astarte's part to get me out. But Astarte, being a mistress of lust and desire, eventually wore out my resistance. Truth be told, I never stood a chance. I doubt Astarte was ever denied anything when she had her heart set on it.

"Come now, it is not even the witching hour and all I ask for is an escort," she said, leaning against my door. "I won't bite. Not unless you ask."

↔

We walked to the East End, past churches, temples and shrines that eventually gave way to taverns, bars and the seedier clubs that offered many off-menu items. I doubt that there was a single vice in Heaven or Hell that wasn't on tap here.

At the heart of Paradise Lot is a hill and on that hill is the Millennium Hotel, a once-upon-a-time castle–turned–chic boutique guest house that used to charge an entrance fee just to walk into the foyer. The building was circular, looking more like a rook chess piece than a hotel. It stood at the crossroads of Paradise Lot, a small courtyard surrounding the five-story building like a moat.

Astarte started up the stairs and I stopped her. "Hold up, the building will be filled with squatters and—"

"Oh, pish-posh," she interrupted, "the building is empty and has been for some days now. No one in Paradise Lot would dare disturb it." She pulled out a key and unlocked the turnstile door at the front.

"How do you know?" I asked.

Astarte ignored my question, leading me inside. She walked to a side door that apparently acted as the utility room. She pulled down on a heavy metal breaker and the inside of the hotel lit up, dusty lamps casting soft embers in a room misty with dust motes.

↔

The Millennium Hotel had an incredible reception, its central dominance huge and inviting, with a large circular reception desk sitting in the middle. I followed Astarte's eyes, looking up, and saw that the interior was empty, each floor landing looking out into the epicenter of the building. There was an elegantly crafted wrought-iron guardrail on each floor that depicted the scene of an elaborate copper garden. From the guardrails, one could look all the way down to the reception area or all the way up the giant stained glass window that made up the Millennium Hotel's roof. The window depicted an unfolding lily, each pane white, yellow or clear, and it reminded me of the flowers on Bella's sundress.

The hollowed center was large enough for Penemue to spread his wings and fly up to the seventh floor unhindered. And for those without wings, a stairwell zigzagged along the floors leading all the way up.

"We didn't have time to clean it all up, and dwarves make the most appalling maids. All they wanted to do was polish the marble and stone."

I looked down and noted that, indeed, the marble floors were immaculately clean, even if the rest of the place could use some work.

"But it's a start," she said, walking into the center of the foyer and pointing up.

"A start for what?" I asked.

"For a second chance." She handed me my black collarless jacket. It had been dry cleaned and still sat in its cellophane wrap. "Remember the humans that you saved that night in your hotel?"

I nodded. "The naked ones."

She smiled. "They are my … ah … most loyal customers. I told them that if they wanted to continue our little romps they had to come back to the One Spire Hotel.

And since that place blew up, we needed somewhere new. Well, voila. Somewhere new."

"Hah," I said, looking at the succubus with marvel and awe. "But you're forgetting one thing. You're my only paying tenant. I couldn't possibly afford the rent."

"Humans will do so much for pleasure. I will take care of rent. And you take care of this place. It is a fair exchange, don't you think?"

"This place is huge, I'll never—"

"I hear you have an employee. Given that your line of business is helping Others, I'm not sure I approve of your choice, but who am I to judge?"

"What, you mean EightBall? How do you know about that?"

The succubus smiled again. "I have my ways."

"Penemue."

"As I said—my ways."

I looked over the hotel and thought to myself that there was no way I could ever manage such a grand place. Astarte was a succubus of near godlike status. She had temples, shrines and luxurious brothels built in her name. She also had minions. Thousands of them. All I had was a drunken angel, a prima-donna succubus, a poltergeist mother-in-law and a former gangbanger human. There was no way. I couldn't do this. I just couldn't.

"I can't—" I started.

"It's too late. The lease is already in your name."

"But—"

"But *nothing*, Jean-Luc," Astarte said, coming in close to me. "It is done. The lease is in your name, the hotel will need work, but right now you have so much goodwill in the Other communities that I'm sure they will help for a fraction of their normal price. Besides, how expensive is glitter anyway?" She winked at me.

"How did you manage this, Astarte?" I asked in wonder as I looked around.

"Never underestimate the power of lust." She strolled over to me as she spoke, her lips dangerously close to mine. I could feel my own lust stirring in me and she knew it. Before I could turn away, Astarte walked over to the reception desk—a real desk, unlike the IKEA marvel I had at the One Spire Hotel. "Speaking of lust, I hear you have a date with a certain snake lady."

"What?"

"Medusa. She knows you're back in town. You better call her."

"But—"

"Again with the 'but' … But *nothing*, Jean-Luc. You better call, lest she does to you what she did to her last boyfriend."

"I'm not her boyfriend."

"I know, lover—just let her down easy, OK? Medusa and I are old friends and I would hate to see her hurt."

"I'll do my best." I was still looking around the massive room. There was much potential, so much good we could do for Paradise Lot. "Thank you," I said to Astarte.

The succubus nodded. "You have quite the reputation, Jean-Luc. The Others know what you did for Joseph and how you killed the Avatar of Gravity. Already your story is being turned from current event into legend. This will both aid and hinder you in the days to come. Play your hand wisely and … Where did this come from?" she interrupted herself, showing me a framed picture resting on the reception desk. "I didn't order this."

I picked it up, removing the fabric covering from its square frame. Underneath was an image of two silhouetted figures watching the sunrise from atop a hill. The larger figure was an undefined, hulking man, the other a three-inch-tall fairy that sat on the first's shoulders. And although you couldn't see their faces, you just knew those two were very happy, having found companionship and joy in each other.

CaCa and TinkerBelle! I guessed the pile of poo survived after all. And why not? When you lived in the very substance you were made of, regeneration must have been pretty much a matter of course.

I was so happy I actually did a little dance right there in the foyer.

"Get a hold of yourself," a voice said from behind. "There's a lot of work still to be done."

Miral walked in with her typical characteristic grace, surveying the hotel entrance. "This place is much nicer than One Spire Hotel. What will you call it?" Behind her hovered Judith, surveying her new surroundings with her typical judgmental look.

"The Two Spire Hotel," I said.

Judith snorted. "You must be joking."

I just shrugged in response.

"Oh, Human Jean-Luc," tutted Miral, "you are nothing if not—"

"Tenacious?"

"I was going to say static. Anyway, how do you plan on paying for this place?"

"The rent's free," I said, pointing at a sultry Astarte, who eyed the angel with a lustful, predatory gaze. By the GoneGods, Miral and Astarte together would be a sight erotic enough to coax the gods themselves to return.

"Rent may be free," Miral said, "but bills are not. Keeping this place open will cost you four times what it cost for the One Spire Hotel."

Damn, everything was happening so fast that I hadn't considered that. The angel was right: electricity, gas, heat— this place was so huge, it would cost a small fortune to run. I had a sudden urge to go around the place and turn off all the lights.

Miral gave me an uncharacteristically devilish smile and said, "Don't worry. I have a solution for all your problems. Funding is still open and in a place like this we can throw twice as many seminars. Three times, even. We can do this. If, that is, you are willing to …"

"Don't say it!"

"… bake."

"Arrgh!"

I hated baking, but I loved Bella more.

Before I could answer, a baritone voice bellowed in from the stairwell, "Of course he will."

Penemue walked in the foyer, taking Miral's hand in his. "Ahhh, Miral … of all the unFallen, you, my dear, are the only one I can stomach." He kissed her hand in an exaggerated motion. "Dear Human Jean-Luc will bake your cookies, conduct your seminars and take in our lost brethren without a peep of protest from his lips or hint of grumble in his heart."

"How can you be so sure?" Miral asked, her smile touching her eyes.

"Because he has motivations compelling him to do distasteful tasks that stem from the most base and vile of human emotions … Love."

To that, Astarte rolled her eyes.

I looked around and saw the picture of Tink and CaCa again, back where I had placed it. I thought about Bella and how proud she would be of this place, and I nodded. Why fight it? Penemue was right, might as well die doing something worthwhile.

"And why will you do it?" Penemue said, pressing the issue.

"You know why," I said.

"I do, but they do not. Please indulge us. Why will you do it?"

"Because I made a promise," I said, the words catching in my throat.

"And what promise was that?" Penemue asked, a hand cupped behind his ear.

I cleared my throat. "I made a promise to help Others."

"That's not a promise," Penemue bellowed out, his hands flaring out in an arch. "You would never hear Hamlet merely say, 'I need to get that guy who killed my father,' or Othello say, 'I'm jealous!' A true promise requires flair, theatrics. Passion!"

"Really?" I said. "And how does one make a good promise?"

Penemue gave me a dismissing gesture as if he were bored by the whole thing. "You choose your words. Ye, thee, vow, sweareth ..."

"Fine," I said, unwrapping my collarless black jacket and putting it on. It felt good. Right. Then, not wanting to disappoint my audience, I walked into the middle of the large room and summoned all my high-school Shakespeare training—which was none—and raised my hand before me.

In a deep and resolute voice I declared, "My name is Jean-Luc Matthias and my doors shall forever be open to the lost and frightened, the poor and homeless. And as for those with evil in their hearts? Beware! For the Human Jean-Luc stands watch.

"How was that?" I asked two angels, a ghost and a succubus.

Penemue nodded. "Now *that* is more like it."

(Not) THE END

On the next episode of Paradise Lot...

The night before the gods left, Dionysus—god of wine, ecstasy, ritual madness and theatrical pursuits—threw the greatest party the divine world had ever known. Sparing no expense, he tapped into the then unlimited well of magic and burned tens of thousands of years, ensuring that every drink, light, cushion, chair, party-streamer and cocktail-wiener was perfect. No detail was too small for his attention. And why not? After all, the world as everyone knew it was ending.

"Let us party like there is no tomorrow ... for there truly is not!" He cried out, raising a glass of ambrosia poured from a bottle he saved for a very special occasion. And what could be a more special that all the gods leaving? He drank heavily from its rim. Smacking his lips as he examined the iridescent, green bottle with great pride. It was delicious. No—delicious was too meager a word to describe the fluid that passed through his lips. It was exquisite, enchanting, divine. And far stronger than anything he had ever distilled before. As it should be—this ambrosia was corked at the dawn of time.

Looking down at his party, he watched as his brothers and sisters danced, sang, made love—each of them enjoying their last moments on Olympus. Truly this is my greatest achievement to date, he mused. And what an achievement it was ... he was, after all, responsible for some of the classics—Pompeii's Inauguration, the Sinking of Atlantis, Y2K ... and who could forget Sodom and Gomorrah?

Dionysus did not know what tomorrow held. All he did know was that after tomorrow, he would no longer live on Mount Olympus. He would live with the gods somewhere new.

"For a tomorrow that never will be," he cried out drinking deeply again—this time straight from the bottle.

308

↔

But tomorrow did come. At least it did for Dionysus. Waking up in the stirred remnants of his perfect party—a party in which he passed out far too early—he looked around and saw that everyone was gone. The gods had left. And what was worse, they had left him behind. At least his bottle of special ambrosia was only half drunk.

Then it started: "Thank you for believing in us, but it is not enough. We're leaving. Good Luck." Damn Hermes—always so economical with his words. An event like this deserved flare, piazza. Joy. Something like—

Dionysus did not have time to mull over the message he would have delivered—not with all the shaking. Olympus trembled. Or was it his head? Dionysus was honestly not sure.

Staggering to his feet, he tried to remember where they went and if there was a chance for him to catch up. He tried to burn time and connect with them, but there was no connection, no way to reach them. They had already left.

"Damn it!" he cursed aloud. If only Dionysus had listened to Zeus when he explained where they were going, he could have followed. But instead, Dionysus was drunk and let's be honest … when that old static fart started talking, he could just go on and on and on. Blah, blah, blah—GrandExodus this, new beginning, that. Who could sit through that dribble? Certainly not Dionysus and that was why he planned to latch onto Athena and follow that diligent little godly pet into the 'Place Beyond'.

But you have to be awake to latch on, and his sister was probably so busy preparing how she was going to kiss the

Lightening Bearer's ass in a new setting that she forgot all about him. Or he forgot to tell her…

He honestly couldn't remember.

The halls of Olympus started to crumble.

They'll be back, he thought.

The pillars that once held up the Great Hall cracked.

I'm the life of the party.

The darkness from beyond was approaching, consuming Olympus in a tidal wave of nothingness.

They wouldn't leave me behind?

A platoon of talos centurions entered the Great Hall, confusion on their bronze metal faces. "My lord," the lead guard said, "What is going on?"

"Don't you know?" Dionysus said, "Olympus is over. Now is the time of the mortals!" As the words left his lips, he knew that was the message Hermes should have delivered. Now is the time of the mortals. That was exactly what was happening.

"What do we do, Lord?" the guard asked, his copper colored face showing signs of rust—a sure sign of fear for the metal soldiers.

"What any good mortal does," Dionysus said, waving his hands and opening a portal between Olympus and Earth. "We run!"

Dionysus is not a leader. Never was, never will be. He jumped through first, followed by thirty very scared talos centurions who fell to Earth like pennies from the sky.

↔

For the first three years of mortality, the talos centurions followed Dionysus around like lost puppies. They defended him during the Great War between the AlwaysMortals and

310

the newly-made ones. Some even died, defending their once-upon-a-time god, believing Dionysus stayed behind because he was loyal to them. After all, he was the youngest of the gods and the only one with a mortal mother. Perhaps he embraced the part of him that was always meant to die. None of them knew the truth and Heaven forbid that Dionysus would ever correct them.

When the war settled down to distrust and malice, the centurions hid him. They knew that AlwaysMortals and Others alike would like nothing more than to capture the only god amongst their midst. They would pester him for answers he did not have and when he refused to answer because he could not, they would use torture. Or worst—force him to sober up. And for what purpose? To find out why the gods left and where they went. Dionysus may be a god, but he had absolutely no idea where they went. As for their other question—who knows why the gods do what they do?

Dionysus and his whittled down platoon moved from hiding place to hiding place, until eventually they settled on a dire little slum called Paradise Lot. It was the only place on this godless green earth that seemed to accept them and their kind. They found accommodation and did the best with the little they had.

The talos centurions stuck around for a while, but Dionysus was no leader and one by one they abandoned him, seeking to make a go at what the AlwaysMortals called life. Still, they were a loyal bunch—each giving him a monthly tithe from something they referred to as their salary. They even brought him a flat, all-seeing window called an iPad so that he could order food and what passed as wine in this dimension without having to leave his apartment.

Occasionally Dionysus would put on his coat, fedora and sunglasses, and wander the streets of Paradise Lot incognito. But that did little to alleviate his boredom.

Alone and imprisoned by his once-god status, Dionysus was not only devastated by his new mortal existence, wrecked by his brothers and sisters abandoning him and traumatized by the drivel AlwaysMortals drank ... He was also bored beyond belief.

↔

That was then and this is now ...

Dionysus sips his wine as he wanders the streets of Paradise Lot, hiding his face from the world around him. He is not an unusual sight here. Alone, drunk and wearing far too much clothing seems to be the typical uniform to these lost Others.

As he walks, he occasionally catches the eye of another Other and sees what he always sees—no joy, no happiness. No hope.

He pulls hard on his bottle. Cider, they call it. More like fermented piss. Bahhh—he misses his wine cellars, his liquor cabinets, his fields of grapes and barley, wheat and a thousand other fruits that he would distill, ferment and brew to make his drink. But on this realm ...

He pushes the thought out of his mind. It is too depressing and Dionysus doesn't do depressing.

Instead his mind wanders to the lost creatures of Paradise Lot. They are so unhappy, living a life without delight, without ecstasy, without revelry. Each of them crying out in silent, tearless misery ... But why?

Why has their existence become so damn miserable?

Is it because they miss their gods? That might have been the case before, but now that the world knows the gods abandoned them, missing them was long ago replaced by anger. No, it was something else.

They, like he, mourn the loss of their once carefree life. They, like he, age under the strain of incessant worry over silly little things like money and food and shelter. And drink.

They worry about survival.

They worry about tomorrow.

Well, what if tomorrow will never be? Would that bring them joy?

Author Bio:

R.E. Vance lives in Edinburgh with his wife, recently born child and imaginary dog where he enjoys a beautiful city, whisky (Scottish spelling, not mine) and long walks. All he really wants is to quit his job and write stories based in Paradise Lot. All he really hopes for is that his child is healthy (ten fingers, ten toes and at least two eyes is a good start) and that eventually he can can get a real dog so that he can have an excuse to go on even more long walks.

Dedication:

As many of you know, June 20th (coincidently my birthday) saw the birth of my son.

Well, four months on and I can say without question that these last few months have been the best time of my life.

So, as with everything I write, this book is dedicated to my muse and angel, my banshee and Yara-Ma-Yha-Who …

Wee John.

Parenting, writing, my 'day' job …
It's all under control.

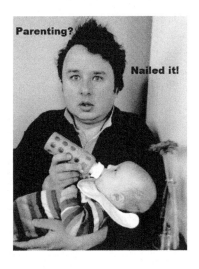

Made in the USA
Coppell, TX
24 November 2020

42012897R00177